"I gave birth to the twentieth century."

Jack the Ripper,
in *From Hell* by Alan Moore and Eddie Campbell (1989)

THE CANVAS OF THE WORLD

ANTONIN VARENNE

THE CANVAS
OF THE WORLD

*Translated from the French
by Sam Taylor*

MACLEHOSE PRESS
QUERCUS · LONDON

First published as *La toile du monde*
by Éditions Albin Michel, Paris, 2019
First published in Great Britain in 2021 by

MacLehose Press
An imprint of Quercus Publishing Ltd
Carmelite House
50 Victoria Embankment
London EC4Y 0DZ
An Hachette UK company

ISBN (MMP) 978 1 52940 386 2
ISBN (Ebook) 978 1 52940 384 8

Designed and typeset in Monotype Haarlemmer by CC Book Production
Printed and bound in Great Britain by Clays Ltd, Elcograf S.p.A.

"This problem in dynamics gravely perplexed an American historian. The Woman had once been supreme; in France she still seemed potent, not merely as a sentiment, but as a force. Why was she unknown in America? For evidently America was ashamed of her, and she was ashamed of herself, otherwise they would not have strewn fig-leaves so profusely all over her. When she was a true force, she was ignorant of fig-leaves, but the monthly-magazine-made American female had not a feature that would have been recognised by Adam. The trait was notorious, and often humorous, but anyone brought up among Puritans knew that sex was sin. In any previous age, sex was strength. Neither art nor beauty was needed. Everyone, even among the Puritans, knew that neither Diana of the Ephesians nor any of the Oriental goddesses was worshipped for her beauty. She was goddess because of her force; she was the animated dynamo; she was reproduction – the greatest and most mysterious of all energies."

Henry Adams, "The Dynamo and the Virgin"
in *The Education of Henry Adams* (1901)

New York Tribune, March 1900
By our special correspondent, Aileen Bowman

THE WIND OF CHANGE

We set sail on a French liner, along with a thousand other passengers bound for Paris, the city soon to be illuminated by millions of lights.

By a curious coincidence, the *Touraine* is the last vessel belonging to the Compagnie Générale Transatlantique still to be rigged. While steam engines roar invisibly below, the ship's sails cast their round shadows onto the metal deck. As we make our way towards the biggest world's fair ever imagined – the Paris Exposition – those canvas sails remain as a sort of tribute to tradition, to a glorious maritime past. The white cotton of our South, the wealth of empires, with the black plume from the chimneys drifting up above it. The sound of the wind is drowned out by the whistling of the boiler. In tandem, these two very different powers propel the *Touraine* onward, the ship's prow cutting relentlessly through the waves of the Atlantic.

I had an old uncle – a rough pioneer from a vanished epoch – who would tell me stories about the heroic conquest of the American continent. All his tales would end in the same way: my uncle would smile and recite the words that – to me, as a child – had the ring of a magic incantation: "There's only one direction in America: west." And yet, for the next six months, the planet's compasses will have only one pole, a shining and ephemeral north: Paris.

For us citizens of the young American nation, this crossing to Europe is a journey back to our origins. Such ideas – or perhaps the ship's sails – give rise to a surprising feeling as we voyage towards that gigantic exhibition of new technologies: nostalgia. A strange emotion, an attachment to something forever beyond our reach. The past. If memory were an apple, nostalgia would be the worm inside, devouring its own home.

The evidence is there: by celebrating a new century, we will lock behind us the door to the century in which we were born. We feel threatened by the idea that progress, in its constant rush forward, will sweep away our memories. Among the passengers of the *Touraine*, however, not everyone is burdened by such doubts.

There are entrepreneurs here, determined to take their place at the Paris Exposition. I listened to the opinions of a weaving-loom manufacturer, a Californian sawmill owner, and a Pennsylvania representative of the great Standard Oil Company. Despite their disparate backgrounds and interests, these men all had two things in common: the same smile when I asked them what they thought of the liner's sails, and a refusal to be overawed by the achievements of European engineers. They all mentioned the brilliant inventor Thomas Edison, the unchallenged star of this Exposition, who alone has registered as many patents as ten German, French and British companies put together. "Yes," they told me, "we're going to Paris to make discoveries and seal deals. But anyone who thinks we'll just be admiring visitors is kidding themselves. The western part of the world is American now. We are trading partners with Europe in our own right. I mean, our country is as big as their whole continent!"

Some travellers are irritated by France's paternalistic attitudes, but the French also have a nickname for us that should make us proud: they call us the "sister republic" of the United States of America, a budding Republic of Enlightenment. But doesn't such a heritage imply a certain degree of moral and political responsibility? The United States is vast enough that we could rely solely on its domestic market, but what meaning would the principles of openness and tolerance enshrined in our Constitution have if we didn't apply them?

"We will satisfy those demands, we will meet this challenge," the Californian businessman declares.

And the proof, both symbolic and material, is this: our involvement in this unique event, the Paris Exposition, and the million-dollar budget approved by Congress, four times more than was invested in the previous Exposition of 1889 (memorable for the construction of the fabulous Eiffel Tower). Other than our French hosts, the United States will have more artworks and artists than any other country. Not to mention the wives of these distinguished entrepreneurs, arrayed in the most beautiful dresses from New York, Boston, and Chicago, determined to prove that Paris does not have a monopoly on high fashion and good taste.

Historic rivalries prevented some countries from taking part in the 1889 celebration of the centenary of the French Revolution, but this year's Paris Exposition will bring together all the nations of the world, a symbol of a new era of collaboration. That is the central message from all the conversations I had aboard the *Touraine*, a French liner that is, in spirit, international.

Aboard a ship still lit by quaint, old-fashioned oil lamps, the enthusiastic, determined representatives of the new America are en route to connect with the electrified world.

I

At the businessmen's table, Aileen was treated like a whore at a family dinner, tolerated only because she was a journalist. The first dinner, in the main dining room of the luxurious *Touraine*, had been enough to convince her that she was aboard a floating circus, transporting only animals and clowns, with the troupe's real artists presumably on a different ship.

In her presence, husbands did not let their wives speak, probably out of fear that they would stupidly, inadvertently express the curiosity they felt for this scandalous woman: the woman in trousers, the *New York Tribune* socialist, the notorious redhead Aileen Bowman.

When the conversation turned to Thomas Edison, she mentioned the current war between Tesla's alternating current and Edison's direct current, and how Edison – to prove the dangers of his rival's invention – had eagerly promoted Brown and Southwick's electric chair. Aileen asked whether anyone at the table had attended one of Edison's demonstrations, which had taken place at fairgrounds all over the United States and involved the electrocution of dogs and orang-utans using alternating current. Then she described the execution of William Kemmler at Auburn Prison – the first use of the electric chair on a human being, and the subject of one of her first published articles. The smoke pouring from the condemned man's blackened orifices, the muscles convulsing, the tendons snapping, the smell of burned flesh. Aileen declared that she was also going to Paris to hear Edison's phonograph. America had to export its greatest inventions.

Afterwards she started drinking, ignoring their hostile arguments, and distracted herself by mentally undressing the women at the table. She imagined their breasts, in all shapes and sizes and ages, swaying from side to side above the flower-patterned porcelain plates in time with the pitching of the ship. The young wife of the Standard Oil man glanced contemptuously at the two undone buttons on the journalist's blouse, perhaps wondering what the bust of a 35-year-old spinster who'd never breastfed a baby would look like. Aileen sat up tall when their eyes met. The young woman had been the only moment of love in that entire evening.

The greatest scandal of all was her loneliness.

When they arrived in Le Havre, Aileen waited on deck, leaning on the rail and observing the other passengers as they rushed towards the station to catch their trains to Paris.

It had a bigger effect on her than she'd imagined. Was she the only one feeling the nostalgia that she'd described in the article she would telegraph to New York as soon as she reached land?

Forty years earlier, her parents had made this journey in the opposite direction, with no idea that they would meet each other over there. They'd never talked about this continent as a place they wanted to see again. Aileen was following the tracks they'd attempted to cover.

They had died that winter, both of them within the space of a few months, as if the new century had forbidden them entry. Arthur had gone first, an old and weakened man, followed by Alexandra, who couldn't go on without him. Aileen had thought her mother would become a serene widow, grateful for the past but continuing alone. She'd imagined her inexhaustible energy carrying her into the coming years, imagined her managing the ranch and fighting her political battles. But she had died very soon after Arthur. Their love had proved fatal.

One year earlier, Aunt Maria and Uncle Pete had also departed this world, frozen together in Oregon by the great blizzard.

The Fitzpatrick Ranch, which her parents had founded, had from its beginnings been a refuge for immigrants, deserters and fugitives, a tribe brought together by chance and adoptions. Her tribe, swept away in a single year. In the West, which ground down bones and teeth, winter made quick work of tired old pioneers.

All these deaths and memories were carried in the knapsack on her shoulder and the little travelling bag at her feet on the deck of the *Touraine*, and they suddenly felt too heavy.

Her father's past was a mystery kept intact by his long, silent life. Like the ranch employees and the people of Carson City, all she knew of his military career were a few snippets of information, and the fact that he'd been a sergeant in the East India Company. His body and face had been covered with terrifying scars. He'd had fingers missing. But his silence was the symptom of his real pain. He'd been a policeman in London, after leaving the Company, then he'd boarded a ship to America. Aileen imagined her father, before he met Alexandra, as a ghost wandering the globe.

Alexandra and Arthur had built their ranch by the edge of Lake Tahoe. An estate torn from the grip of the wild Sierra Nevada, taken from old Indian lands. The ranch was all that remained of Alexandra's idealistic dreams, a golden prison for her husband's nightmares of war.

During the winter of 1865, at the end of the fiercest, deadliest and most absurd civil war ever fought, two brothers – having deserted the Northern army – had crossed the mountains and hidden at the ranch, curled up in the warmth of manure inside a barn: Oliver and Pete Ferguson. The first in a long list of marginals, poor criminals and rebels to spend a few days, weeks or months at the Fitzpatrick Ranch. Oliver and Pete stayed longer than most. Alexandra, the utopian, and Arthur Bowman, the insomniac veteran, had protected and adopted them once the war was over. Aileen had been only one year old at the time.

Pete Ferguson became her favourite uncle and she became the princess of that kingdom. Uncle Pete hated everybody except for his younger brother and this adopted niece. He burned and broke everything he touched. He made too many enemies in the county, then fled the ranch. Three years later, after a long journey, he returned; Aileen was ten. That part of his life, like Arthur Bowman's past, became one of the mysteries at the heart of that community of misfits.

Pete had been in a state of exhaustion when he returned, crippled in one leg, his body covered not with scars but tattoos. But Uncle Pete had not come back alone. He was leaning on the shoulder of a young Indian woman who spoke an unknown language, Guatemalan Spanish and a smattering of English. Maria – her Aunt Maria – wanted nothing to do with that white family. And so the two of them, too marginal even for the ranch, had found refuge with some other homeless Americans, in the last resort possible for a deserter and an exile: an Indian reserve. Warm Springs, Oregon, where they had frozen to death.

Uncle Oliver had remained at the ranch with his wife Lylia and their three children – those cousins whom Aileen barely knew. They had been the branch of the family that had taken root, notable people whose fortune – as dictated by the American Dream – had made their humble origins unimportant. When Aileen saw them for the last time, at Alexandra's funeral, they had looked at her from a distance, she and they isolated by their thoughts and the clouds of steam that escaped their mouths. It was Oliver's family now who ran the ranch.

The Ferguson brothers had given birth to two distinct dynasties of Americans: the majority strain of solid entrepreneurs and defenders of property law, and the minority strain of confined nomads.

After her mother's funeral, Aileen – now an orphan – had returned to New York with a settlement that made her a rich woman and the horrible feeling that the ranch, the lake, the horses and even Alexandra and Arthur were now nothing more than a child's dream.

Perhaps nostalgia, at first so painful, would end up becoming a remedy, once the past had been recycled into oblivion.

Le Havre was bathed in sunlight. Crowds swarmed along the wharf and cranes leaned over the moored ships. The houses on the seafront, tall and narrow and squeezed close together, looked like cabaret dancers, elbows joined in a chaste but joyful line dance. Aileen imagined the houses' legs high-kicking to show a flash of thigh, suspenders and knickers to the calm, imperturbable sea. The weather had been perfect during the crossing and she regretted not landing in France with her hair dishevelled and the liner in a state of disarray after facing the wrath of the Atlantic.

The Standard Oil man's wife went down the gangway. Aileen waved and the young woman became entangled in the folds of her long dress.

She decided that Paris could wait another day. She would spend the night here, eat in the city's best restaurant and sleep in a room with a view of the port.

The tide was high. That evening, the swell increased and the waves crashed onto the jetty. The wind blew salty spray against the houses' windows, bringing a scent of seaweed and splashed granite. Aileen ate seafood with her hands. Her greasy fingers left smears on her wine glass. The Exposition would open its doors in less than a week; all the restaurants and hotels within 120 miles of Paris were fully booked. But for a woman travelling alone, they found a room and a table. She changed her dollars to francs.

She listened curiously to the customers and the waiters and was surprised when she understood them. She was anxious to know if she could answer them correctly. She had only ever spoken French with her mother, who was born in a village in Alsace. Since Alexandra's death, Aileen had forced herself to think in French, out of fear that she would forget what her mother had taught her. Growing up in a country where they were the only two people who could understand each other, Aileen had imagined herself the last guardian of a secret language. But, here, everybody spoke it.

The existence of this mysterious land had confirmed what little Aileen always supposed: that she was a princess from another world, and her mother a sorceress who had chosen Arthur Bowman, the strongest of men, to be her husband on this earth.

And this evening, she was finally here. In the place she'd come from.

This was why she'd persuaded her employer to send her to Europe. And Whitelaw Reid, owner of the *New York Tribune*, was not the kind of man who was easily influenced. He campaigned for an opinionated press, but was not at all keen on dialectics unless he got the last word.

"Royal Cortissoz will already be there. There's no point having two of you."

"There's no comparison! Royal is a stubborn man who can only speak New York English. Who will cover what's happening in Paris when he leaves France after the inauguration?"

"Two weeks is enough to get what we need. Nobody cares about the rest of the Exposition."

"I'll stay there six months and write in-depth articles."

"Six months? Are you crazy? That would be a gigantic waste of time and money."

"I'll stay until 1901. The start of the new century."

"Out of the question. This Exposition is just a trumped-up tourist attraction. The French think it's way more important than it actually is."

"They're expecting millions of visitors. Princes from Asia,

kings from Africa, politicians from all over Europe, the world's greatest intellectuals will all be there. If you don't have anyone there who can speak French, how will you find out anything that's happening? Are you planning to reprint Mr Bennett's articles from the *New York Herald*?"

Whitelaw Reid frowned. Not only was the *Herald* his newspaper's toughest competitor, but Bennett was his enemy. Aileen drove home her advantage:

"I'm sure Mr Bennett has hired an army of reporters who speak French and English. Did you know he even has an office on the first floor of the Eiffel Tower, just like he did in '89?"

"Are you threatening to go and work for that purveyor of cheap thrills and bad news, Miss Bowman?"

"No."

"No?"

"No. Quite the contrary: I'm promising to be a thorn in his side. I can write articles in English for New York and French versions that can be shared out among the Parisian newspapers. That way, the *Tribune* will have a presence on both sides of the Atlantic."

She'd had him at the first mention of James Gordon Bennett, but Whitelaw Reid continued to argue just to save face.

"I am not going to pay you to take a six-month vacation in that crazy city."

"I'll pay half of my rent and expenses myself."

"Putting one over on Bennett is one thing, but I don't want any of your incendiary, provocative articles. It has to be reasonable or I'm not publishing it."

"But if I find French newspapers interested in what you've rejected, I have carte blanche, right?"

"Not under your own byline. As long as you're in France, your name belongs to my newspaper."

"You're right – I'll choose a male pseudonym so I can write about women's rights."

"Oh, don't start!"

"Until 1901?"

"Wire me a weekly column, plus news articles if anything important happens."

"I won't write about fashion."

"Agreed. You'd scare the poor designers. As long as Royal Cortissoz is in Paris, you'll be his assistant for arts and culture."

"Absolutely not."

"Get out of my office."

He watched her smile as she stuffed herself with oysters, which were already milky even though it was only early April. She congratulated herself on arriving in Paris a day late and provoking the wrath of Royal Cortissoz, who was never more ridiculous than when he lost his temper. Strong emotions revealed his inaptitude for passion, against which – as a champion of the most conservative American art (which imitated the most conservative European art) – he considered himself one of the last bulwarks.

Aileen spread a thick layer of butter on her bread and poured herself more wine.

Later, standing by her bedroom window and searching for stars in the cloudy sky above the Channel, Aileen cried as she thought about all the opportunities she had missed to visit her aged parents. She would have liked to write them a letter now, to tell them about the taste of the seafood and the port of Le Havre, from where, she'd been told, for a few days every year, when the air was pure and the sun at a certain angle, it was possible to make out the dark line of the English coastline – her father's land. She went to bed late, worried that this stay in France would end up nothing more than a long, guilty period of mourning. "Tiredness does strange things to your mind – go to sleep," her father used to say, even though his own nights were scarred by bad dreams.

Would this mourning be like a drogue, holding her back, just as the ship's old-fashioned sails slowed down the *Touraine*? It would be a sad way to celebrate a new century in Paris, but perhaps not an unreasonable one given that she planned to question the engineers here on the place that would be reserved, in their glorious future, for women like her and for people of mixed blood like her cousin Joseph.

The Fitzpatrick Ranch had three heirs: Aileen Bowman, Oliver Ferguson and – following the deaths of Uncle Pete and Aunt Maria – their son Joseph.

Of all the ranch's offspring, Joseph, the bastard son of an Indian woman and a deserter, was the most tragic and the most dangerous in that lineage of dangerous men. He was also the one that Aileen understood best.

After the burial, instead of going straight back to New York, Aileen had visited the reserve at Warm Springs. At the Indian Affairs Office, she questioned a government employee. The man hummed and hawed, so Aileen held a ten-dollar bill under his nose to convince him to look up Joseph Ferguson in his register.

"He was hired."

"Hired?"

"For a show."

"What show?"

"Pawnee Bill's Show."

"And where would I find that?"

The answer to that question cost her another ten dollars.

"It'll cost you a lot more than that if you want to see the show! Because Pawnee Bill has hired a whole load of redskins to replace old Buffalo Bill in Paris!"

"Paris, France?"

"I think so, yeah!"

"For the Exposition?"

"The what now?"

She took a train back to the east and spent the journey writing a list of reasons for travelling to France, in order of importance, and sketching out some arguments likely to convince the owner of the *New York Tribune* to send her there.

2

As they draw closer, each Exposition appears like a mountaintop from which we can look back over the distance already covered. The visitor emerges feeling reassured, encouraged and optimistic about the future. That joyful optimism – the prerogative, in the previous century, of a few noble minds – is now spreading much more widely; in this fertile cult, the Expositions appear as majestic but useful ceremonies, necessary for the existence of a hard-working nation driven by an irresistible urge to expand, like companies distinguished less by the material profits they offer than by the injection of vigour they give to the human mind.

Aileen studied the Exposition map, read the names of the main buildings, then put the booklet back on the bench. This extract from the official decree had made her ill at ease. There was something violent, naive and oppressive about the bombastic syntax. Something vainglorious, like wartime propaganda.

Through the window of the train, as it rounded a long curve, she looked out at the vivid green Normandy countryside – forests, fields, fences, cattle – cut in two equal parts by the long curve of the shining railway tracks. The Pereire brothers had founded the Compagnie Générale Transatlantique, linking New York to Le Havre, and then the Compagnie des Chemins de Fer de l'Ouest, linking Le Havre to Paris. They had been inspired by the writings of Henri de Saint-Simon, who had laid down the blueprint for a peaceful, united world, run by benevolent scientists and industrialists; a dream shared by his peer, Fourier, who hoped to achieve it through hard-working communitarian companies where everything would be shared and human passions would exist in harmony. The Pereire brothers, paternalistic messiahs of the industrial age, building on the ruins of the past, had created a company to fund their theories: Crédit Mobilier, which invested individuals' money in long-term public development projects. Their idealism and greed led this bastard bank into bankruptcy. After that resounding failure, Europe's utopian dreamers focused on more modest objectives: communities that, although still ideal, were much smaller in size. Some of them, to escape the reactionary forces of their home continent, exported their visions to a new land with no past: America. Newspaper articles, speeches and adverts convinced hundreds of people to sell their goods and set off in search of adventure: followers of Saint-Simon and Fourier, apprentice sorcerers and bumbling messiahs went to build phalansteries in the United States. There, once again, some badly applied ideals and the betrayals of certain financier friends led to these communities falling into bankruptcy. One of these ephemeral towns, named Reunion, was located in Texas, by the Trinity River, and was created by two men: Victor Considerant, a graduate of the prestigious Ecole Polytechnique in Paris, and Jean-Baptiste Godin, a manufacturer of wood-burning stoves and a champion of human progress. After surviving for three years, the small town tragically collapsed. Aileen's mother, Alexandra Desmond, aged nineteen at the time, had been one of the three hundred colonists who'd settled in Reunion in 1858, with her husband, who – weakened by malnutrition – caught a fever and died.

As she stared out at the Pereire brothers' railway tracks, Aileen tried to remember that Frenchman's name. She had seen it once on the flyleaf of a book at the ranch. Alexandra's first husband had written her a note: a few lines, scrawled in a cramped, slanting calligraphy, ending with the words "With all my love", followed by the name that she couldn't quite recall. "With all my love" . . . The first time she read that note, Aileen knew nothing about the Reunion debacle and wouldn't have cared if Alexandra had told her about it then and there: she had just discovered that her mother had once loved another man. She'd discovered that it was possible to live more than one life.

For a long time she was afraid of that book, which stood among others on a shelf in the living room, visible to everyone, but particularly to her father, like a horrible secret that she was forced to share with her mother. Later, Alexandra had explained that love is free, that it can die like everything else, but also survive. She told her daughter how Arthur, the ex-soldier, had arrived in the ruins of Reunion, carrying a book that he would read while carefully tracing the lines with his finger. She'd described how this terrified, terrifying man had become her new and last love. Arthur knew about the existence of that book, that note, that other man. "Don't worry, it's not a secret," her mother had told her. "The real danger comes from me telling you about it. Because the rest of the world doesn't like to hear about free love, passion, pleasure."

Jerome. Jerome Desmond gave his surname to Alexandra, who kept it afterwards, when she was with Arthur. The name came to Aileen after she abandoned her observation of the landscape and turned her attention to the passengers in the first-class carriage, some of whom glared back or looked away.

The villages grew bigger and more closely spaced as the Le Havre express sped without stopping through the little suburban stations, whistling and smoking and catching the eyes of the curious locals as they waited for a slower train.

The men took the suitcases down from the luggage racks, the children stuck their snotty noses to the windows, and the women adjusted their outfits. Aileen jammed the sagging black wool hat further onto her head; she'd been wearing it ever since leaving Nevada for New York. She caught other passengers staring at her disapprovingly or curiously, perhaps imagining that she worked for one of those cowboy-and-Indian shows that Joseph had joined.

Aileen had interviewed William Cody, after he had started calling himself Buffalo Bill, at a time when the public was starting to take seriously his ridiculous version of how the West was won. But Aileen was no wide-eyed Fenimore Cooper fan. She'd grown up in the West. After that article, there was no way Cody would think about hiring her, despite her riding boots and trousers and her skill with a gun. Her father used to say, half-jokingly, that while it was better to live surrounded by friends, dying without a few enemies should be a source of shame. Aileen was glad to have the famous Buffalo Bill for an enemy.

The train shook as the points slowed it down, the tracks converging on the station. The buildings lining the route were blackened by locomotive smoke. Behind the upstairs windows, she glimpsed the silhouettes of her first Parisians, indifferent to the rumble of the trains. The sky disappeared behind glass panes and a metal skeleton.

She slung her knapsack – as tired-looking as her hat – over her shoulder and stood up. Made of waterproof oilcloth, its leather parts blackened by use and still smelling of horsehair, this bag did not contain any beauty products, hairbrushes or bicarbonate of soda to be smeared in her armpits. Aileen used it to carry her notebooks, pencils and books, a sanitary belt, a few changes of underwear, and a Smith & Wesson Ladysmith. The knapsack had belonged to her father. She'd always viewed it as a sort of magic bag from which he could pull whatever they needed while they were out hunting together in the Sierra. Ammunition, equipment for cleaning guns, water, bread, dried meat, a book to read by the fire, tobacco for the pipe that he let her smoke, and – when she was hungry and thought all their food was gone – always one last dried apricot or slice of apple. Arthur Bowman, a taciturn man, was obsessed by impermeability. One night, he told his daughter about a magnificent and perfectly waterproof powder horn, carved from ivory, the inside coated with rubber-tree sap, which had saved his life in India. As he was describing this fantastical object, little Aileen realised he was actually talking about something else, that her father was giving her advice about the way she should deal with the world: know when to shut up, keep your powder dry, always be ready. And be beautiful too, maybe. In the way that Arthur Bowman appreciated beauty: when it arose from a harmony between an object and its usefulness, from a person and the place she occupied in the world. Her father's knapsack and her mother's French were Aileen's most precious heirlooms.

The carriages juddered to a halt. She had pins and needles in her feet from four hours of vibrations. The riveted posts of the station kept moving backwards in a slow optical translation. She felt dizzy and her swollen heart seemed to bang against her ribs and the flesh of her breasts.

On the platform, the other passengers streamed past like a fabric landscape behind a theatre stage. Her fingers fiddled with the paper at the bottom of her pocket, the address that she had memorised long ago: 14, rue Saint-Georges, in the ninth arrondissement of Paris.

Before venturing into the streets, she sat down at a café terrace on the main concourse to catch her breath.

"What can I get you, madame?"

"A glass of red wine."

The waiter observed her outfit.

"Madame is American?"

"No, I'm French."

The waiter thought this a joke in bad taste. He brought her wine and told her the price: five centimes.

The vast concourse, perpendicular to the platforms, was filled with sunlight. The brightness highlighted the contrasts between the dark suits and the garish colours of the advertisements that covered every surface. They were on pillars, over arches, on hanging signs, drowning out the smaller signs indicating platform numbers and destinations. The slogans extolled the taste of chocolates, the quality of furniture, the expertise of wine merchants, the elegance of shoes and gloves, the sophistication of restaurants and patisseries. The SALE sign above a large door competed with the huge letters, painted on the ceiling, of Galeries

Lafayette. Posters were plastered everywhere, publicising all the new products available at the Paris Exposition: electric light bulbs and latex utensils, bicycles, hot-water tanks and hard-wearing fabrics. The coloured lettering gave the names and addresses of the buildings where these wonders could be found: the pavilion of agriculture, of mechanics and chemical industries, the pavilion of water, of fabrics and clothing, of metallurgy.

Beneath this fireworks display of names and products, the fashion of the day – full-length dresses, corseted waists, sheathed backs – outlined the figures of the women more clearly than those of the men, who all wore long, shapeless coats. The women's breasts were lifted by underwiring and crammed inside short jackets like the marble chests of classical statues. Rows of buttons rose up from valley-like bellies, passed between those steep mountainsides and continued up to the pale throats with their bulging veins; Aileen found herself wanting to unfasten them so those poor ladies could breathe.

The women were designed to be picked up by their waists and spun around like tops. The more elegant they were, the more thoroughly their flesh and blood was enveloped and oppressed. As for the slumped, blurred figures of working-class women, they could almost be confused with the figures of men leaning on their walking sticks. That warlike accessory gave the men an elderly look, like schoolmasters ready to whack the bottoms of noisy children, or inspectors who might – with the steel tip of their cane – lift up a dress to check the number of skirts beneath. The men paraded around as if they each had the right to examine every woman they saw.

Aileen finished her wine, left a coin on the table, and got to her feet. The back of her riding jacket, with its leather-patched elbows, only half covered her buttocks, moulded inside the jodhpurs she wore. Her riding boots snapped loudly on the ground when she walked. In this shopping arcade of a train station, whispers followed in her wake.

People rushed along rue Saint-Lazare, and they ran on rue de Rome. She took refuge from the crowds in a nook within a wall, stood still and watched intently for long enough to transform these first sensations into a lasting memory, as she sometimes did for a sunset or a beautiful morning on a New York avenue. It wasn't easy, to really look; to prevent this sun or that image slipping into the mass grave of indistinct memories; those drawers of the mind where all the pretty sunsets and landscapes end up, piled on top of one another, no longer truly seen or remembered but only accumulated.

The pedestrians crossed the road by zigzagging between carts, omnibuses and hansom cabs driven by whip-happy men, while a few steam-powered vehicles made the horses jump. There were bicycles, tricycles and handcarts, hawkers and newspaper vendors, policemen blowing into their whistles. Here, too, advertisements covered every surface: newspaper kiosks, wagon tarpaulins, walls and buildings.

She concentrated on what she was feeling, the sum of her impressions – of this architecture, of the sounds she could hear, of the presence, still invisible, of that unparalleled Exposition: everything making up the mental photograph taken by an Aileen Bowman who had never before been this woman leaning against this wall, with this sensation finding a new, yet oddly familiar pathway inside her brain. She felt at home in this strange city.

3

It was only a ten-minute walk from the train station to the offices of *La Fronde*, along rue Saint-Lazare, then rue de la Chaussée-d'Antin and rue de la Victoire. The three-storey building at 14, rue Saint-Georges was elegant, discreet and surrounded by other buildings in the same style and of the same size. Nothing on the building's facade suggested that it was a feminist bastion or even a newspaper office. Aileen had imagined something in a working-class district, half-hidden near a factory perhaps, a single-storey wooden building where socialist pamphlets were printed in secret. *La Fronde* was situated at the end of a street in a prosperous neighbourhood. Inside the entrance hall, the walls were white and pale green, the lighting was electric, and the floor tiles shone. Behind the reception desk, a young woman was reading a book beside a telephone that looked just like the ones in the *New York Tribune*'s office. Behind her was a cloakroom large enough for two hundred coats, then some glass doors opening onto a reception room where some women were clearing away the remains of a party from tables standing in front of a theatre stage. From the entrance hall, Aileen could smell the mingled odours of wine and stale tobacco.

"Is this the office of *La Fronde*?"

The receptionist nodded. "How can I help you?"

"I don't have an appointment, but I telegraphed Mme Durand

to say I'd be in Paris this week. She told me to come here as soon as I arrived."

"Your name, please?"

"Aileen Bowman. I'm a journalist at the *New York Tribune*."

"Mme Durand will see you now. Her office is on the first floor. Second door on your left."

The walls were decorated not with front pages of the newspaper but with modern paintings: scenes from Parisian life, busy streets, markets, all of them populated with women. Aileen announced herself to a secretary as elegantly dressed as the receptionist downstairs, and who knocked at her boss's door.

The editor of *La Fronde*, a blonde woman with the smile of an actress, was dressed and bejewelled like a princess. Her appearance was enough to convince Aileen that she'd made a mistake. Their conversation would be the usual polite drivel about charity, moral principles, and the right of women to wear feathers in their hats.

Marguerite Durand's smile froze when she saw what her visitor was wearing.

"My God, where have you come from?"

"A ship and then a train."

"Without being arrested? Then again, the way you're dressed, I imagine the police thought you rode here on a horse."

"I beg your pardon?"

"I was under the impression that in New York, too, women are not allowed to wear trousers?"

"Nobody ever stopped me. I grew up on a ranch, so I wouldn't even know which end of a dress to put on first."

Marguerite Durand burst out laughing, then instantly composed herself.

"Well, that's a shame. With a bath and a change of clothes, you would brush up so beautifully that – on my arm at a fundraising party – you'd earn us enough money to keep the paper going for the next six months. Your French is remarkable. You should know, however, that the only women in our country allowed to wear trousers are those riding a bicycle or a horse. And, even then, they have to be those horrible puffed-up knickerbockers that don't show" – here she waved a finger in front of Aileen's abdomen and hips – "all that."

Mme Durand was a tall woman with broad, straight, handsome shoulders. Her blonde hair was darkening slightly as she approached her forties.

"I've never ridden a bicycle, but I can stay on a horse for a day and a night before I need to soak my butt in a stream."

"An arresting image . . ."

"I'll let you get back to work. I think I made a mistake."

Marguerite Durand's voice lost its urbane pomposity and she spoke in simple, clear tones. "I remember your telegram. You said that you were going to stay in Paris for the whole six months of the Exposition, and that you would be sending articles to New York, but that you were also looking for French newspapers who would be interested in publishing some more personal articles. If you leave before you've even told me what you want to write, how will I be able to offer you work at *La Fronde*?"

"I don't know what I'm going to write yet."

"How did you learn to speak French so fluently?"

"My mother was French."

"Your accent is delightful, which is not always the case for your compatriots."

"Oh, I have an accent?"

Mme Durand laughed like an actress again.

"What do you have to offer me?"

"What are you willing to publish?"

"Let's get things straight, Mrs Bowman."

"Miss, not Mrs."

"Miss Bowman. One of our employees here is the first woman in this country to have earned her living as a professional journalist. Our friend Séverine has contacts among politicians, judges and union leaders. Her opinion matters in the nest of vipers that is French politics and she is a fervent advocate of your American method of on-the-ground reporting. We have the first female doctor at a French hospital specialising in modern psychiatry. Walk through the corridors here and you might also bump into the first female lawyer ever allowed to plead a case in a French courtroom. We have the only female economics journalist in the country. We work with the woman who translates Charles Darwin. Some of our other contributors are critically acclaimed artists. A number of them have been fighting since I was a child to improve living conditions, education and work opportunities for women. We are all fighting, step by step, for a new law that will grant women the right to vote. Even though we don't have that right at the moment, we present candidates at every election and publicly champion manifestos for the advancement of women's causes, so that we can remind everyone of our presence and legitimise our arguments. The journalists at this paper are socialists, anarchists, libertarians, religious believers and atheists, married women, single women, young women, old women, women who love to dress up and women who are horrified by the idea of make-up. Nobody here loves to dress up more than I do, and I ask the women who work behind the reception desk to dress tastefully. I organise parties, concerts and shows that attract everybody who's anybody, and I shower them with champagne. I'm the only feminist in France to be sent flowers by the most conservative cabinet ministers and businessmen. Since the start of the scandalous Dreyfus Affair, which I am sure you've heard all about, we have been among the few newspapers to demand justice for that innocent man. We lost half our readers over that issue, but I am a free-thinker and the first duty of all free-thinkers is to let others think freely too. Don't make the mistake of imagining that I am not fully committed to our cause just because I have played ingénues at the Comédie-Française. I know how to put on a show. All the rest is a matter of personal preference. Do I reproach you for supporting women's rights while dressing like a man? No. However, I do reproach you, my friend, for so inelegantly hiding your beauty, and I also worry – after hearing some of the things you've told me – that you spent your entire childhood suffering from colds after soaking your bottom in streams. I will publish everything you bring me if it's up to standard and I can afford it. You're not going to have debates with me, but with your colleagues at La Fronde."

Aileen's teeth were still gritted. She was not going to apologise for thinking that La Fronde was a cocoon for luxury mistresses, because it was. Nor would she admit that this little history lesson had impressed her, even if it was written all over her face. The editor smiled at the American's stubbornness. Obstinacy was a character trait whose excesses did not diminish its usefulness.

"Do you know where you're staying?"

"I'll find a hotel."

"I doubt it. Paris is full. All you'll find now are a few third-rate boarding houses. Things will calm down after the inauguration, but for now I would suggest that you take one of the bedrooms on the top floor of this building."

"I'll pay whatever rent you usually charge."

"Nonsense! I'll just take it out of your pay. We have a fencing room, a tea room, an art gallery and a library. You are welcome to use them all. Make yourself at home. But I must go now, as I have other meetings scheduled. Eloise will accompany you. Eloise?"

The secretary entered, quick as a hunting dog.

"Would you be so kind as to show Miss Bowman to the unoccupied room on the top floor? Miss Bowman is a journalist from New York. I've convinced her to work with us for the duration of the Exposition. One last thing, Miss Bowman. The police station in Paris can grant you an authorisation to wear trousers. The police commissioner, M. Lépine, is an acquaintance of mine and a regular guest at our soirées. I will make sure you receive that document very soon, but in the meantime would you please wear a dress? For your own protection."

"I don't have one."

"Eloise will make the necessary arrangements. I hope you and I will find time to eat lunch together soon, so you can tell me all about the ranch where you grew up. Welcome to Paris, Miss Bowman."

The interview ended there, with one last actress's smile and a firm handshake, followed by the rustling of silk and the clinking of jewellery as she left the room. Aileen hadn't had time to thank her, but she felt sure that Marguerite Durand was not the sort of woman to worry about that kind of thing.

The small attic room was decorated with the same care as the rest of the building. From beneath her feet, on the newspaper's second floor, Aileen could hear the noises of the typesetting room. *La Fronde* was a morning daily. The typographers would be busy all night long. Aileen would sleep perfectly. But late. As late as possible. Through the dormer window, she saw the rooftops of the surrounding houses and, high above them, M. Eiffel's tower, already lit up. Night was falling and the electrified city was white.

She stopped outside the door of the typesetting room and watched the employees. Everything was the same as at the *New York Tribune*: the same gestures, a combination of concentration and hurry, tiredness and repetition, but here all the employees were women, their sleeves rolled up, their wrists slender and supple, their faces – if anything – even more determined.

As she was walking through the entrance hall, Eloise, the secretary, ran after her and handed her an envelope.

"Mme Durand told me to give you this letter. It may be useful if you have any problems with the police."

"The police?"

The beautifully dressed secretary looked at Aileen's manly clothing.

"Mme Durand suspected you wouldn't change your outfit."

So apparently her trousers were more dangerous than her Ladysmith. Nobody had demanded an authorisation for that.

4

Aileen was not a fan of poetry. Instead of being soothed by the music of the words, instead of accepting the images without question, she would lose herself in intellectual musings. She couldn't help dissecting the contents of the too-dense verses, challenging the arbitrary nature of the word choices. But while she couldn't ever finish reading a poem, she did acknowledge that poets had a particular talent and shared the pleasure that they took in long, aimless walks, the cadence of her footsteps giving birth to ideas. And there was nowhere better than in the streets of a city to hear the click-click-click of heels. Sometimes, on dry ground, the hooves of a horse could also draw her into that meditative hypnosis. But it was in New York that she'd discovered the hobby of slowly wandering around a city that became a backdrop and echo chamber to her thoughts.

She tried to find the right tempo for her boot heels.

In that erotic rhythm was conceived the first article that she would write in France. It wouldn't be a column for Whitelaw Reid, but for the hive of activity that was *La Fronde*. A story for those women, in which she would allow herself a little of the poetry forbidden to journalists.

On the island of Manhattan, half of the buildings had been built during the fifteen years that she'd been living there. Here, almost every building she saw was older than her country. As she walked vaguely towards place de la Concorde, she savoured this contradiction – of being here to write about an Exposition constructed in wood and plaster, doomed to destruction within a few months, in the middle of a city that had already existed two thousand years before, when the Roman army conquered Europe.

To compensate for the brevity of their history and use glory as a shield against the inferiority complexes it produced, Americans sought constantly to prove their identity, reforging it in exaggerated nationalist postures. The Parisian streets, under her leather soles, obtained the same result simply through their presence and a little noise. America was still struggling to build enduring myths for itself. The ones about its foundation, by the fathers of the Constitution, had been smashed less than one hundred years after independence when the country had torn itself to pieces in the rage of civil war. The dubious fable about the abolition of slavery was the only myth that could be salvaged from that wreck. There weren't any old, cobbled streets in the United States, only the graves of half a million Americans to prove that unity had a price, that their history was not a blank slate after all.

The French, by contrast, had so much past beneath their feet that they probably knew almost nothing about it. It was the echo of the forgotten catacombs that gave the granite streets their resonance. Whether too long or too short, timelines always give rise to incomplete memories. The control of time – education – is in the hands of the powerful. Ordinary people, too busy surviving, do not have enough time to capitalise on it, to bend it to their will. They merely pile up the stones of buildings that will outlive them.

Aileen was seventeen when she first travelled a long way from the ranch. It was springtime; she was armed and riding a fast mare. It took her ten days to reach the Warm Springs reserve, and she stayed there until the summer. During one of those evenings around the fire that invite the sharing of secrets, her Uncle Pete – a half-mad hermit, living with Maria in isolation from the other Indians – had shown her his tepee. "This is how the world is made," he'd said. "It's a pyramid. The force of gravity issues from the point at the top, flattening itself with all its power against those at ground level – us. In a just world, the point would be the base: it would be planted in the earth and it would raise us towards the sky." Seven-year-old Joseph was there, between his parents, trying to understand what the grown-ups were talking about, observing his cousin, who was not yet old enough to be a mother but already a woman, white like his father but dressed like an Indian. Joseph compared the colour of his own skin to hers.

Aileen heard the crackle of Uncle Pete's fire, in unison with her footsteps.

Books are too long for those who have no time; newspapers are better for them. Journalism, thought Aileen, would perhaps become a new force in the pyramid, capable of transforming it, as Marguerite Durand had said, if you could write about things as they were on the ground. No more begging for information from the summit. What she had to do was find her subjects here, at the base, and lift them up. She had to discover the truth by pounding the streets, not by spreading second-hand myths.

There were fewer Parisians on the streets tonight. The shops had closed, and only restaurants, cafés and bars were open now. During the day, it was objects that were sold; at night, it was time, for those who needed to take it. Alcohol slowed it down, lengthened it, and the workers with no free time wanted more and more of it.

Between the headquarters of *La Fronde* and place de la Concorde, the streets were wide and clean, the buildings well lit. From the entrances of narrower side streets, Aileen glimpsed doorways illuminated only by gas lanterns, beyond the reach of the electric streetlamps. The exploration of those parallel streets would wait, however; first, she wanted to see the Exposition in the dark, in its last moments of silence before the crowds and the booming speeches.

But she found no peace or darkness. As soon as she had crossed the square with its mighty obelisk, she heard the hubbub of voices. She'd been expecting fences, closed ticket counters, men in uniform guarding attractions hidden behind screens, covered with tarps. Instead, it was chaos. From the Champs-Elysées to the west and the docks to the east, hundreds of carts were converging on the main entrance, transporting beams, bags of lime and rocks, bricklayers, carpenters and painters. She saw lit-up stalls where vendors yelled out the prices of the soup, tobacco, bread and wine they were selling. Nobody was guarding the Exposition: people simply shoved past one another to get in. The heart of Paris was a tumult of hammering and sawing, creaking cranes and rumbling steam engines, clattering horseshoes and lowing cattle. People called out, shouldered past one another, all of them trying – amid the rushing, tired bodies – to achieve their aim: unload this cart, squeeze through that crowd, get something to eat, make themselves heard.

Aileen weaved between the animals and carts. Dressed as

she was, men took her for another man and pushed her around unceremoniously. She elbowed her way through the Cours-la-Reine and reached the Pont de la Concorde.

She laughed.

Both banks of the Seine were swarming with boats, and with people emptying their holds. Steamboats went up and down the river, their engines echoing as they passed under bridges, the parapets and streetlamps half-disappearing under a fog of black clouds. She could make out the outlines of domes and towers, spheres, belltowers and minarets, complex constructions with criss-crossed rooftops, all seeming to merge together. Every building was clothed in the dark lace of scaffolding. They were trying out the lights and, for a few seconds, hundreds of kilowatts of electricity illuminated the facade of a building before suddenly going out, the facade dissolving once again into the night as her pupils dilated. The magnificent entrance in the Cours-la-Reine was illuminated in turn. It was framed by two 60-foot minarets covered with light bulbs, while thousands of other bulbs shone from the pillars of its three giant arches, dazzling a dozen roped-up painters, caught in the act of brightening the stucco with bold colours. Above them, the skyline was dominated by the immense sculpture of La Parisienne, looking serious in her long coat, its edges blowing in a breeze. The bustle in the square below slowed for a moment as men, bathed in electric light, looked up at her and fell silent. The light bulbs went out and the buzzing of their filaments was replaced once again by the murmur of the workers' conversations, the sounds of movement, quiet at first, then gradually increasing in volume until they had regained their previous intensity, as if nothing had happened, as if the sudden appearance of the arches and that giant woman had been mere figments of the collective imagination.

How long had Paris been like this, an insomniac city? How many labourers had been working day and night, harried by foremen and architects, to finish the project in time? It was obvious that they were well behind schedule: the rooftops of three-storey buildings were still bare and the paint on the entrance hadn't dried yet, even though the Exposition was due to open in a week's time.

Aileen assumed that the United States pavilion was in a similar state. She imagined Royal Cortissoz fulminating amid the clouds of sawdust, watching in terror as valuable artworks were hung roughly on walls by boorish men in helmets and boots.

She stayed on the bridge for an hour, thinking, while she stared down at the black Seine and the furrows left on it by passing boats. She lifted her head to observe the vast construction site flickering in electric light, smiled briefly, and concentrated on the phrases circling her head, trying to remember what she would write in her article. The lighthouse beam from the Eiffel Tower swept the sky, moving over rooftops and illuminating low clouds. This projection of light, though regular as clockwork, had something panic-stricken about it, like a navigator seeking safe passage through dark horizons. If you stared at it too long, the lighthouse no longer seemed designed to light up Paris, but to call for help.

On the way back she stopped at a coalman's bar in rue Cambon. The place was almost deserted. She drank a few glasses of wine at a table in the corner.

It was gone midnight when she arrived at rue Saint-Georges. A different receptionist, just as well dressed as the previous one,

44

was working the night shift. On the top floor, Aileen saw light coming under the door of the room next to hers.

The little desk beneath the dormer window was lit by an oil lamp and furnished with a fountain pen, an inkwell and a sheaf of good-quality writing paper.

Aileen took off her boots and her jacket and sat in front of the paper. Before starting to write, she listened to the noises coming from the typesetting room below her feet, then got up and put her ear to the wall she shared with the room next door. She couldn't hear anything, so she went back to her desk.

Just before dawn, lamp in hand, she tiptoed across the landing to the communal bathroom, which had hot running water.

She ran water into the hip bath then lay in it, rubbing at her pale skin with a horsehair glove. Her skin turned red and Aileen felt aroused. She rubbed the rough fibres against her breasts while her other hand vibrated between her legs, the movement stopping abruptly when the waves in the bathtub splashed too loudly onto the floorboards. Her neighbour's room was just the other side of the dividing wall and she thought she'd heard a noise from there. She got out of the tub and dried herself.

"Do you want to publish your articles under your own name?"

"What matters to me is that they're published, not the name."

"We're not afraid of rocking the boat or causing a scandal, as long as the results are good. I have nothing against your writing and the subject of your article meets *La Fronde*'s requirements, even if it's a little more literary than most of our pieces. I'm just asking if you'd prefer to use a pseudonym for your own peace of mind. Your article will be in tomorrow's paper. It will provoke a reaction. If you want to write a series of articles, we could give you a weekly column."

"I would like to do more, but two columns per month will be enough."

"All right then. And the pseudonym?"

"Alexandra Desmond."

La Fronde, 6 April 1900
A column by Mme Alexandra Desmond

THE ILLUMINATED CITY

They call me the despots' whore. They say I've had more kings and emperors in my bed than elected representatives of the people. Because they only remember my most powerful lovers, the ones who built bridges and golden domes and palaces for their own glory, the stones that history leaves standing longest. But I also sleep with the starving masses, the masses wild with celebration or rage, the masses that flay alive other masses. In my secret backstreets, I have comforted young soldiers speaking many languages as they've hidden momentarily, trembling with fear, pissing their pants, praying not to die for me, before venturing out again to conquer me. I have slept with barbarians, Vikings, Roman legions and the executioners of the Terror. I am the whore of Versailles and the bastard child of revolution.

But people confuse me with those few men who have tried to redraw me in their image.

The neighbourhoods and buildings do not tell who I am. Only one witness would be credible, one witness who knows everything but will never say. Because she forgets it all. The Seine, my discreet sister, my perfect elder sister, the saint, the peaceful hypocrite ... I exist because she flows through here, because some savages decided to build their first huts by her banks. My embryo. If she could speak, my sister would tell you that we gave ourselves to everyone, men and women alike. But she is silent, and nobody judges her; she leaves me to take the blame alone. She is an old maid, grey and virginal and bored, unchanging through seasons and centuries. But she drinks blood and she, too, is a whore, like all saints who clean the wounds of victims and murderers. The good, brave Seine cleans me too, washing all the blood from my streets and carrying it to the ocean. I have dirty hands and clean feet: she makes them shine.

I am the vain strumpet, the brothel madam of kingdoms, indifferent, protective, tyrannical. I am losing my passion for men and women. I am inconstant, susceptible not only to the megalomania of dictators. I can give myself away over a trifle: a small park, a glass roof, a song.

Today they are organising a new baptism for me. They are painting my portrait, and in pictures

I must look forever young. After bathing in the waters of progress, I will emerge resuscitated, beautified, photographed! They will even film me . . . The Lumière brothers, whose name is – by a coincidence too perfect to be mere coincidence – the same as the name I will wear from now on, have invented a machine that places photographs side by side and moves them past so fast that they give the viewer the illusion of movement. But I am disappointed and sad to see myself posing, motionless, a mere background to the movements of people. I look too stiff, too serious. I am jealous when I see my sister the Seine, the eternal Seine, moving so easily on film while I – like a wooden actress – simply stand and watch her flow past, no more than a piece of scenery.

But I don't care. I may not be as good an actress as that hypocrite, but I am illuminated.

For some time now, I have had new lovers.

Not poets or triumphant knights, but hard-working fathers whom I rarely see laughing. The passions and infidelities of these virtuous husbands are only for their work, their mission. They do not pursue power, but the future. In their hands, I am no longer a conquest, I am a laboratory. I have become the engineers' mistress and guinea pig. They manipulate me, redraw me, some even disfigure me – like the awful Baron Haussmann, the architect of wide boulevards where the troops' bullets whistle. But there are also some who, often inadvertently, make poetry of me. My favourites? The magicians of electric waves. My new costumiers.

When night falls, my streets become luminous scarves. Rivers flowing with thousands of bulbs, neural pathways, new erogenous zones, an erotic acupuncture. And for eleven years now, I have had the perfect spot from which to contemplate them each evening. Birdcage or perch, it is the wildest gift from my sensible new lovers: Gustave and his formidable tower, at the top of which he has built an apartment so that we can meet whenever we like. He goes there alone, looks out at me, does the sums, makes new plans for my future. I surround him and sleep at his feet. Recently I have been spending more and more time there.

Because I am weary of the spectacle of myself – that is the fate of vain strumpets – and of seeing myself once again tarted up. I no longer recognise myself. There are too many of them this time – builders, shopkeepers, politicians and ambassadors, fighting over square feet of me. That is why Gustave's tower has become my refuge, that construction to the glory of his talent, the favourite monument of meteorologists and children.

I have another lover that I will tell you about, but I mustn't mention him in front of Gustave because he is prone to jealousy. From the tower, I see the mouths of his works and the traces of his passing on the paved streets ... That man touched me more deeply than the others. His passion is furious and our rendezvous are more secret than my dates with Gustave, which are now widely known.

The sun is rising on the final preparations for the great Exposition. I see people gathering at my feet and I only feel like myself at the top of the tower, far from the ground and all of them. I watch my sister the Seine flow past and it frustrates me that I cannot follow her, far from here. I see them coming from all directions, with their black smoke and their whistles, the trains loaded with machines and workers converging on me. They are coming from Marseilles, Spain, Italy, Germany, Hungary and Russia. It's a clear morning and I can see the liners being unloaded in the Channel ports. I watch my sister's silver meanderings as she flows west across green Normandy. She's always telling me about our little cousin, Honfleur, and her estuary where the washed blood of history is diluted in the silver sea.

Since Gustave gave me this view of myself, I have grown nostalgic. I turn my eyes away as I am filled with the sadness of altitude: loneliness.

I no longer know if I am a free woman or a whore. There is a ticket counter on every street corner now. In these times of peace, I am no longer conquered, only sold.

5

A believer in the latest evolutionary theories of politics, Royal Cortissoz was convinced that political entities and nations, like biological organisms, have natural lifespans. Because of its youth, the United States was destined to become the next great cultural empire. Consequently, its artists should devote themselves to authentically American subjects, vehicles for this new pinnacle of civilisation, while continuing, of course, to follow the classical principles of "great art", of which the French school offered the most commendable example. And so you can understand Royal's nervousness – the multiplication of his many complexes – during his temporary exile in Paris.

Porters walked past with wrapped paintings under their arms, pushing carts loaded with marble statues. Decorators, carrying paint pots and stepladders, went back and forth through the rooms. They hung curtains, rolled out carpets, screwed legs into velvet benches. The Grand Palais was in a state of uproar, behind schedule, trampled in every direction, filled with diplomatic crises and national disasters. Amid the agitation and the noise, the group of big-mouthed Americans could be heard loud and clear.

In theory, Royal had no right to oversee the positioning of artworks at the Grand Palais des Beaux-Arts. But such was his influence that, despite not being part of the selection committee, his taste was decisive when it came to the fates of the artists and their works. He assessed the pieces' quality according to criteria that Aileen considered barely relevant: background, architecture, fashion, colours. Royal was terrified by change, eaten away by the fear that things and people should be anywhere other than in their rightful place, that libraries should not be ordered alphabetically, that cars might drive on the wrong side of the road, that children should speak without being spoken to, and that beauty could be born of chance. A sculpture might have a tragic theme, but it was out of the question that it should express sadness, an emotion that demanded atonement, care, intimacy. An oil painting could be glorious, it could elevate the viewer's soul, but on no account must it be joyous – an unpredictable, chaotic feeling. For Royal, art could leave no room for doubt. Tragedy was fine, but not ambiguity; portraits could show human dignity, but they should never seduce. Art should be allegorical, should represent life without letting it escape; art should contain life without ever talking about it or imitating it. It was the art of fear, which Royal called the "American Renaissance".

The day before, Aileen had seen him enraptured by a William Henry Howe painting. The huge portrait of a bull lying on a bed of hay inside a wooden barn. The animal, in profile, was turning its calm, bovine head towards the viewer, its eyes half-closed. Royal and a gathering of his admirers had stood in front of the canvas for a good twenty minutes.

"Powerful," the critic had declared. "Simple and strong. Balanced. About nothing but itself. This animal embodies the calm strength and perseverance of American farmers."

It was the portrait of a well-fed, comfortably housed,

thoroughly bourgeois male – the sole male in a troop of females that one could imagine mooing peacefully under the gaze of their master. In terms of allegory, the painter hadn't beaten around the bush: "The Monarch of the Farm" . . . Aileen had refrained from pointing out the royalist overtone in the title of this masterpiece of republican art.

"Wholesome and popular," Royal had concluded. "Classicism applied to an authentically American subject."

"Male supremacy?" she'd asked.

Royal Cortissoz, the monarch of patriotic art in Paris, had already been irritated by her presence; now he was openly offended.

Since the publication of her column in *La Fronde*, Aileen was always the last to arrive at the Grand Palais. She smelled of alcohol and sweat, of nights spent walking from café to bar in search of subjects that were solid, social, political, real: better excuses for her nocturnal wanderings than poetry, that pursuit of the rich and powerful. In the anonymity of working-class bistros, with the aid of alcohol, she convinced herself she was staying awake for the cause of her profession, rather than merely fleeing the immobility of sleep and too many questions. She had felt weary recently, less comfortable with her solitude, although still incapable of going out in search of Joseph. She had gone from aesthetic ambulation to a sort of anaesthetic drift. It was nothing too worrying as yet, but the more unkempt she became, the more Royal Cortissoz – whether by contrast or from a desire to provoke her – seemed to take care of his appearance.

After the wholesome pleasures of bovine portraits for the glorification of men, today Cortissoz was supervising the hanging of nudes. It was hard to squeeze them in on the already overloaded walls of the American galleries. The frames were practically touching and all it took was a single bump to one of them and all the others would be sent swaying perilously from side to side. The selection committee had decided that quantity was at least as important as quality.

The curators, glancing anxiously at Royal, nervously picked up a large canvas showing two nymphs in their birthday suits, painted by Julius LeBlanc Stewart. The two women were smiling as they emerged from some shady undergrowth, as if they'd just done something naughty in there, or perhaps gone for a pee, and they lacked the usual elegance of ancient models: they actually looked like women, with their round hips and attractive busts. A ray of golden sunlight was like a hand cupped around a pink-budded breast. The other nymph, in response to the sun's caress of her colleague, was laughing as she held one of her breasts in her own hand, her fingernails digging lightly into the flesh. She was turned to her friend and a strand of her hair fell down over her eyes, half-concealing her expression, but you could tell that she was biting her lower lip. Stewart had entitled his painting "The Nymphs of Nysa" after those second-rate divinities who had elevated Dionysus, the god of winemaking, vegetation (including, presumably, shady undergrowth with patches of nice soft moss) and excess.

Royal declared to his little court – loud enough that the man hanging the canvas could hear – that Mr Stewart's talent was being employed in the dubious commemoration of models who were frankly ugly. The painting was immediately relegated to the dimmest part of the room. Stewart was exactly the sort of

American artist likely to provoke the ire of Cortissoz, a man of modest origins who had become a guardian of the traditionalist art of the powerful: Julius LeBlanc Stewart was the son of a billionaire, who lived in Paris and gave classical titles to his nudes so that he could enjoy the pleasures of painting models recruited from local whorehouses.

Next was a work by Joseph DeCamp, a more chaste nude called "Woman Drying Her Hair". Viewed from behind, she lifted up her long hair with one arm, creating a brown wave that poured from the nape of her neck and mirrored the line of her back down to a single exposed buttock. The roundness of that lone buttock made Aileen want to pull the sheet away to reveal its hidden partner.

"A beautiful picture of a feminine gesture," breathed Royal. "But it lacks naturalness and is too obviously posed. A mistake that DeCamp, with his experience, ought to have been able to avoid."

Royal was quite clearly wrong. DeCamp had not intended to paint the innocent, natural gesture of a woman who believes she is alone, drying her hair after taking a bath, blithely unaware of her uncovered buttock. He'd painted a woman who knew she was being watched. It wasn't a private scene, contemplated by art enthusiasts as through a keyhole. DeCamp's painting was at once an invitation and – this was legible in the way the model was turning her back on the viewer – a declaration of contempt for the hypocrisy of "specialists" dressing their sexual arousal in the dry vocabulary of criticism. The canvas was affirmation that, in the game of desire, women hold all the aces. But to Royal Cortissoz, this was inconceivable, therefore he was blind to it. All the same, this nude was, to him, obviously preferable to the carnal crudeness of Stewart's nymphs. To satisfy M. Cortissoz, the curators found a better place for DeCamp's oil painting.

Next came some relief. A small canvas by Charles Courtney Curran, "The Peris", a charming sketch of five tiny fairies, one of them naked, the others in long transparent dresses, playing in a grove of white roses, the flowers as large as their heads. These little angels – fallen and then redeemed – looked a little bored as they sniffed the flowers, intoxicated by their scent, each fairy as languid as the petals around her. Presumably they were waiting for the appearance of a manly monarch or an art critic to rouse them from their torpor. They numbed the senses the same way that a feather pillow invites sleep. Royal smiled when he saw this painting, which elevated the tone of the day. No doubt these perfect little women were entirely the products of Curran's imagination; he, at least, hadn't found his models in a brothel. And if his painting had been inspired by real women, they must have been his mother and sisters. It was possible to contemplate these allegories of femininity without feeling any troubling emotion, attributing to them the ideal qualities that might be expected of the fairer sex: discretion, fertility and grace.

Royal Cortissoz smoothed his moustache as Curran's small canvas was given a prominent place in the arrangement of paintings, now complete, in Room D of the Grand Palais. As on the walls of other nations, portraits of aristocratic wives rubbed shoulders with naked whores paid three sous to bring vicarious pleasure to art critics and faithful husbands. Aileen wondered if Marguerite Durand and the journalists at *La Fronde*, fighters for the feminist cause, would have something to say about all this.

Should they ban female nudes or make it fashionable for queens and ministers' wives to strip off for their portraits? What effect would these paintings have on bourgeois men visiting the exhibitions on their spouses' arms? Did the women have two discrete kinds of understanding, one for looking at nudes and the other for judging the portrait of Mme So-and-So in her salon? Would they recognise themselves in any of these works?

Aileen went to see Stewart's "The Nymphs of Nysa" again and found herself imagining Marguerite Durand emerging naked from some undergrowth, brandishing a copy of *La Fronde* in one hand and playfully cupping a breast in the other. Cortissoz approached her. He looked like he had a bad taste in his mouth and a stick up his back.

"The selection committee is sometimes influenced by factors other than the quality of the work."

He was talking about Stewart's wealth.

"What do you think of this painting?"

Aileen smiled at the nymphs.

"I grew up surrounded by cows, I like paintings of women. But you live surrounded by women, don't you, Royal?"

The critic, blushing, recoiled as if the creatures on the canvas and his colleague had some contagious disease.

"I sent a telegram to Mr Reid yesterday, informing him that I had no need of your assistance. He will contact you directly, but you may as well concentrate on writing articles about social issues. That's your specialism, isn't it?"

"I'll leave you to your cattle. If anything happens outside the Grand Palais – a revolt or a war, for example – I'll try to let you know."

Before leaving the American section, Aileen found out Julius LeBlanc Stewart's address in Paris.

An heir to his father's sugar cane plantations in Cuba, Stewart lived in an apartment building in the sixteenth arrondissement, on rue Copernic, and he'd had his studio built in the inner courtyard: a long, high-ceilinged rectangle with a glass roof, the underside draped with billowing white sheets that diffused the daylight uniformly about the room. The windows were blocked by thick curtains and only one of them was open, giving a view of some leafy treetops. It looked like the greenhouse of a botanical garden, nestled between six-storey buildings. The sounds of the city were muffled and the artist, in this vast, barely furnished space, seemed perfectly alone with his materials and his blocked-out canvases. Julius LeBlanc Stewart was a tall, solid-looking man who seemed to have a sort of natural physical strength despite never having worked with his hands or done any outdoor activity at all. He looked like the descendant not of landowners but of coalminers.

When he learned that an American journalist wanted to see him, he received Aileen without hesitation; a servant guided her through the ground floor of the apartment, then along the gravel path that led to his studio. Stewart the millionaire was not generally impressed by journalists, but he seemed delighted when he saw this redheaded woman whose age he couldn't guess, with her non-childbearing hips.

There were several nudes on the walls, along with scenes of bourgeois life: some smartly dressed couples eating lunch on a lawn; two women and an enormous white dog in a motor car; a baptism; a group of men and women on the deck of a yacht in full sail. Next to the yacht was a picture of two nymphs – you could tell that was what they were from the spears in their hands – which reminded Aileen of the ones in the Grand Palais, with their rounded buttocks and firm thighs; they were laughing as they walked through a small clearing, holding the leashes of two white, muscular, dangerous-looking dogs that were dragging the women forward. Aileen wondered if Stewart mentally undressed every woman he met and how many of them, imagining themselves stripped before him, were tempted or horrified.

"I'm lucky enough to be friends with James Gordon Bennett, owner of the *New York Herald*. I'm sure he'd be happy to meet you, Mrs Bowman. None of his journalists are as pretty as you."

Stewart was not an attractive man, but the naturalness with which he greeted her, surrounded by these powerfully erotic images, had an uncomfortable sensual effect on Aileen. His austere beard and suit were typical of men of his era and class. The feelings that Aileen had experienced in front of "The Nymphs of Nysa" were not reproduced in his presence.

"My employer, Mr Reid, believes that your friend Bennett is a purveyor of bad news and misinformation."

He smiled and pointed at the painting of the boat.

"That's his yacht, the *Namouna*. Maybe you recognise the woman reclining on the deck chair?"

Aileen stepped closer.

"It looks like Lillie Langtry."

"That's exactly who it is."

She moved on to the next canvas, the scene of the baptism, in a private chapel with large bay windows; in the foreground were two women lying languidly on loveseats, in positions similar to that of Lillie Langtry on the yacht. The actress had looked somewhat ill on the boat, but Aileen had put that down to seasickness. However, the two women at the baptism seemed ill too. The contrast with the healthiness of the nymphs surrounded by nature was quite striking. The bourgeois women appeared pale and weak on their sickbeds, the world arranged silently around them, as if in mourning.

"I saw Mrs Langtry on the stage, two years ago in New York. A vain woman. You made her look younger than she is."

"You make a strange society journalist, Mrs Bowman. Perhaps your employer, who seems to know Mr Bennett very well, should be more concerned about his envoy's work in Paris."

He was increasingly amused by her, and Aileen found herself interested in this aristocrat with a peasant's body, who sought among the whores of Paris the good health that the women of his own world had lost.

"*Miss* Bowman. And I do not write about society or about fashion. I've just come from the Grand Palais where Royal Cortissoz kindly dismissed me from his service. I'm here for the entire duration of the Exposition and I plan to write about social issues. I saw one of your paintings at the American section and I wanted to meet you. My mother once told me that if I was ever in a strange city and feeling lost, I should knock at a writer's door. Do you think her dictum could apply to painters too?"

"You don't seem in the slightest bit lost to me."

"No."

"And I am certainly not a social issue. Your company is a thousand times more enjoyable than that of Cortissoz, but I would still like to know why you're here."

"I don't know yet."

He gestured to two armchairs, facing each other, on a rectangular oriental rug, like a miniature reproduction of the dimensions of the studio itself. Aileen smiled as she caressed the velvet armrests.

"Is this how you receive your models?"

"Sometimes."

"Why is it, do you think, that some women are offended by the idea of posing nude but find it perfectly acceptable to hang paintings of other nude women in their salons?"

He was not surprised by this question.

"I am often amused by that paradox: the houses of respectable people decorated with the bodies of prostitutes. But perhaps respectable women don't pose nude because they're not allowed to. Perhaps they'd jump at the chance if they could. What do you think?"

"Do you often see your critics in the brothels where you find your models?"

He burst out laughing and she could tell from his amused look that this was something that did occasionally happen. Aileen crossed her arms – her forearms pressed against her breasts, her fingers tucked into her hot, damp armpits – and peered into the painter's eyes, which looked very dark against the white background of the studio.

"Would you agree to paint a portrait of me, Mr Stewart?"

The amusement on his face gave way to curiosity.

"A nude?"

"Without any pointless mythological references. A portrait of Aileen Bowman, journalist and Nevada landowner."

This time, he methodically undressed her with his eyes, with a sensuality that eased her discomfort. Stewart painted nudes because he was afraid of all those sick-looking women lying on divans. He protected himself from them with prostitutes whom he transformed into ideal, desirable women, without fear of being judged by them or infected by their lowliness. Aileen Bowman was visibly in perfect health and had the very pale skin of his favourite models.

"If I agree, what will you do with the painting?"

"Nothing. I just want to pose without hiding my identity. You could exhibit the painting if you wanted. Do you think your work will endure, Mr Stewart? Will your paintings still be exhibited a hundred years from now?"

"What is it that interests you, Miss Bowman – posterity or eternal youth?"

"I just want to create a precedent. A landmark case, if you like."

"Do you have a particular setting in mind?"

"No. I didn't know when I came here that I was going to make this proposition."

"Well, Miss Bowman, I'd be honoured to accept."

Back in her room, Aileen found a dress on her bed, along with a corset and petticoats. The gift was accompanied by a note from *La Fronde*'s editor:

Please accept this dress, in celebration of your first column. I'm sure it will suit you perfectly. If you're free tomorrow, I would like to introduce you to Paris, because the entire city is wondering: who is this Alexandra Desmond?

Your friend,

Marguerite D.

Inside a second envelope, she found a document, signed and stamped by the Paris police. As Marguerite Durand had promised, the commissioner, Lépine, was granting Miss Aileen Bowman, American citizen and journalist, the exceptional right to wear her riding outfit in public. The authorisation, which could be renewed upon request, was valid until 7 October 1900.

Aileen heard the floorboard creaking in the room next door. She opened the little cupboard built into the dividing wall: between the wooden slats, behind the objects on the shelves, the light from that room filtered through. A shadow kept passing back and forth. She heard the rustle of clothes, then the squeak of bedsprings. The light went out.

6

A telegram from New York – whose staccato rhythms reproduced perfectly a dialogue with Whitelaw Reid – instructed Aileen on what subjects she should be writing about most urgently. But it was the part of the message that mentioned Royal Cortissoz that made her laugh:

> Heard R.C. unhappy. Concur. Problems to come? Paris in danger? To work!

The United States pavilion was at the very top of the list of articles her editor was demanding.

It was an architectural melange of the White House, the Library of Congress, and a millionaire's family vault; it was stuck between the enormous rectangle of the Austrian pavilion to the right and a taller, narrower building to the left, which belonged to Turkey. The architect, Charles Coolidge, whose success had not been built on understatement, had given it the full works. His aim, clearly, was to provide the highest possible number of pedestals for the stone eagles with their magnificent wingspan. There was also a forest of flagpoles, flying the Stars and Stripes, each desperately trying to overshadow the minaret next door. The entire street of nations was an exhibition of flags, horses and eagles. On a horse raising one hoof towards the Seine, a triumphant George Washington, sculpted from marble with the nobility of an ancient hero, saluted the Right Bank with one arm. Aileen walked through his shadow and stopped on the steps of the semi-circular porch, then twisted her neck to look up at the long fresco that would welcome the pavilion's visitors. The committee had chosen Robert Reid, known for his portraits of women in fields of flowers, to paint "America Unveiling Her Natural Strength": a semi-circular frieze about 25 feet long, full of feminine allegories with Renaissance ambitions, including a particularly voluptuous Agriculture, holding a scythe, breasts bared, who would certainly have been a popular figure among the farmers near Carson City. Aileen stood stock-still, incapable of taking another step.

She crossed the Pont de l'Alma back to the other side of the Seine and hurried towards the Champs-Elysées, where she sat on a bench at the back of a brasserie, ordered some beer and food, and took out her writing paper, her inkwell and her fountain pen. In two hours, she had finished a column for the *New York Tribune* describing the rushed preparations of the committee's members, the last touches of paint, the hanging of works in the Grand Palais, the importance of the American presence, the growing excitement all over Paris, the lights, the flags, and the harmonious entente of nations come together to celebrate peace and commerce.

She finished her meal and blinked, still submerged in the music of her sentences, the concentration required to choose the right words, so she didn't recognise the man standing in front of her table and speaking to her.

"Our friends in New York told us that your article went down very well and that they recognised my wife and myself from the description you made of the passengers. I'm glad to be able to thank you."

As he held out his hand, the bald man realised that the journalist was struggling to place him.

"From the *Touraine*!" he exclaimed. "We dined together on the first night of the crossing. Don't you remember? Eugene Stanford?"

"The *Touraine*?"

"Oh, I'm sorry, ma'am. You were writing and I'm disturbing you. I'll leave you in peace. I hope we bump into each other again sometime."

"Wait. Yes, of course, I remember you."

She looked behind the man, at the nearby tables.

"You work for Standard Oil, right? How's your wife?"

He looked intimidated but proud to have been recognised by a journalist, even if it was this strange woman.

"She's right here! Would you like to join us for a drink? I can see you're busy, but maybe you could spare a few minutes?"

She stuffed her writing paper, the ink still damp, into her bag and followed the Standard Oil man. His young wife stood up to greet her. The husband ordered a bottle of champagne and bombarded the journalist with questions. Had she visited the fabulous American pavilion? Had she had time to see the American section in the gallery of machines and the Industry pavilion? Did she know that there was a show about the Wild West – almost as spectacular as Mr Cody's – taking place in the Bois de Vincennes? Yes, Aileen knew that. The oil salesman was high on optimism again. Revolutionary inventions, he explained, would be presented at the inauguration and they would probably revive his business.

"Have you heard about M. Diesel's internal combustion engine? It has much greater power and capacity than a steam engine. It's comparable to an electric engine, but more compact and autonomous. And it needs oil to work! It's a revolution, Mrs Bowman, a revolution! I've heard talk of a European automobile capable of speeds up to sixty miles per hour. Can you imagine?"

The champagne foamed in their glasses and Aileen gave yes or no answers. Catching the wife's eye, she finally interrupted the man, who was red-faced with alcohol and enthusiasm.

"And what about you, Mrs Stanford? What have you visited?"

Her husband answered for her, pouring more champagne for Aileen, who was drinking quickly.

"The shops, Mrs Bowman, the shops!"

"Maybe your wife isn't as fascinated by machines as you are?"

"She's not even remotely interested in them!"

"Would the artworks in the Grand Palais be more to your taste? I could get you in, if you wanted."

He spoke for her again.

"Ah, what an excellent idea! Can you believe that my wife doesn't dare walk around Paris on her own? And I don't have time to look after her while I'm busy with meetings. Darling, please accept Mrs Bowman's offer – it'll keep you entertained and it'll finally give me some free time. What do you say?"

The young woman didn't have time to reply before the whole thing was agreed. Aileen suggested she could pick her up the next morning from their hotel. She left the brasserie before another bottle of champagne could be ordered and walked out into the dazzling sunlight.

La Fronde's reception room was in a state of agitation when she arrived. The newspaper's employees were helping the caterers to set the tables, and there were musical instruments on the stage.

Aileen picked up the corset and turned it in her hands in front of the dormer window, the daylight rendering the fabric transparent and revealing the boning beneath. She thought about those medical radiographies produced by X-ray machines, which were becoming more and more common in hospitals; those photographs of the body's interior that she couldn't help finding obscene in a way that no nude painting could ever be. She'd written an article on the technological and medical revolution of radiography, and after finishing her report she'd had persistent nightmares about transparent bodies, the horror of glimpsing strangers' organs as she walked down the street. Aileen pointed out in her article that there had been several cases of serious burns suffered by patients who had been exposed to X-rays for too long. Her editor had made her cut that part: baseless rumours, he'd argued, probably spread by rival businesses. She threw the corset on the floor. It was an instrument of torture, and women only submitted to it in the hope of pleasing men.

The dry Paris air and champagne had made her thirsty. She could feel her anger growing, accelerating the cycle of truncated arguments, her contempt for the female gender, so servile and submissive that Aileen was almost inclined to excuse the men who abused it. Those roast turkeys in their corsets, which had killed more than one of them . . . they got what they deserved.

Those bourgeois women who didn't care whether they had the right to go to university as long as their wardrobes were full; those brood mares who complained about the number of mouths to feed yet let themselves get pregnant without protest; the mass of those ordinary women, drowning in their daily chores, busy cooking and earning money, always grumbling but terrified by the idea of rebelling against their condition. Aileen's anger swelled to contain her hypocrisy. In men, anger triggers violence and masks helplessness, doubt and guilt – those shamefully feminine feelings. You don't approach a man when he's angry; you tremble before his ire, never daring to interrupt. Aileen had inherited her father's rages. When she lost her temper, it was Arthur's voice she heard inside her. She began to mutter through gritted teeth, railing at those nymphettes who rolled around in flowers, at Marguerite Durand and her evening gown, at the statue of La Parisienne, which men lit up whenever they liked, guarding the Exposition like a madam at the entrance of a brothel, at socialites who collected lovers like victories, at young girls who believed in marriage, at women who took beatings from their husbands before redistributing them to their kids like sweets. She took out her anger on the dress lying limp on the bed, which passively absorbed her punches, crumpling and entangling itself around her arms. She struggled against the fabric, kicking out at the bed until she hurt herself and suddenly stopped, realising the pointlessness of her violence.

Anger gave way to sadness then, another masquerade to hide her stupidity behind the shield of noble tragedy. When this happened to men, they would drown their sorrows in alcohol, deny and forget, go drinking with their brothers, who would advise them not to worry about it. But Aileen was past the age when she would negotiate fake peace treaties with herself, justifying violence and its end, the unjust and the just, reconciling everything but changing nothing. She had learned to quickly admit her hypocrisy so she could identify the feeling that had caused the explosion, the emotion beyond her control, the fuse of her rage. It was often the same fuse. Most people, after all, have only a few such triggers in their entire life.

It had started the day before with Julius Stewart, the painter of nudes who was afraid of women. Then, today, the allegorical women on the fresco at the American pavilion. The wife of the Standard Oil man, that beautiful idiot who knew nothing about men or women. The contradiction of Aileen's simultaneous desires for women and for men, the absence in one of what she loved in the other, the qualities of women that were so lacking in men, and her in the middle of it all, with her father's anger and her childless womb.

She tossed the dress onto the bed and was smoothing down her clothes when someone knocked at her door. A woman in her early forties, her hair tousled and curly, frowned as she spoke.

"I'm in the room next door. I heard noises . . . Are you okay?"

"Yes, I just tripped and fell. Thank you for your concern."

The woman observed Aileen's appearance. She herself was very elegant, apart from her hair. Her high cheekbones, her long mobile eyebrows, her unwrinkled forehead, even the lines around her eyes and mouth . . . they all accentuated the determination in her pale eyes. A beautiful woman, on the threshold of the changes wrought by age.

"You're the American journalist?"

"Yes, I work for the *New York Tribune*."

"And *La Fronde* too, Marguerite tells me. I didn't like your column about Paris. I'm a journalist too."

"My column wasn't supposed to be liked. Good evening, madame. Thank you again for your solicitude."

The woman simply ignored this dismissal. A true journalist, she didn't budge.

"Your article was literature, not information. I'm more interested in the methods used by your colleague at the *New York World*, Nellie Bly."

"You know what Nellie did when she got back from her world tour last winter? She became engaged to a millionaire older than her father."

The woman's laughter emphasised her cheekbones and made her hair shake.

"I'm Séverine. I write for *La Fronde* and other Parisian newspapers."

"I read some of your articles about the Dreyfus trial. My colleagues in Manhattan and I are aware of your work."

They shook hands.

"Will you be at Marguerite's party tonight?" the woman asked.

"I doubt it."

"That's a shame. I'd have enjoyed pursuing this discussion. If you come downstairs around ten, there won't be many people left. It's just some food and drink with a bit of music. I think everyone's going to some minister or ambassador's house afterwards. We could chat, and you wouldn't have to wear the dress that Marguerite had delivered to you."

*

Aileen stopped writing at eleven o'clock, late enough to prove that she had no interest in the party. She realised when she went downstairs that she'd probably waited too long. The orchestra had packed up and left, and the room was being cleaned. But in the library parlour she found Séverine, talking to a man who sat, glass in hand, listening to her, while the journalist's own drink stood untouched on a low table. She got to her feet and invited Aileen to join them. The man, who was in his fifties, with a soft face and direct gaze, stood up too, unsteadily, either because he'd had too much to drink or because he was still stunned by Séverine's rhetoric. The journalist introduced him.

"M. René Viviani, lawyer and socialist deputy. M. Viviani is working with a few of his colleagues on a new law that will allow women to take the Bar exam."

"An exam for a bar? What do you mean?"

"Sorry, your French is so good that I forgot you were American . . ."

The deputy interrupted Séverine: "We want all women to have the right to become lawyers, just as they can now become doctors."

"And when we save men from diseases and the guillotine, perhaps they'll grant us the right to vote for them," Séverine added dryly.

Viviani gave an embarrassed smile. The French journalist glared at him and started speaking again before he had time to respond and before Aileen had time to sit down.

"But many men are still resistant to that idea, even among so-called progressives. And that's not even mentioning the conservatives and all those old men terrified by their wives' intelligence."

Viviani remained silent in the face of this approaching storm. Séverine brandished a newspaper, and now Aileen felt certain that it was her fury, and not the wine, that was making the politician stagger.

"Take the great 'poet of the humble' – your friend François Coppée, M. Viviani – and this column that he wrote for *Le Figaro . . .*"

She raised her voice as she read from the newspaper:

"To quote your friend, M. Viviani: 'the female lawyer, already a monstrous figure in the emotional and personal realms – how do you declare your love for a lady who will reply with a defence speech? – the female lawyer, a forerunner of that most dangerous beast, the female voter, is a circus freak, a fairground attraction, and should not be allowed anywhere near a courtroom'."

Viviani did his best to meet Séverine's gaze.

"François exaggerates for effect. Those lines are just cheap jibes. He's playing to the gallery. He doesn't believe half of what he writes."

"Even half of that would be overwhelming proof of his stupidity."

"The law will pass, Séverine. Nobody can stop it now. Our cause has sufficient backing."

"*Our* cause?"

"Let's leave it there for tonight, please. It was an enjoyable evening, but I have a long day tomorrow."

He shook the French journalist's hand and she let him keep the remnants of his dignity. Then he turned to the American woman as if to an ally.

"I hope we will have another opportunity to talk, madame. In fact, now I think about it, would you like to accompany the presidential procession at the inauguration the day after tomorrow?"

"Thank you, M. Viviani, but my newspaper has already arranged that."

"In that case, I will leave you. If you need anything, let me know through our mutual friends Séverine and Marguerite."

After seeing her adversary leave with his tail between his legs, Séverine sat down and drank a mouthful of champagne. A young waiter brought a glass and poured some for Aileen, who sat in the deputy's vacated chair and felt momentarily repulsed by the warmth left behind by his buttocks.

"You were pretty rough on him."

"Viviani is an honest politician, one of the most supportive of women's causes, but he sometimes lacks the courage to shake up his own camp, and they're often as pitted against us as men on the Right."

She took a long swig from her glass, then a deep breath. Aileen listened in amusement to the well-rehearsed but still passionate tirade that followed.

"Nothing exasperates me more than men who ask women to be patient a little longer before they become fully fledged citizens, when they have been in power for three thousand years! Men who can't read or write, can't tell left from right unless the army put hay in one boot and straw in the other to help them remember . . . those men have the vote! Tramps who never sober up, who dissolve their few remaining brain cells in alcohol every day . . . they have the vote too. Lazy men who let their wives do all the work . . . pimps who live off their daughters . . . all of them have the vote. Senile old men? Sure, let them vote. Murderers? Absolutely – why not? But when it comes to women, who are considered inferior to all these men, the Republic grants them only one right: let them pay tax. Yes, we have to pay income tax on the salaries that our husbands can legally bank in their accounts! Do men own the fruit of women's labours in your country too?"

"The condition of women in the United States isn't much better, but there are maybe a few more notable exceptions – more Nellie Bys and Séverines, if you like. The most committed activists often belong to temperance leagues, which fight for the protection of women against their husbands' excesses, whether related to alcoholism or gambling. But they also fight for religious, Puritan principles. Essentially, they're not opposed to women's domestic role; they just want us to be able to perform our duties without seeing our housekeeping budget pissed away in the gutter."

"Marguerite told me you grew up on a ranch. Is that true?"

Aileen wondered what Séverine, the feminist journalist, would think if she told her about the nights she'd spent in New York in the beds of other women. About the risks she took to find her female lovers. About all those men and women who dragged people like her through the streets by their hair to punish and humiliate them. She wondered if Séverine, and her well-dressed friend Marguerite Durand, would still let her sleep under the roof of *La Fronde* if they knew the truth. And she wondered what was stopping her from telling them.

"When my parents died, I inherited more than twelve thousand acres of land and a large house by Lake Tahoe, with thirty employees, hundreds of horses, and cattle in even greater numbers. My father always hated being a landowner. He was convinced that, while it gave him comfort and safety, it also took away his freedom. My mother told me before she died that I should rid myself of all of it. I decided to leave the running of the family business to an uncle. I still own a lot, but I'm unwilling to fight for my right to have as much as the others. Because the others only ever give you what is yours if they're sure that you're one of them. If the differences between them and you are swept away. Men will only give women the vote when they're sure that women will vote the same way they do. I have no desire to join the ranks of American or French women who want to be men's equals. No men or women are going to decide who I am or if I'm being that person in the right way. My parents taught me very bad manners on our ranch."

Aileen raised the champagne to her lips and the rounded edge of the glass took the place of the polite smile that she no longer felt like giving. When she put the glass down, Séverine noticed the tension in her expression and changed the subject.

"So you said you know Nellie Bly? You must have read her work on women's asylums . . . What did you think?"

Wrenched from her memories of the Fitzpatrick Ranch, it took Aileen a few moments to sort out her thoughts in French and in English.

"I made fun of Nellie before, but I have to admit it was incredibly brave of her to get admitted to an asylum by pretending to be crazy."

"Did her articles have any effect?"

"They made her famous. Their publication led to a federal inquiry, a major increase in the budget allotted to psychiatric hospitals and some reforms in the ways that doctors made their diagnoses."

Séverine turned her glass around in her fingers, without drinking. Clearly, the conversation about Nellie Bly was a diversion and she wanted to talk about something else.

"What do you want to know, Séverine?"

The French journalist didn't hesitate for long.

"Your article on Paris bothers me. You see, I'm the kind of person who needs to categorise everyone I encounter. I'm Marxist, libertarian, anti-parliamentarian, and feminist – a long list of labels, all of them open to discussion, obviously – but I need to see the colours hoisted above the camp before I decide what strategy to employ. Did you come to Paris to drink on café terraces and sample the zeitgeist, Miss Bowman, or to use your words to advance the cause of people oppressed by wealth and power?"

Séverine's unrelenting seriousness and the hints of intolerance in her tone made Aileen want to get up and leave. She signalled to the young waiter, who was standing close by, attending to the wishes of the party's last guests. He poured her more champagne and she watched his long, clean hands as they gripped the bottle.

"I didn't come here with any set plans. I'd never set foot in Paris or even France before. My article was just the beginning; a summary of my first impressions. But I'm also interested in the fate of the people who built this Exposition, if that reassures you a little. Not only in the ministers and the powers-that-be. I'm sorry I don't fit into any of your little pigeonholes, but the bad manners I learned in Nevada also lead me to believe that there's no wrong or right kind of writing. I believe all forms and genres can be bent and blended, and that they can all contain what we need to discover. Not just information, but something deeper. The truth, if that's what you want to call it, when it really touches us. We can find it just as easily in a newspaper article as in an autobiography or a biography or a sketch or a novel. It's just as real in a novel as it is in a fable, perhaps as real as it is in our dreams. When the truth is a guide and not an order, knowledge an asset and not an obligation, they can take any form that we want them to."

The Frenchwoman pursed her lips. She wasn't prepared to discuss this, and her refusal spoiled her beauty. She was also not at all amused by the American woman's lingering looks at the waiter, who was yawning in his corner.

"If you want to write reports on the reality of life in Paris, Miss Bowman, I can put you in touch with some useful people."

Séverine stood up, stiffened by her unbending principles and the first signs of arthritis. This woman wrote for six or seven different newspapers whose political range – for paradoxical reasons that only she could justify – ran from the most red-blooded socialism to the most rabid nationalism.

"I have work to do and I've spent too long at this party. Please excuse me. Good night, Miss Bowman."

Aileen didn't have time to get to her feet and politely accompany the departing Frenchwoman. The waiter came over without being asked and refilled her glass. She drained it quickly. She was always so harsh on submissive women and slaves to fashion, yet when she met an intelligent, independent, talented, combative woman, with an intellect worthy of her mother, she immediately made an enemy of her.

The last to arrive and the last to leave, Aileen explained to the blushing waiter how he could find her room on the top floor once his shift was over.

An hour later, lying on her bed, she listened to the young man's quiet footsteps on the landing, heard him stop in front of her door, imagined him holding his breath as he worked up the nerve, then heard the three little knocks. She didn't move, letting him knock again, louder this time, and started laughing when Séverine, in the next room, got out of bed to open the door. She wished she could have seen the Frenchwoman's face as she insulted the poor, embarrassed waiter, who ran downstairs as fast as he could.

7

The Stanfords had rented an apartment on the Champs-Elysées, in the ultra-modern Elysée Palace so beloved of American visitors. The hotel lobby, like everything else on this day before the inauguration, was in chaos. Bellboys, backs slumped like workhorses, pushed trolleys piled high with luggage, the wheels getting caught in the rugs and the employees' shoes skidding on the floorboards. The reception desk was under siege from angry guests demanding the rooms they'd reserved months before and which still weren't ready. Cab drivers came inside, trying to find their passengers, shouting out English names rendered almost unrecognisable by their accents. Some of the guests were offended, some too timid to protest, while others were already regretting having come all this way. Some wore frayed clothes and matching expressions, others were arrayed in all their finery.

Aileen waited her turn, observing the merry-go-round of suitcases and hats, before asking the receptionist to inform Mrs Stanford that she was here. Not long after that, the young woman appeared between the brass doors of the lift, in a pale dress, and cut a swathe through the crowd of curious men. Not quite the shrinking violet Aileen had imagined. Her cheeks were a little red, but she had dressed to impress and she was clearly enjoying the effect she'd produced. She greeted Miss Bowman with a low curtsey. In contrast to her behaviour on board the liner and at the brasserie, she did not seem embarrassed to be seen with the female journalist in her infamous trousers, about whom there were so many rumours in New York that some were bound to be true.

"Please call me Aileen. And tell me your name."

"Mary."

"Let's get out of here – it's too loud for a conversation!"

Mary Stanford's corset was so tight around her waist that each time she breathed her chest swelled for a long time.

"Do you think we'll be able to get into the Grand Palais, with all these crowds?"

Aileen smiled.

"You know what, Mary? I think you're right. We wouldn't get in and the whole visit would be a waste of time. I have a more amusing idea."

"Amusing?"

"Follow me."

"Where are we going?"

"To a place where there's no chance of bumping into your husband."

They walked for ten minutes from rue Galilée to rue Copernic. When they reached Julius LeBlanc Stewart's house, a servant led them through the inner courtyard to the studio.

Young Mary found it especially hard to breathe when she saw the great artist – dressed in shirtsleeves in the sun-baked glasshouse – working on a canvas. A naked woman, standing on a small stage, was leaning on a broom that, in the painting, would be transformed into a spear held by a voluptuous warrior nymph.

"Miss Bowman, what a pleasant surprise!"

As he walked towards the two women, Julius mentally undressed the deeply blushing Mary Stanford, who – suffocating in her corset – suddenly fainted. He rushed over and caught her in his arms before she could collapse on the carpet. When Mary awoke, the prostitute dressed as a goddess had a shawl tied under her arms and was gently patting her cheek while holding smelling salts under her nose.

"I always keep them on me in heat like this. The girls drop like flies where I work. I undid your corset – that thing'll kill you, my lady! Oh . . . you're not pregnant, are you?"

Mary Stanford replied in English. The kneeling woman didn't understand her, but she wasn't discouraged and continued speaking, articulating her words more slowly and clearly than before: "If you've got a bun in the oven, you mustn't squish it like that! The poor little thing'll come out with a flat head!"

Julius came to the young American woman's rescue.

"All right, Charlotte, that's enough. She doesn't understand. Miss Bowman, could you . . . ask Mrs Stanford?"

Aileen, a little disappointed by this beautiful woman who had proved herself too fragile to be amusing, posed the question in English. Mary Stanford, still very pale, swore that she wasn't pregnant. They brought her some water and a glass of cognac and she lay on a sofa, looking just like one of those sick bourgeois women in Stewart's paintings. The artist bade farewell to Charlotte: they'd overrun the allotted time and she had to get back to her day-job.

"Have you thought about your painting, Miss Bowman?"

Aileen had thrown her jacket over the back of a chair and poured herself some cognac. She leaned close to the canvas he was working on: the freshly daubed oil paint made Charlotte's curves shine and gave off a strong smell of thinner.

"Not really."

"Do you know Courbet?"

"By name and reputation."

"And the legend of 'L'Origine du Monde'? It's a painting that Courbet did in the late 1860s. The story is that it was a commission from an Ottoman diplomat, a sort of portrait of his mistress, which he ended up selling a few years later – along with the rest of his art collection – to pay off some gambling debts. After that, the painting passed from owner to owner – antique dealers, art enthusiasts, professional collectors – before disappearing. A few people in Paris swear they've seen it in this house or that."

"Why is it such a mystery? And what does this portrait of a mistress and the creation of the universe have to do with our painting?"

Julius Stewart laughed. Mary Stanford, looking a little more like herself, was listening closely now.

"'L'Origine du Monde' – 'The Origin of the World', Mrs Stanford – is not a religious painting. Some claim to have seen it, and I've been given a credible description. It's not about the creation of the universe, but the creation of human life. The painting shows a woman's belly, splayed thighs and vulva, on a bed with rumpled sheets. You can't see her face, only her genitalia, and the image is rendered with perfect realism."

Mary Stanford swallowed noisily as she drank a long swig of cognac. A smile played on Aileen's lips for an instant.

"Well, I don't want my head cut off, but I do find the idea

interesting. What might our own origin of the world look like, Mr Stewart?"

There was a silence then in the sunlit studio, as if all three of them were thinking for a moment about that future painting, Mary lying on the sofa, Aileen standing in front of the unfinished nymph, Julius in an armchair, one hand resting on the table covered with drinks. Aileen put down her glass among the pots of paintbrushes and crushed tubes.

"There's something else you should know. Or see, rather."

She unbuttoned her shirt and tossed it onto the chair over her jacket. She was wearing one of those new brassieres, which Mary Stanford would have happily exchanged for her corset. But it wasn't this scandalous accessory that fascinated the young woman and the painter. On the journalist's arms and shoulders, beneath the lacy underwear and on her white hips, were black geometric lines and shapes: triangles, rectangles, circles.

"You'll have to paint this too."

Aileen turned around; the dark lines continued on her back, reaching down to the waistline of her trousers.

Julius stood up and reached out with his hand.

"Where did . . . What is it?"

"I had an uncle who lived on an Indian reserve called Warm Springs, in Oregon. He'd been accepted by the tribes there and he'd become the tattoo artist for their warriors and women. These drawings are the Paiute symbols for the elements that make up the universe. It is, in a sense, their origin of the world, Mr Stewart."

The lines had been traced with a precision that immediately impressed the painter. The ink shapes supported the shapes of Aileen's body, making her look stronger and monstrously beautiful.

"Do you . . . Are they on your legs as well?"

"Only a few lines."

Mary Stanford blinked. The warm air of the studio had dried out her eyes. She turned away from and then back to the tattoos, which reminded her of a piece of pottery painted by savages that her husband had insisted on putting in their living room – as a decoration, he said.

"I should go back to the hotel."

Hesitantly, she left the room. The other two seemed unconcerned. In the doorway, she glimpsed Aileen Bowman dropping her trousers to her ankles, her diaphanous skin in the white studio, her blazing red hair: the she-devil of the *New York Tribune*, with those terrifying, fascinating ink lines on her body, even under her knickers, which she slid down her muscular thighs, revealing her pubic hair, the same colour as the hair on her head.

Mary rushed back to the Elysée Palace. In her room she took off her dress, her corset, her petticoats, and lay naked on the bed, massaging the red marks left on her belly, her breasts and her ribs. When she'd got her breath back, she kicked away the sheets, spread her lightly trembling knees, and imagined that there was an artist in the room, his eyes flickering from her genitals to the canvas he was working on. Hearing footsteps in the corridor, she felt suddenly afraid that her husband would walk in on her, so she ran to the bathroom to rinse the sweat from her skin.

Refreshed, in a dressing gown, she wrote a few words on a sheet of monogrammed hotel writing paper. Then she called the reception desk and asked a courier to take a message to the *La Fronde* newspaper.

After quickly putting on a long coat and a hat, Julius Stewart left his apartment in the sixteenth arrondissement, his dark figure accompanied by another smaller figure, dressed in a man's cape, a wide-brimmed, floppy hat obscuring the person's forehead. The two figures skimmed the stone walls as they turned on street corners, they hurried between streetlamps, quick and discreet in the insomniac city. They seemed to be advancing against the tide, with a sort of cynical drunkenness, shoulders twitching as if they were laughing mockingly at the great whore of kings and tyrants dolling herself up for the Exposition.

Julius and Aileen had drunk cognac and absinthe, that liquorice-flavoured liquor into which you dipped sugar cubes before setting fire to them and melting them in the glass. It was a sickening, neon-coloured drink, which Julius called the "green fairy"; it lay heavy in your mouth but it made your feet and thoughts lighter than air. They crossed the cobbled roads, laughing as they ran between hansom cabs, the great artist holding the hand of the cross-dressing woman. She let him drag her along, paying no attention to crossroads or the names of the streets, until they reached a black-painted door, lit by a small lantern in its lintel. Julius knocked three times and a cylinder of light shone through the spyhole, as if from a film projector, before the door opened.

The doorman greeted the painter by name; Julius presented his "*ami américain*" who was staying in Paris for the Exposition, and Aileen stifled her laughter at being designated – and accepted as – a man. They walked through a corridor, the walls filled with poor-quality nudes that reminded her of the American section in the Grand Palais, until they reached a small hallway with two spiral staircases, both covered in thick, flower-patterned carpets. Everything was flower-patterned here, in fact: rugs, lampshades, furniture, the curtains separating this hallway from a room echoing with voices, clinking glasses and piano music; even the dress of the cloakroom girl was printed with enormous roses, while her extravagant hairstyle was held in place with the aid of combs sculpted from ivory in the shapes of stems and petals. Her make-up dazzled like a flowerbed of thoughts and worries, but her teeth betrayed more difficult times.

"Mr Stewart, we hardly ever see you these days! Charlotte spends more time posing for you than you spend here!"

She cooed compliments at him and told him about some of her new recruits, who'd come for the Exposition and would be certain to please him. From the corner of her eye, without ever losing her smile, she observed the young man accompanying Stewart, who hid his face between a silk scarf and the brim of his hat.

"And I'm sure your friend will find a companion to his taste. Monsieur . . .?"

The elegant Julius laughed bawdily, linked arms with Aileen and led her through the curtains.

Grey smoke from cigars and pipes filled the air. Grey beards were tugged by bare-shouldered girls, their skirts and petticoats pulled up to their silky knees.

A curvy woman curtsied to the painter and, without a word, slipped through the customers towards the back of the room, beckoning the newcomers to follow her. Men leaning on the bar or sunk deep in armchairs, their eyes heavy with wine and champagne, noted Julius' presence with a raised eyebrow here, a half-smile there, and he responded with discreet signs of complicity. Among them there must have been art critics who admired or loathed Stewart's work, men in business with the Stewart family, city officials and art collectors: hard-working breadwinners deservedly granting themselves a little relaxation. Friends did not greet each other in loud voices; acquaintances ignored each other; rivals cohabited in hypocritical diplomacy: even between enemies, there was a male solidarity that would never betray the secret of their presence here. Each of these old men with their wavering erections was with a girl, a girl who – despite all the other men surrounding her – had eyes only for her man, who laughed only at his jokes. The bureaucrats with their unbuttoned suits glanced furtively at the little man who'd accompanied Stewart, the richest of all the establishment's customers. The fleshy hostess led them to a purple velvet alcove in a discreet corner, from where they had a clear view of the rest of the room. For their comfort, a private door in the wall of this carpeted bastion led to some upstairs rooms. Aileen sat on the banquette, her face concealed behind a curtain with a golden fringe. Facing her, Julius looked relaxed, the perfect companion for her first visit to a brothel.

As aboard the *Touraine*, Aileen began mentally undressing the guests, but this time it was the men whom she stripped in her mind. Champagne glass and cigar in hand, swaggering like emperors, they stood naked in front of the girls, who laughed at them. She imagined their white bodies back to back, the flesh slumping without the support of their clothing, their penises shrinking inwards like snails, their old scrotums sagging halfway down their legs; she imagined them in all shapes and sizes, swaying in time with their gesticulations, their voices booming to signal to each other the presence of those great wild beasts. What a fine sight they would have made if they'd really paraded around with their testicles in the air! The image reminded Aileen, with a sort of perfect reversal, of those paintings of dogs playing cards in tailored suits. She finally burst out laughing after holding in her hilarity ever since their arrival, her inhibitions swept away by a long rush of absinthe euphoria. A bucket of champagne had been brought to their nook and the glasses filled. She drank some to dampen the effect of the green fairy, which changed simple thoughts into wild hallucinations. She caught Julius watching her.

"Are you satisfied, *mon ami*? You were so keen to come here. Are you taking notes for an article? I'm afraid you will find nothing else to do in this place. It's not the kind of establishment that offers boys as well as girls. Those places are more clandestine and my reputation would suffer too much if I went with you."

Aileen was no longer listening; she was looking at a framed photograph above her, and she noticed that there were three others on the wall of their alcove. The pictures had a softer tint than the usual black and white of photographs. They must have been developed with a different chemical formula because they were all an attractive sea-blue colour. The subjects, however . . . Aileen stood up, forgetting to conceal herself under her hat. Julius leaned towards her, pouring more champagne into her glass as he murmured: "My friend, I fear that we can see a little too much of your face."

Aileen, suffocating with heat under her clothes and scarf, slumped back down on the bench and asked where those photographs were from.

"They're cyanotypes by Jeandel, an unsuccessful painter, scorned by the critics. He worked from photographs taken in his studio. In the end, he gave up painting and just sold his photographs to places like this one or to curious collectors. His reputation suffered and he was driven from the capital. Nobody knows where he is now. As for the addresses of the places where you can . . . do that . . . well, I don't know them myself . . . if you were interested."

Above Julius, in a small frame like a window overlooking a pale blue dawn sky, a woman was lying on her side, turned towards the viewer, on a raised wooden stage, in front of a coarse linen sheet nailed to the wall. She was naked, her head thrown back and her eyes pointing upwards. Her legs were tied up in ropes, from her ankles to her knees. Her arms were tied behind her back, and another rope – whose fibrous hemp reminded Aileen of her horsehair glove – was digging into the flesh of her breasts. Her vulva was squeezed between her thighs like a gagged mouth. She looked terrified, at the mercy of everyone who was watching her, as if begging to be released. But not from the ropes. To be released by being touched.

In the next image, a wooden gantry stood on the same stage. Another naked woman, with large, firm breasts, was hung with her arms behind her back, a horizontal beam underneath them, her knees bent and her ankles tied behind her to her wrists. She was lifting her head as far as she could to face the photographer, the spectator, Aileen. She looked like a saint, or a martyr, kneeling on a prayer bench, but twenty inches off the ground, in violation of Newton's laws, held in the air by some mystical force, pain and pleasure.

The third cyanotype, which had an identical setting and colours, showed the same woman, this time tied on her back to a plank angled like a guillotine blade, arms painfully twisted underneath her, her spine forced into an arch, breasts pointing in the air. The ropes were tied tightly around her legs, her belly and her neck. A man in a long cape, with a pointed hood like an executioner, was kneeling on the woman's ribcage; in one hand he held a funnel, in the other a jug, from which he was pouring into the metallic cone shoved down the woman's throat.

Aileen, mesmerised, the champagne glass shaking slightly in her hand, moved on to the next photograph. Two women were lying, one on top of the other, arms outstretched like Tantalus beneath the fruit tree, faces hooded, their legs, vulvas, bellies and breasts crushed together, their wrists and ankles bound. A blind embrace, like the symmetry of a body lying on a mirror.

Julius' voice came to her as if from the bottom of a well, above the hum of the brothel, which had been pushed into the distant background.

"Jeandel, though a very bad painter, discovered – or revealed – some powerful truths about what we are. Beings that desire and suffer, fragile and strong, on the verge of tears and radiant with happiness. He showed us truths about the sexes and their relationships, about that inner reality masked by our clothes and social conventions. I love the architecture of those tortured bodies, torn by the revelation of the true secret of confession: that we feel pain and pleasure only on earth, that we must admit our desires without asking for forgiveness."

He smiled at the journalist, before his face crumpled in a frown of sadness and disgust.

"It's not painting but modern photography that has captured those desires."

Alcohol and fatigue were overpowering the artist. Aileen slid towards him and took his large hand in hers. It was cold in this overheated place and – despite the risk of being caught – Julius accepted her caress. Aileen thought about the ropes in the photographs and the lines of her tattoos, about all the powers and needs that a body could contain, and how few of them we ever let out. About all the things that had to be forbidden to human beings to make them human. About Julius and his listless bourgeois women, into whose mouths he dreamed of shoving a funnel that might rejuvenate them, whose bodies he wished to pierce with spears so that he could see inside, as with X-rays, to discover what remained of their desires and freedoms. That was all Jeandel's cyanotypes told us, really: that the decadence so feared by the tamers of human nature – teachers, philosophers and politicians finding their pleasures at a brothel – was a desire to play with corrupting time, to convince it to become an ally.

"Don't let it get you down. I love your muses."

Julius accepted the compliment, even if he didn't want to believe it. Aileen squeezed his hand.

"You're here to enjoy yourself. Why don't you ask for Charlotte?"

"Yes, that's an idea. But I don't think I'm in the mood. Let's go home. Please."

She leaned closer and the brim of her hat brushed the artist's cheek.

"What are you doing?" he asked in a panic. "They're watching."

She held his now-warm hand and pressed herself more closely to him. Her absinthe breath whirled from her mouth into Julius' ear, into his nostrils, making him shiver.

"Ask for Charlotte. I'll go with you."

The billionaire Stewart and his mysterious friend disappeared through the secret door of the alcove.

8

La Fronde, 14 April 1900
A column by Mme Alexandra Desmond

THE VISITED CITY

It went everywhere, the procession of men with their rigid backs and stiff legs, in their black suits, in a long line behind President Loubet. No ordinary people. The anonymous citizens of Paris will have to wait until tomorrow to buy their ticket to visit the vast building site of the Exposition. The line of officials snaked between the piles of sand and wood covered with tarpaulins, the sledgehammers and chisels, the scaffolding abandoned for a few hours by the workers.

There were kings, archdukes, princes, ministers, captains of industry and a swarm of journalists, speaking a score of languages. My architects and my engineers were there, many men and very few women other than trophy wives. At the ends of the barricaded streets, crowds gathered in the hope of glimpsing something.

First they passed through the majestic entrance,

the effect of its painted colours dimmed by the absence of electric light in those thousands of bulbs. The banners flapped only at the tops of the domes; lower down, the breeze was too gentle to raise them from their lethargy, so they just hung there limply. But the men's formal suits shone in the light of the generous sun.

At the inauguration ball in the Petit Palais, it was art from France that was first on the itinerary, and – minds curious, feet still fresh – they took their time to admire it. Then they went to the Grand Palais, opposite, to devote more or less the same amount of time to the art of thirty other nations. There weren't enough visitors to look at all these artworks. The ambassadors tried to slow down when they stood before their own country's art, but then President Loubet and his ministers disappeared into another room and they had no choice but to follow. The glass roof of the Grand Palais, with its windows opened, was like a giant translucent whale spitting out a plume of hot air, and the procession emerged dizzy and sweating. From there, they went to the Pont Alexandre III, that technical marvel of marvels, which the Russian delegation had been invited to open. In a single 300-foot stride, the bridge steps over the river. Four golden statues guard it proudly: Art and Science on the Right Bank, Battle and War on the Left Bank, where hansom cabs and horse-drawn carriages await to carry the illustrious guests to the foreign powers' private pavilions. These constructions, dedicated to various companies and their works, are as lavish and extravagant as those of the States facing them across the river, on the street of nations: on one side, a political consecration; on the other, import and export. There, once again, the ambassadors, nudged by their industrialist friends, tried to slow down the procession before the pavilions that interested them, but all this did was create a traffic jam. The presence of kings and presidents was barely enough to halt the flow of insults from the mouths of frustrated cab drivers. The disgusted dignitaries, political and military leaders, descended from the blocked carriages, in the shadow of the Schneider Company's cannons. Perched on turrets a hundred feet above the ground, their metal domes painted bright red, the guns from the Creusot steelworks spun around 360 degrees, sweeping the rooftops, the country beyond, and the horizon of borders.

The procession came to a stop by the side of the two-mile-long moving walkway that goes up avenue de la Bourdonnais to the Champ de Mars and the Machines pavilion.

Amid a noise of gears, belts and connecting rods, the visitors passed between the giant dynamos with wheels the size of houses, mills that produce an invisible energy. The generators of

French, German, English and Russian electricity are moved by good old steam power, spurted forth by boilers that, every hour, gobble up 200 tons of coal and 40,000 gallons of water. The copper wires then carry the magical current to the attractions and the pumps for the enchanting, light bulb-strewn fountains in the Electricity pavilion. They are everywhere, those little glass teardrops, lifeless in sunlight, like a skin disease disfiguring the constructions of the Exposition.

After the excitement of the machines, the dignitaries and politicians crossed the Champ de Mars, where the greenery and aromatic refreshments made a pleasant change. There, a spectacle awaited them: another procession, organised for the pleasure of theirs. A celebration of Woman. On carts pulled by Negroes dressed in loincloths and animal skins, the white-winged Allegories of Family and Education were fanned by Caribbean savages waving palm leaves. The drums of five continents gave a beat to the parade. Everybody applauded very loudly, enjoying the respite offered by this break.

Then they passed between the legs of my tower, the bridal dress that Gustave built for me from riveted lace. The old gentlemen, necks stretching backwards, stared up, hoping for a glimpse of my garter and knickers, before crossing the Seine over the Pont d'Iena. Their feet ached as they climbed the Trocadéro hill and I lost them from sight in the back alleys of the plaster medinas that lead to the colonial village.

There, the masters of the world watched an oriental belly dance, some graceful dancers from Indochina, then some tattooed women from the mountains of North Africa; they listened to tambourines and the strange notes produced by stringed instruments made from goats' intestines; they inhaled the perfume of the Empire's teas and spices.

They didn't have time to stop at the giant, 60-foot telescope in the Optics pavilion, designed to make the moon look as though it is only 40 miles away. From a distance, they saw the big wheel that can carry 1,600 people in its carriages; they passed without slowing outside the reception hall with a capacity of 20,000 spectators, and the Swiss village with its fake rocks and rivers, and the rebuilt neighbourhood of my medieval childhood, and the great celestial globe where you can admire the movements of the stars in a blue-and-gold sphere 200 feet high. They didn't have time.

In the evening, the officials attended their nations' private parties, where they discussed their impressions, as well as the latest rumours and information about their political or commercial rivals.

I am illuminated again, and from my lofty perch I can admire the millions of kilowatts produced by the dynamos highlighting my lines and contours.

While they wait for tomorrow morning's public opening, the hordes of visitors who have already arrived have spread themselves throughout my quarters, taking over restaurants and hotels, eating, drinking, loving and fornicating, stealing, snoring and dreaming. Others have gone to the Bois de Vincennes to enjoy the warm evening. In the aerostat field, the lucky first-comers have been able to stand in the basket of a tethered balloon. Thousands of cubic feet of hot air, held close to the ground by a steel cable, rose 1,000 feet into the air, as high up as my birdcage. In the night and the cold air of altitude, the women pressing their noses into fur collars, the men wearing scarves round their necks, they shared – for a few moments – my own vision of myself. When they floated back down to earth, their eyes were shining.

That was where my night ended. I ignored the festivities in the centre and did not get home until dawn, with the swollen feet of someone who has danced too much and walked for miles and miles.

It had been Julius' idea: that nocturnal ascension in Vincennes. Up there, Paris was reduced to the proportions of a map, its streets dotted with electric lights.

Since their sexual games, inspired by Jeandel's cyanotypes, with the professional nymph Charlotte, they had become certain that they didn't really love each other. But Julius Stewart, in whom women inspired guilt and terror, was happy to have found, in Aileen, a partner for the release of his desires. For her part, she was glad to have a companion who did not try to make money or take power from the world, only to create paintings. She'd held his hand in the tethered balloon and had sensed him blushing, worried that someone would catch them in this breach of etiquette. The other passengers, busy staring out at the capital, or drinking a glass of Mercier champagne – whose logo was emblazoned on the side of the balloon – couldn't have cared less about the woman in trousers and the bourgeois painter holding hands.

Tying up bodies to free them. Like the balloon tethered to a winch. A symmetrical response to the social laws that chain up individual liberty to guarantee the liberty of the group. Those forbidden games were individualistic, selfish, but genuinely shared since they were impossible without others. No morals were sullied; that was a lie. They emerged from them feeling lightened, their fears of the others erased. But after their loud orgasms, after paying Charlotte for her participation, they became themselves once again.

In the basket of the tethered balloon, above a Paris swept by the Eiffel Tower's lighthouse, they had formed a more peaceful – and, they hoped, a more lasting – relationship. They held hands until their feet touched the ground.

For a few minutes they strolled around open-air cafés and bars, watching the dancers and listening to the musicians, then Julius wanted to go back to his studio to paint. They parted ways at the Porte de Vincennes. A cab took Aileen to *La Fronde*'s headquarters in the ninth arrondissement.

After writing her column and taking it down to the typesetters, she fell asleep listening to the women making the special edition that would, the next day, join the printed clamour of all the other newspapers hailing the opening of the greatest exhibition of human creations ever imagined.

In the morning, Aileen decided to give up Marguerite Durand's hospitality and find another lodging. Then she went back to the Bois de Vincennes.

It had become dangerous to wait any longer. Despite all the diversions, Joseph had never left her thoughts. She just kept pushing back the moment, exhausting herself in finding false excuses.

The automobile manufacturers had built hangars as long as stadiums. The machines, on their supple tyres made from rubber taken from the trees of the colonies, were surrounded by the smells of oil, grease and polished metal: copper, brass, chrome steel. France, as the leading producer of motor cars, was presenting models by thirty different manufacturers, using fuel or electric combustion. At the centre of the Exposition was the stunning vehicle made by Camille Jenatzy, the Belgian engineer who'd just beaten the land speed record in his Jamais Contente, an electric car that resembled a giant artillery shell. Jenatzy had become a global celebrity after smashing the 100 kmph barrier, a feat that some scientists had claimed was impossible: the human body could not bear such speeds, they said, and would disintegrate. He was now a hero and a god. The French engineers, Panhard, Renault, Peugeot and Berliet, discomfited on the eve of the Exhibition, boldly declared that they were working on prototypes that would soon beat Jenatzy's record.

The Michelin brothers, to encourage everyone to drive around on their tyres – which were, they said, unsurpassed for comfort and grip – had published a guide, cataloguing the addresses of the best restaurants in each region, which they would give away for free with every purchased bicycle or car tyre. Aileen leafed through it, wondering if, in the pages for Alsace, a restaurant might be recommended in the village of Thannenkirch.

She walked away from the kinetic feats and the dead, mineral odours of these machines of the future, affordable for now only by the world's wealthiest men. Other scents lured her, swelling her chest with a richer air: the smells of leather, animals, dung and straw, which transported her in a single leap to America, to the banks of Lake Tahoe, the stables, the ranch.

Several "Wild West shows" had followed in the footsteps of William Cody's, and – with Buffalo Bill absent from Paris – Pawnee Bill was the main attraction. Between two stakes hammered into the ground, a painted banner announced the grand-sounding Pawnee Bill's Historic Wild West Show, Indian Museum and Encampment. The troupe had set up camp on the periphery of the city, close to the Olympic stadium and the hangars full of automobiles and aeroplanes. For two francs, you could visit an authentic Sioux camp; for four francs, you could watch Mexican Joe's horse show, a reconstruction of an Indian war, Bill Pickett's steer-wrestling exploits, and May Lillie's demonstration of sharpshooting. The shows were to take place twice a day, six days a week, for four months.

When she reached the hut at the entrance, Aileen asked to meet Pawnee Bill. The little shack was covered in the stars of the American flag, but the man inside was French.

"I'll ask if Mr Gordon has time to see you. There are already a lot of people. Stay here."

Pawnee Bill – whose real name was Gordon William Lillie – was no pale imitator of Cody; in fact, they had once been partners, together putting on the greatest show ever known. Lillie was also a person of importance in the country, for other reasons. He'd been a leader of the Oklahoma Boomers movement, when some pioneers, wishing to settle on land belonging to the Creek and Seminole reserve, had been opposed by the American army. In the late 1880s, the government found in favour of the farmers. The Boomers took over the land, pushing the tribes even further away. Lillie, an American hero, had boasted of his country's greatness while taking up arms against his government and had been rewarded with a large portion of the conquered territory. There, he'd built his ranch, next to the town of Pawnee, and afterwards nobody had been able to work out which had given its name to which: the show to the town or the town to the show. Next, Lillie had invested in banking and the extraction of kerosene for oil lamps. While Buffalo Bill had frittered away his fortune on spectacular hunts, women and drinking, Pawnee Bill had proved himself a shrewd businessman, and he was here in Paris to celebrate with his peers the birth of a new century of money-making.

He posed for photographs in front of a Panhard & Levassor that he'd just bought himself. A dozen other journalists were already asking him questions, and – since her article on Buffalo Bill – Aileen knew that the *New York Tribune* wouldn't publish anything she wrote about Pawnee Bill. Not that it mattered. She hadn't come here for that. She headed towards the corrals and the horses, extras in the Indian Wars part of the show.

The animals, fresh from the hold of a transatlantic liner, had already eaten and trampled all the grass in their little patch of Parisian pastureland. Men brought them cartloads of French hay. On one side of the camp's main pathway were English saddle horses, belonging to the white men; on the other, painted mustangs. Aileen smiled when she saw the coloured patterns on their hair. The green shapes were prayers for the healing of sick horses or their owners. But white was the dominant colour – the colour of mourning and peace. For the tourists, the painted horses were merely decorative, but for the Indians they were weighed down with important meaning. Some of the symbols and colours, like the red and the black, were forbidden in the United States. They summoned spirits to the dance of the dead, a religious ceremony that on the reservations had been the occasion of a brief spiritual rebirth, a burst of solidarity and the emergence of some charismatic leaders. Fearing a wave of rebellion, Washington had banned it. The Indian extras in Pawnee Bill's Show were making money from this strange journey over the great sea to practise ceremonies that had become clandestine back home.

But it was not those forbidden colours and patterns that held Aileen's attention, but some others decorating the black coat of a beautiful stallion. One of those animals highly prized at the Fitzpatrick Ranch as studs. Against the dark background of the stallion's coat, lightning bolts of orange fire and downward-pointing hands, painted yellow, the colour of death, burst forth amid the green and white of the messages of peace.

Like Aileen, the Indians in the camp – and probably a few of the old pioneers, cowboys and bison hunters employed by Pawnee Bill's Show – knew what this really meant.

The downturned hands were the most prestigious symbols that warriors could use to protect their body and their horse. The ones reserved for the elite braves' missions, from which they had to return either victorious or dead. The word "symbol", the word "white" . . . these words were nowhere near the order imposed by an inverted hand. European art, however sacred it might appear, could never attain the degree of urgency and reality of this image. An inverted hand contained death. It *was* death. The black mustang, grazing on French grass, was a tool of destruction, a declaration of war without mercy. It was a poisonous plant in a pretty flowerbed, a loaded weapon in the hands of an actor on a theatre stage, the barrel aimed at the audience.

Aileen stood by the fence, blinking as she contemplated the stallion's muscles between the lightning bolts and the sun-coloured hands and the pale-violet geometric lines and forms. Designs that she knew well, in negative: pale on the mustang's black coat. She had the same, in black ink on her white skin. That animal belonged to Joseph Ferguson. On its flanks he had traced the same lines that Aunt Maria and Uncle Pete had tattooed on Aileen's body that summer when she'd gone to visit them.

She passed the closed stands of fairground attractions and sweet shops, painted in bright colours, the symbols of pleasure and buying. On the tepees in the Indian village, other paintings in black and green secretly communicated to visitors the same message of reparation and grief, lending the camp the atmosphere of a spring festival and moving Aileen to tears.

The first tepee she approached didn't even stink, a sign that the Indians living there were no longer themselves: they'd been forced to clean the camp for the comfort of visitors. In reality, the West stank. Not only the Indian camps. Cowboys, stagecoach drivers, mule drivers, hunters, men, women and children on farms . . . they all stank. They spent their lives in the same patched clothes, handed down from brothers to sisters to brothers. They washed once a week at most, washing their clothes at the same time. The Indians always had their hands in dead animal flesh, tanning hides, working the bones, tendons, guts; they smelled of the fish that they ate from their hands, the animal grease that they used to protect their skin and their horses' coats from the sun. The camps' refuse was cleared by dogs, ants and worms. In the Bois de Vincennes, the Indians swept the ground outside their tepees and defecated in holes in the ground.

Outside the tepee, Aileen greeted the Lakota woman who emerged from it, using the few words she knew. If Aileen heard her father's voice when she was angry and her mother's voice when she spoke French, it was Aunt Maria's voice that echoed in her head when she spoke Sioux.

The Indian woman didn't understand what the white woman wanted; she replied that she had nothing to sell, that the show was later that evening. Aileen shook her head; she wasn't here for the show, she was looking for the warrior with the black horse, the animal covered in yellow hands. The woman went back into her tepee and a man came out. He looked angry as he waved the white woman away. Aileen asked her question again, in English this time, hoping that the man would understand her but not the other Indians who had drawn close. The strategy seemed to work: the warrior looked proud as he replied, so as not to lose face, more anxious than he wanted to admit.

"It is important problem. The bastard warrior is crazy. Go

away from here, woman-man, it is dangerous. Or tell your white brothers to lock up the bastard. Not Indian police. White police." He lowered his voice, almost whispering as he went back into his tent: "On his tent are yellow hands also."

There were about forty tepees in the camp, in a triangle of forest between the velodrome, the large greenhouses for the agricultural exhibitions, and the hangars of the automobile clubs. She found Joseph's tent at the southernmost point of this triangle, away from the others at the edge of the woods.

From the branches of the nearby oaks hung amulets, wind harps and mobiles crafted from little whitened bones. Here, the refuse wasn't buried and the smell of Indian life wasn't camouflaged. A pan was heating on four stones, an odour of boiled chicken rising from it. The tent was covered with the same symbols as the black horse; the same ones she'd shown Julius in the studio on rue Copernic. But the canvas was also covered with more complex designs: objects and figures arranged around a railway that rose in a spiral towards the top of the tepee; a train, its wagons, its locomotive and its plume of black smoke. The cone of the tent, held in place by wooden poles, had become a fresco that followed the upward movements of the rails. Near the ground, some horses were painted standing on green grass, Indian families gathered, grazing cattle, scenes of dancing and hunting: a peaceful life around the edges of a large pale-blue lake. It was summer. Then, higher up the tepee, it was autumn; a season that separated people, an atmosphere of desolation, bare trees, a cannon, a battle, fallen bodies.

Aileen imagined Royal Cortissoz examining this naive, disturbing, powerfully evocative artwork: the cries of horror that the critic and the members of the selection committee would have emitted at the idea of exhibiting this canvas in the Grand Palais, with the other work of American artists. Even higher up the tent, at eye level, came winter. Mountains white with snow, their peaks sharp and menacing.

Aileen had no difficulty understanding the story behind Joseph's fresco. It was a tale about solitude, abandonment and lost time. She knew that lake and those mountains. She walked around the tent to read the rest of the story. A snowstorm turned grey and mingled with the smoke from the train. She stood a little closer. At the foot of the mountains, there was a tepee, its flaps open to offer a peek inside; in the circle of its base lay two bodies; simple figures sleeping pressed together, like two spoons in a drawer. The painter had used a dark blue to trace these two slender forms, a blue of hurt. Of frozen flesh. The snow, darkened by the soot from the locomotive, fell on these two dead beings and, all around them, yellow hands pointed at the earth. She felt suddenly dizzy.

One winter, when she was eleven or twelve, Aileen had gone to the Warm Springs reserve with her parents. Since that visit, the name of that frozen, deadly place had always made her grimace. They'd taken clothing, ammunition and food for Uncle Pete and Aunt Maria. Joseph had been a baby at the time, not yet able to walk. Some of the Indian families had already lost children and older relatives. Aileen remembered the bodies lying on the ground, outside the tepees, covered by blankets as stiff as marble, glued to the ground by ice. Pete Ferguson, the white man, and Maria, the South American Indian woman, had died like that, two years ago, both of them older than their years. Aileen often imagined them, nestled together inside their tepee, watching the last pieces of wood burn up in the hearth, the last embers dying, leaving them with only the heat from their bodies, shared until their last breaths, each one desperately trying to stay alive to keep the other warm. The cold had preserved them for days on end, sealing their Indian smells beneath the frozen furs. No one had been able to find Joseph to give him the news. For a long time, his whereabouts were unknown, the boy with the mixed blood and the disturbed mind. But he had seen them, his parents, lovers until the end, solidified by death. He had painted them.

Above the two little blue silhouettes, at the top of the tent, the train's smoke cloud covered everything, turning the whole world black. Only one white eye pierced this darkness, ending in two points like spread fingers, a triangle from which emerged, in a spiral movement, the poles of the tepee: the coal-grey plumage of a crow – spirit thief of light – its open eye and beak expelling the wooden poles. Or perhaps the poles, now become spears, were sinking into the crow's throat.

Raising her head, she looked around the tepee, seeking the presence of a watcher in the branches, behind the fleshy green leaves of spring.

"Joseph?"

She listened . . . and heard the distant sounds of fairground shows from the Bois de Vincennes, the yells of the crowd in the velodrome, the whinnying of the horses in Pawnee Bill's Show.

"Joseph?"

"Not stay there! Go now, woman-man!"

She jumped. The warrior who had talked to her before had come up behind her without her realising. He'd stopped a good distance from her, his body tensed, and he was waving frantically.

"Not stay there!"

Aileen moved between the charms and mobiles hanging from the branches, avoiding their touch. The Lakota warrior urged her to leave. She turned back to look at the tepee and its black spiral before leaving the camp. On a forest pathway, she stopped in front of the stand for a French département whose name she'd never heard before, run by men and women in traditional costumes. They were selling local products and, on a stage, some musicians were playing folk songs. France, too, was showing the world its traditions and history.

Aunt Maria always used to say that her son was like those stones split by cold or fire, one of those pebbles that appear intact but are actually cut in half, irredeemably cracked, that break as soon as you touch them. Two worlds in one, separated. "Too many worlds coexist in Joseph," said the Indian woman who had given birth to him. "He is broken."

Joseph painted. To glue the pieces back together. To suture the wound.

9

She didn't fall asleep until dawn, so she woke up late for her first meeting, on rue des Saints-Pères. While her body had rested for a few hours, her mind had continued working. Upon waking, she had chosen to forget the truths brought to the surface by her dreams, like someone stubbornly ignoring good advice, but she couldn't rid herself of their effects: the echo of that inaudible message left her anxious and tense.

The furnished apartment on rue des Saints-Pères belonged to friends of the Stewart family. In the capital, where every square foot with a roof was rented at ridiculous prices, the luxury – and the snobbery – of possessing vacant lodgings was the sole preserve of Julius and his friends. In this case, it was a third-floor apartment, recently renovated, with three rooms – bedroom, living room and office – and central heating, which would perhaps be useful in the autumn. Aileen quickly visited the premises. The maid who serviced the rest of the building could spare three or four hours a week to take care of Aileen's apartment. The concierge told her to come back late that afternoon so she could meet this young woman. With her first meeting over, she ran to the second.

She was expected at the German pavilion, which had, unsurprisingly, divided the French critics. For Aileen, there was nothing there but the ugliness of the Exposition's grand pomp:

an assemblage of mismatched bells and belfries tastelessly tacked onto some existing buildings. The Germans – close enemies of the French – had returned to Paris for the first time since the 1870 Exposition. The two nations regarded each other stonily. But Kaiser Wilhelm had been shrewd enough to exhibit, in this temporary pavilion, the French art of his ancestor Frederick the Great, who – as a student of Voltaire – was the only German sovereign it was acceptable to love unreservedly. Kaiser Wilhelm was widely suspected of being a scheming hypocrite.

Rudolf Diesel was strolling beside a wall of Dürer engravings on the ground floor when Aileen arrived. His English was academic and butchered by his German accent. A little over forty, tall, well built and already almost bald, Diesel looked like a solid American, chosen by migratory selection: selection through hunger on the third-class boats, where passengers dropped like flies, ensuring that the migrants who made it to the United States were the strongest or the most ruthless. Rudolf Diesel had the body of a tough, straight-toothed Teutonic survivor, and yet his expression was both weary and anxious, the stigmata of a melancholic temperament. He didn't want to stay in the pavilion, so they went outside, where Diesel immediately felt better.

"My parents were German, but I was born here, you know. In Paris. I spent my childhood here."

Aileen replied in French: "My mother was French."

"Ah? Would you mind if we walked to the Champ de Mars, Mrs Bowman? I have business there. And, if you have time, you could see the engine. It's a beautiful day – why not make the most of it?"

He was more interested in the benefits of the walk than in

their interview. Aileen turned back to the facade of the German pavilion, another victim of the Exposition's architectural leprosy, with its allegorical and nationalist frescos. A few phrases were painted on it, just in case the symbols were too subtle for some.

"Would you translate for me, M. Diesel?"

He frowned.

"'German genius full of gravity and duty, bloom in God's light-filled air.' And the one next to it says: 'German hand that wields the hammer, forge in fire the ploughshare and the sword.' Let's get away from here, Mrs Bowman."

"How do you feel about receiving the Grand Prix de l'Exposition?"

Rudolf Diesel could have made an effort, but he seemed incapable of smiling, or even of displaying the false candour of declaring that his fortune was made or that he was delighted his hard work had been rewarded. Instead, he looked up at the sky as if to contemplate the pointlessness of the good weather.

"I beg your pardon?"

"Are you happy to be given the prize?"

"Yes, of course. Very happy."

"What are your objectives, or your hopes, for the future of the engine?"

The engineer spoke in well-oiled, mechanical phrases: "The Diesel-Krupp engine will supply small businesses that do not have the resources to afford large steam engines, which are in any case far less efficient than ours. Our engine is small, powerful and economical, capable of working the dynamos of small- and medium-sized workshops, using vegetable oil as fuel."

"Vegetable oil?"

"If put under high pressure, sufficiently heated and then lit, a melted block of butter would be enough to make it work. But the most economical fuel, for small businesses competing with large factories, is peanut oil."

"Can you envisage adapting your engine, as other engineers have done, to contemporary electric or steam-powered vehicles?"

"It's not the primary aim of our engine, but of course it's perfectly possible. As yet, automobile vehicles are not particularly useful."

He had muttered the end of that last sentence, before falling into a silence that lasted for several footsteps. Then a new idea came to him and he turned to the journalist.

"Did you say that your mother was French? Why did she emigrate to the United States?"

"She wanted to start a new community there, with political and economic ideals. An expedition partly financed by an industrialist whom you perhaps know . . . M. Godin?"

"Yes, I know about M. Godin's business – and his commitment to humanity. I am myself working on a book about social and economic issues, based on the principle of solidarity. But my work as an engineer prevents me from giving it as much time as I would like."

"Solidarity?"

Diesel did not elaborate. They were approaching the Esplanade des Invalides, with its long electric walkway. Aileen suggested they take it.

"Your company is agreeable to me, Mrs Bowman. Would it bother you if we continued on foot?"

They walked in the shadow of the mechanical walkway on

avenue de la Motte-Picquet, approaching the Champ de Mars and the gallery of machines, where the Krupp enterprises were headquartered and where the famous engine, the centre of everybody's attention, was on display. But the engineer slowed down again and, at the crossroads of avenue Duquesne, without a word, he took Aileen's arm and turned away from the crowds. For a while, they walked in silence, alongside the wall of the Military School, then crossed through the barriers and ticket counters separating the Exposition from the rest of the city.

"If your engine was a metaphor, in this Exposition, in this year, what would it be?"

The engineer smiled and thought for a moment, gazing vacantly down the avenue.

"I have often wondered about the forces that traverse and define our human communities. Those forces, like the tendons of muscles, that set our skeletons in motion. I've often thought about the periods that have marked our history. From the ancient empires to the nations of the Renaissance, from the Enlightenment to the technological revolution of our own century. When I say our century, I mean the nineteenth. I don't yet feel at home in the twentieth . . . I wonder if there are intellectual vortices, in the same way that there are certain places in the world where magnetic fields are concentrated. If there are epochs that bring together ideas, concentrate human creativity, human discovery. That's the impression that this Exposition gives. Perhaps it's just an illusion. Perhaps movement and change are permanent but we don't always pay attention, so certain moments are highlighted more than others. But if we imagine being in the heart of one of those vortices, the fuel-injected combustion engine could be the metaphor – or the updated myth – of Promethean fire. A power that goes beyond those developed by biological forces. Our engine may still be small, but there is no doubt that other, bigger engines will soon be created, that their power will only increase, as is the case for all the inventions on display here. This Grand Prize-winner, our engine, poses the question of power and its mastery. My conviction is that creations – or creatures – always escape their creator."

"Like in Mary Shelley's novel?"

"Yes. *Frankenstein or the Modern Prometheus.* I like that story. Mrs Shelley was inspired by Aldini's wild dreams to re-create life using electricity. He used to terrify the public by electrocuting dead animals until their bodies quivered."

Rudolf Diesel's arm leaned more heavily on Aileen's.

"The gathering of so many human inventions is a cause for celebration, but all the steel of these machines – including my engine – also contains a threat. When the engine turns, the metal is hot. When it stops, seeing and feeling it cool down always give me a strange sensation. As if it were rediscovering its true, insensible nature, as if it were hatching some dark plot in its sleep."

"So you don't believe, like Saint-Simon, that engineers will be the great men of this new century? That technology will bring peace and prosperity?"

It took him another moment of silence to find the right words, or perhaps to find the courage to answer her.

"I'm a pacifist, Mrs Bowman, but I know it's not the workers or the poor masses who send nations into war. It takes a politician's power to do that. And politicians wouldn't enter into armed conflict if they didn't have the support of scientists, who increase the chances of victory with their discoveries and inventions. No, I do not share the optimism of Henri de Saint-Simon."

Diesel was lost in his thoughts again, and this time he couldn't find his way out of them. Aileen suggested that they retrace their steps. He hesitated.

"I'm going to cancel my other meetings," he said. "I'll go home and get some rest. My wife didn't want to come with me to Paris – she doesn't like crowds. I think I'll make the most of my stay and buy an apartment here. That way, we can come as a family in the future. I like this place."

He was too tired to walk now. Aileen hailed a cab, which took the inventor of the internal combustion engine to his hotel. She waved to him for a long time, until Rudolf Diesel's hand disappeared back inside the carriage.

She walked to Quai Voltaire, where she got on a steamboat. Watching the city flow past from the calm Seine soothed her thoughts, which had been rendered even more anxious by the engineer's worries.

She was amused by the fortifications of the medieval Ile de la Cité and Ile Saint-Louis, imagining them growing higher and thicker through time as the bows, crossbows and catapults became ever more powerful. The cannons from the Creusot steelworks could now send shells flying through the air for miles.

The maid was a girl of fourteen, although nobody thought of her as a girl anymore since she was so hard-working. She had a strange French accent.

"I'm from Brittany, madame."

The concierge suddenly sounded like a brothel madam as she explained that many cleaning girls were from that region.

"The girls are servants and the men work on building sites, many of them in the tunnels of the Métropolitain. They have hostels here, madame, respectable hostels run by clerics from their province."

Aileen suspected there must be some sophisticated organisation recruiting those girls from distant farms. This one had a hardened look: a hint of resignation, but still with the spark of some remaining hope that she might one day achieve something here. She was blonde and graceless, but highly competent. Aileen hired her. Three sets of bedding, her travel bag, some food and wine . . . all this had been delivered to her apartment, just as Julius had promised. The concierge asked Aileen to follow her and they went down to the building's inner courtyard.

"Another gift from Mr Stewart, madame."

And the concierge, whose Breton accent had been almost completely worn away by life in Paris, added in a tone of envious complicity:

"You're lucky, madame, to have such a generous friend."

A brand-new Peugeot velocipede. An envelope was tied to the saddle with string, which had been wrapped around it several times, like the ropes in Jeandel's cyanotypes. On a card, Julius had sketched a bottle of absinthe and a few flowers from the brothel's wallpaper. He'd written a short note:

So that you can cross the Seine and come to see me whenever you like, dear friend.

*

That first night on rue des Saint-Pères, Aileen didn't sleep; she filled a succession of pages – without pausing or rereading what she'd written – with the beginning of the story she'd been meaning to write for a long time. The story of the Fitzpatrick Ranch and America, as told between the landmarks and fences of that estate, whose ownership weighed so heavily on her.

At dawn, she went back to the Bois de Vincennes, pushing the bicycle through the streets since it gave her – in addition to the police commissioner's special permit – another excuse to wear trousers.

Around the velodrome, food stands and gift shops were opening. It was the ideal place to try out Julius' present. She sat astride the Peugeot and, legs spread, rolled down a gentle slope before putting her feet on the pedals, instantly losing control of the bicycle and crashing to the ground. She wiped her grazed palms and, learning her lesson, tried again, this time taking care not to press too hard on the pedals, her feet as light as in a stirrup. But the handlebars started shaking and swaying uncontrollably between her tensed hands. She jumped off before the bicycle ran into a tree, bounced off it, rolled a few feet and then lay down in the grass.

"Do you need any help?"

"Don't worry, I've had plenty of experience falling off horses – and they're higher and more dangerous than these machines."

"But a bike doesn't stay up on its own."

The man had a bicycle too, with curved handlebars like the horns of a bull. He was wearing tights cut off above his knee and a vest that showed off the lines of his chest and shoulders. He was hatless and sweating and – in the air shaded by foliage where the night's coolness still remained – his breath, warmed by strenuous exercise, came out in little clouds of steam. He was a good-looking man. Or at least he had a nice smile. Or perhaps the sunlight, grazing his blond hair, flattered him. He looked perfectly at home here, while she looked grotesque.

"I'll manage."

"All right, good luck then."

He waved an imaginary hat in the air and headed towards the gates of the velodrome. The cyclist turned back and saw the woman limping slightly in the direction of the cowboys-and-Indians show.

The little bones, twigs, spoons, empty cans, leaflets and wine-bottle corks swayed and tinkled in the breeze. The gentle wind twisted the smoke from the hearth into a moving vine around the Indian tent and its painted crow vomiting the pillars of the sky. Joseph, sitting cross-legged in front of the fire, was plucking the contorted body of a white hen on his bare thigh. He dropped handfuls of feathers into a hessian sack, as dust motes and scraps of down floated around him, caught in a beam of light. He smiled, unsurprised, and gestured with his head to invite Aileen to sit down.

"Hello, Joseph."

Beside the man's head, the yellow stains of inverted hands, seen through the thin wall of the tent, looked as if they were flying amid all the feathers. Joseph's chest was striped with red, black and white lines: the colours of the forbidden dance of spirits, those distant cousins of Christian souls that have no real translation in English. Their return was supposed to end the white men's oppression and bring the bisons back to life, before gathering the dead and the living in one peaceful world. The brutal repression of this spiritual movement had sounded the death knell of Indian resistance. But the dance of spirits, before it became a revolt, had been a way of communicating with the dead: Joseph, like Aileen, was in mourning.

"I'm happy to see you again, Joseph, even if I bring bad news. After your parents, mine died too."

He took a deep breath, swelling his broad chest, a gift from his stocky white father. This morphology, twinned with that of his tiny Indian mother, had made him a sleek, muscular cube. A sparse beard – another incongruous European inheritance – grew erratically over his brown cheeks and chin. The 24-year-old Joseph was short but he gave an impression of strength and solidity. Hardened by the lifestyle of the Paiute warriors, Joseph's body had become a walking weapon. The last time Aileen had seen him, he'd still been adolescent, his body and face still midway between child and adult, between his white and Indian lineages. His wavy, long black hair was another sign of his mixed blood. The beauty of both his parents had been stolen by their union, leaving only angles and strong lines.

"Where were you, Joseph, when they died?"

He waggled his fingers, as you might in front of a baby's eyes to catch its attention, and another handful of feathers fell slowly into the sack. He was frowning and the greasy skin covering his cheekbones made them gleam like two pebbles fresh out of a river.

"I am happy to see you too, white sister, and sad to learn of the departure of the ranch's parents."

Beneath his paintings, Aileen could make out the lines of his tattoos: the Paiute cosmogony and the story of his birth.

"Where were you, Joseph?"

"It is normal to lose each other in the New World. It is now only a country of ghosts and forgotten roads. Easier to find each other here, in the homeland of white American ancestors. Here, the old paths are still visible."

Aileen looked up at the little blue bodies of Maria and Pete, painted above Joseph's head.

"I'm not sure about that. The ancestors, too, are erasing everything. Have you visited their grave?"

"I saw the stones paid for by the family at the ranch, but I don't need those to talk to them. I find them in the dance."

She tried to imagine this cube of muscles and bones moving in rhythm. His painted body staggering as it gleamed under the rising sun, exuding the familiar smell of alcohol. Joseph had started drinking very young, on the reserve. He suckled those bottles with the same avidity as his Scottish father but collapsed as quickly as the Indians of his mother's race. That deadly alcoholism, the white man's last gift and humiliation, didn't even give the Indians the fleeting joys of intoxication. Nothing but blackouts and painful dreams. In the saloons of Carson City, the men would always laugh when they saw an Indian have a few drinks. Sometimes they would pay for an Indian's round; it was a source of entertainment in the absence of a piano or fiddle. Arthur, Aileen's father, had almost been killed by drink, but he hadn't stopped: he'd learned to control it and carried on drinking in secret for the rest of his life. She knew that smell that the body emanates when it's expelling the poison and demanding more.

The feathers kept falling softly into the sack from Joseph's trembling fingers.

"We looked for you after your parents' death. I looked for you after mine died too."

The eyes give signs to the outside world and reveal the interior world; their surface has the appearance of glass. But sometimes they lose their transparency. Arthur Bowman called those "shark eyes"; he said you should give a wide berth to any man with eyes like that. It was impossible to read anything in Joseph's dark eyes.

"What did you want to tell me, white sister? That I should go back to the reserve so I could die with all the others?"

Joseph's voice was hard-edged. Aileen sought some shelter in comforting memories. Aunt Maria's hands, striking the point of the wood with a round stone, injecting the tattoo ink under her skin. As an adolescent virgin, she'd loved those pains, those sensations. Some had made her eyes wet, others had made her wet between her legs. In a corner of the tepee, little Joseph, just seven or eight years old, had hidden so he could see the white girl's naked flesh. This girl whom he was told to call cousin. Their eyes had met, but Aileen hadn't said anything. She'd let the boy – the one she called her little brother – observe her body.

"No, I was just looking for you, that's all. I wanted to know what you were doing, how you were. I wanted to talk with you."

"A poor white man and an Indian woman . . . My parents died the best way they could. Together. Where they wanted to be. I don't need you to talk to me about them."

"But they'd have wanted to see you again."

"I visit them when I dance."

Aileen's fear turned to anger and came out of hiding.

"Your parents didn't hear you when you were drunk, talking to your feet in a gutter. They froze to death, alone, hungry, in a tepee that the Indians of the tribe didn't want anywhere near theirs."

"They weren't born among the tribe."

"But you were. Right? You – you're a real Indian! Joseph Ferguson, employee of Pawnee Bill's Show!"

He spat in the fire and waved away Aileen's words with the back of his hand.

"I was recruited by the Bureau of Indian Affairs. The administrator at the reserve thought I was a good example of assimilation – me, the bastard. The government supervises the hiring of Indians for the shows . . . so they can make sure we have good working conditions, so they say. Forked tongues. The administrators get a cut of our salaries. They choose men and women who are well behaved, because they want representatives of peace and the white man's civilisation. Your civilisation. They hire families with children, so there'll be more life in the camps. The salaries change with the seasons. In winter, we accept less money because the children are hungry."

He poked the fire, held the chicken's body above the flames. The smell of burning flesh stung Aileen's nostrils.

"I didn't mean to hurt you. I'm happy to see you again, even here."

"The more we agree to understand you, the less Indian we are."

"It's not my civilisation. You know me, Joseph. These ridiculous shows make me sick."

He smiled and spread the chicken over a flat stone. With a knife blade, he opened its belly, removed its guts, and tossed them onto the grass. He stuck the carcass on some sharpened branches above the fire. The heat made the air ripple like water.

"You still live in New York. I've read your articles. That's your world. I visited New York – that city smells of stone and piss. You write white men's stories in a white man's newspaper, read by white men who only believe in white men. You're a show too, you know, ranch sister, with your riding clothes and your life in the wild mountains that no longer exist. You're here to put on a show for your own people."

"I came to Paris because I knew you were here. Since I saw your tepee, three days ago, I've started writing the story that you painted on it. Our family's story."

"You can only talk in your own name, white sister. In your race's name. I'm not part of your story. I'm here to remind the Indians in Pawnee Bill's Show who they really are."

Aileen looked at the yellow hands on the canvas behind him, those coloured slaps to the faces of the Exposition's visitors.

"I saw the black mustang. Your battle mount."

"He's here to remind the circus horses where they're from. That they grew up on the plains and were trained for war."

"The others are afraid of you."

"What about you, white sister?"

"Why would I be afraid of you?"

"Because, like the others, like my mother, you think I'm crazy."

"I don't think you're crazy, Joseph, but I know you're not happy."

"Happy? What does happiness have to do with resistance, ranch sister?"

"I'm fighting too, you know, in New York, even if you don't

believe that. I don't want to go back to the ranch. I want to keep writing and publishing, denouncing the sins and mistakes made by white people. But you could go back to Fitzpatrick, Joseph. It's your home. That's what I came here to tell you. That I want to give you my share of the inheritance – all those lands. They're yours."

He smiled.

"We see each other at the end of the world, in the continent of the grasshoppers that invaded mine, and you dare to give me land? White sister, are you seriously giving land to an Indian?"

"Yes, and you know perfectly well what that means. Don't treat me like an idiot. I'm not doing this out of guilt. I don't want those acres, but you could do something with them. Live the life you want there. You'd be safe there."

"Get out of my tent."

"What are you going to do, Joseph?"

The sun was high in the sky now, beating down directly on the camp. Aileen's shirt stuck to her arms and her breasts. Joseph's pores, blocked by paint, were struggling to rid themselves of it. The colours trickled down his chest and onto his belly. He twitched. He needed a drink, but he wouldn't let himself drink in front of her.

"I don't understand the signs or the reasons for this meeting. Go away."

"We're not blood kin, but we're closer than many cousins. Please, Joseph, don't do anything you'll regret."

He leaped to his feet and his black hair rose to the height of the black crow painted on the tepee; the poles seemed to be woven into his hair. Either that or his head was a target for the spears of spirits.

"There's nothing left to regret! The connection you imagine between us doesn't exist. Go!"

Fear dissolved Aileen's lies like anger melted Joseph's paintings, revealing the warrior lines of his tattoos. They both knew it wasn't Joseph she had come to save, but a part of herself that existed in him, on which she had started to give up: resistance. The refusal to compromise. The beauty of resistance was that it led to defeat. Resistance had forged her life as a journalist and a woman in New York, but she had left it behind when she set sail for France. She hadn't come here to fight, but – as the intransigent Séverine said – to write literature. Joseph, in Aileen's words, would become a character from a novel, the bastard son who resisted the spectacle of his skin sold to the highest bidder.

She had come to recruit him, to rally him to the cause of his abandonment.

She was like a do-gooder, a pioneer from Epinal in Pawnee Bill's Historic Wild West Show, as deadly as smallpox. She was the leprosy of compromise and happiness, that workhorse that willingly pulls the carts bearing cannons, in exchange for rations.

With a gesture of his chin, he bade her goodbye. She stood up, obeying his order.

Aileen took the Peugeot bicycle that she'd left leaning on a tree, and her hair brushed against a bone mobile. Joseph, sitting cross-legged, dug with his bare hands into the flesh of the grilled chicken. A bottle of alcohol appeared beside him.

IO

She was slowed down by her clothes, which were heavy with sweat. She wanted to throw her jacket and trousers onto the grass, to be naked in the open air. When she remembered the white hen on Joseph's thigh, the handfuls of feathers torn from the pink skin of the dead bird, a new wave of perspiration streamed down her back. Bile rose in her throat. Images of the brothel orgy came back to her, items of clothing used as ropes to tie her to the bed. The fear in Julius' and Charlotte's eyes at the sight of her body, opened up to them. Her fear of being a prisoner, then her fear that the ties that bound her weren't solid enough to hold her once the prostitute and the painter grew more frenetic in their movements. Later, they'd freed her, when her defensive reflexes had been dulled.

Ropes tying her to a bed. Alcohol to numb her brain . . . Like Joseph, her father, Uncle Pete, and everyone of their race. She had to find a pathway to unconsciousness, it hardly mattered which one.

But her legs were too weak to carry her to Julius' studio. Leaning on the bike's handlebars, she followed its click-click-click, like an inner clock, to the velodrome. She left her bicycle against a barrier and sat in the stands, in the shade of a metal girder, at the edge of the oval track and the green lawn that surrounded it. Athletes in uniforms moved under the banners of nations she'd never heard of, all of them participants in the coming Olympic games. Women under sunshades were encouraging the sportsmen, coaches were yelling, and, a little further off in the forest, Joseph Ferguson was readying himself for a war, fermenting the sugar of his vengeance. The white world of athletes was whirling around itself when suddenly heaven and earth swapped places and the light blinded her, made her lift her head up to breathe and she fell backwards into the unconsciousness that she'd been wishing for.

Aileen came to in a dazzle of light, amid the vibrations of a gong. There was a circle of hats and moustaches above her. Someone was holding those horrible ammonia salts under her nose, the same ones that Charlotte had used to wake Mary Stanford in the artist's studio. She wanted to see Mary again. To twist her principles, pinch her thighs. She was worrying that she must resemble one of those sick bourgeois women in Julius' paintings when she noticed that one of the faces closest to hers looked familiar.

"Sit up slowly."

She felt the weight of her head in the man's palm. Her mouth tasted of vomit. Ashamed of her malaise, she told him that she was fine.

"What did you say?"

She had seen him somewhere before. He'd leaned over her like this another time. After another fall. Oh yes . . . the cyclist from earlier that morning, in his sports outfit, his bare shoulders sunburned. In a self-assured voice, he told the others to stand back, to give the lady some air. The onlookers receded. The man apologised in advance, then put his other hand behind her back and helped her to her feet. Aileen's half-open mouth touched his sweaty shoulder, her tongue brushed against his salty skin. It tasted better than the bile. She sat on the bench, leaning against him, and tried again to say something.

"I don't understand what you're saying, madame."

He handed her a battered tin flask. She drank a few mouthfuls of water and wiped her mouth on her sleeve. The taste of the stranger's skin was washed away.

"You don't have a moustache. I noticed that this morning."

"You have quite a bump on the back of your head. I'm going to hail a cab to take you to a doctor."

"I'm fine."

"I'm not sure about that. You're very pale."

Aileen looked down, poured some water into her hand, and rubbed her face. She rinsed out her mouth and spat on the ground like a cowboy.

"I'm just tired. And hungry. That's what you could do, if you want me to get my colour back."

"I'm sorry?"

"I need to eat something."

With her fingertips, she felt the hot bruise at the back of her head. She poured some water on it.

"It's nothing, honestly."

"In that case, I'll hail a cab to take you to a restaurant, if that's what you want."

"Never mind the cab. There's a restaurant in Vincennes, isn't there?"

"You want to walk? In your state?"

"If you're worried that I won't make it, you could just come with me."

The cyclist hesitated.

"There's the Plateau de Gravelle, near the lake. It's only a few minutes from here."

"I should be able to walk that far."

"All right, give me a moment. I'll fetch my belongings."

"Wait . . ."

He was already on his feet.

"Madame?"

"You can put my rudeness down to being an American if you like, but I . . . the idea of pretending is making me feel exhausted already. If we go to that restaurant together, can you promise me we'll have a real conversation?"

"I'm not sure I understand what you mean, madame."

"Do you know Buddhist philosophy? They say that feelings should run over us like water over feathers. I think that's nonsense! We're not waterproof: emotions run through us. I need a real conversation, not just some glib small talk about worldly matters. If you can't manage that, then I'll just thank you for your help and I'll find the restaurant on my own."

The cyclist bent down and offered his hand to the American woman, who scorned convention.

"My name is Jacques. Jacques Huet. I'm an engineer."

He seemed to regret this detail, which seemed too worldly for the pact he'd agreed with this strange woman. But Aileen smiled at him reassuringly.

"My name is Aileen Bowman. Hélène, if that's easier for you to pronounce. So . . . what kind of engineer?"

"Geologist and mechanic."

"Are geology and mechanics enough to get us through a meal?"

"If not, I could tell you about the Métropolitain."

"The Paris Métropolitain?"

"I work for the inspector-general, Fulgence Bienvenüe, who's in charge of the construction work. I'm preparing to tunnel under rivers for the next line with a procedure that involves freezing the earth."

An image of the Paiute corpses frozen to the ground in Warm Springs flashed in her mind.

"Let's go eat."

"Have a rest while I fetch my things. I'll only be a few minutes."

He descended the steps of the terraces, then came back.

"Since you believe in honesty and sincerity, let's just deal with the most obvious things now. I'm married."

"Does that mean you can't talk about the Métropolitain, or have an honest conversation?"

"No, that would be very sad. I just wanted to save time, for this conversation that you wish to be . . . lively. If that's the right term."

"The perfect term. And I'm not married."

"Then I'll be married enough for both of us."

The engineer straddled his bicycle and rode onto the track. He went halfway around it before disappearing under the stands at the other end of the stadium. Jacques Huet reappeared a few minutes later, crossed the strip of lawn with one long stride. He was hatless and his pale summer suit stood out sharply against the grass. Aileen stood up before he arrived, considering it a point of honour to descend the steps alone.

"Take my arm," she said. "I'm not feeling very brave yet, and we'll look suspicious if we walk side by side without touching. If we link arms, we'll look like a couple."

"If you're trying to go unnoticed, wearing trousers probably wasn't your best bet. What did you do with your bicycle?"

Aileen looked around for the Peugeot.

"That treacherous beast? I left it over there, leaning against a barrier."

"I'll push it with one hand. I think you've fallen enough today."

"What does your wife do?"

"She doesn't work."

"So she looks after your children?"

"I thought you wanted to have an original, interesting conversation? But, to answer your question, yes: my wife looks after our house and our daughter. May I, in turn, ask you a boring question? Where are you from and what are you doing in Paris?"

"I'm American and I'm a journalist for the *New York Tribune*. I'm here to cover the Exposition. I also write a column for *La Fronde*, under a pseudonym, where I make the city of Paris write in the voice of a prostitute. It's causing a bit of a scandal. I don't have any children. I got pregnant in New York once, but I employed a woman to give me an abortion. I was bedridden in her apartment for two weeks with an infection."

"Why are you telling me that?"

"To start a real conversation. We now know that, inside our bellies, there isn't a well-lit room full of souls, fairies or cherubic little boys just waiting for our menstruation blood so they can drink it, grow and decide to come out into the world. Every woman who's ever had an abortion or a miscarriage knows that a young foetus isn't a perfect little child babbling away inside us. They're biological magma, formless lumps of flesh. It is incredibly vain of men to believe that their reproduction is of the greatest importance in the animal world. I claim the right not to have children and, if necessary, to interrupt the miracle of conception."

"Don't you think you'd be a good mother?"

"On the contrary, I believe I would. That's why talking about children makes me sad."

"In that case, why take all those risks by having an abortion?"

"It wasn't all that risky getting in contact with the woman who performed it. In New York, there are lots of personal ads in newspapers offering that kind of service, under cover of remedies for female ailments. The authorities pretend not to know what's going on. A few get prosecuted now and then, to set an example and to appease the religious fanatics."

Aileen gave Jacques Huet a serious look.

"You're more courageous in the face of my honesty than anyone I've met in a long time, Mr Engineer. Aren't you afraid of any subject?"

"There are many subjects that we never discuss in our lifetimes, that we almost never think about, but that are always there, in the background. It's as if they're . . . predetermined for us, by books and newspapers, by what other people say. Like the subject you just raised. It's interesting to talk about it in a different way. And I think we can talk about anything, since we don't know each other."

"And have you noticed that spontaneity and honesty don't help you to get to know someone better? Nobody should be afraid to say what he thinks. It's an interesting paradox. Modesty and secrets sometimes teach us as much as frank confessions."

"Another new theory! How do you explain that?"

"Let's see . . . What we think of as being intimate and unique is often completely banal. Everybody has the same secrets; our lives don't leave much room for real differences. In fact, the point of all culture, it seems to me, is to eliminate the differences at its heart. If we talk about the weather, we reveal almost as much about ourselves as we do when confessing our innermost desires."

"I didn't have the impression that our conversation was banal."

"Really? What did we say that was so original?"

"Maybe not much, but beneath the words we were sharing feelings. And they're unique."

"I don't think so. Not one of those feelings is unique."

"But they belong to us!"

"I can prove to you right now that feelings are exchanged, negotiated and shared just like food or money. They're goods to be consumed."

"What do you mean?"

"When you talked about your wife and your daughter, you became more careful, less joyful, because you didn't want to embarrass a single woman with that subject. So you repressed your joy so that I would understand that you're a gentleman. That's very honourable of you. But you also didn't want to sound too happy for another reason: you didn't want to render other scenarios – between the two of us – impossible, by clumsily displaying your love for them. Hence your calculated commiseration. On my side, by agreeing, I accepted your sadness, which helped both of us: it was communicated to me. Then I told you about my abortion, allowing us to dispense with that first little sadness since my story was far more tragic. You were able to become a man with a comforting presence once again, on the arm of a strange woman with whom, in your mind, anything remained possible. Now, my hostility vis-à-vis your status as a naturally strong man is a warning: don't imagine I'm just some poor spinster who's had an abortion and is dying of loneliness. In fact, I'm asking you not to behave like a polite gentleman, but a man proud to walk arm-in-arm with me. That way, you can brave the disapproving stares of passers-by at this hatless man and this woman in trousers. Your diplomatic sadness was exchanged for doubt, then compassion, curiosity, a slight vexation, and then we came to an understanding, establishing a mutual assurance: our solidarity against the others. It was that solidarity I needed when I sat in the stands of the velo-drome, alone and feeling sick. And I manipulated our feelings, redirected our discussions, linked my arm with yours, in order to obtain it. In other words, we made a deal."

Jacques whistled through his teeth.

"A convincing demonstration, but also an arguable one. For example, you had no idea that we would see each other again when you sat in the stands of the velodrome. Your arguments about the objectivity of feelings don't change anything: it was chance that brought us back together. So tell me, rather, what unique result can be produced by us walking arm-in-arm, instead of reducing us to haggling over banalities."

"Well . . . I might be meeting the love of my life. That would be unique, wouldn't it?"

He laughed to cover up his emotion.

"Let's get back to those banalities!"

He continued holding her arm and they turned onto the

gravel path leading to the restaurant, with its wooden walkways, terraces and pergolas. It was still early and the tables were almost all unoccupied. They chose one close to a hedge, where some bees were hovering. The waiter offered them Clacquesin, a Norwegian liqueur made from pine resin that had received a gold medal at the Exposition.

"Apparently it's the best drink around for your health."

They both refused. Jacques ordered Armagnac.

"Bring us a carafe of water too, please. Do you have ice? Natural or artificial?"

"Natural, sir. From the Swiss Alps."

"The making of ice is a commercial revolution, but the stuff they get from lakes and mountains is far superior," he added to Aileen, who was observing the starving bees as they drank from the flowers, their feet heavy with pollen.

"Do you know the names of any plants or insects, Mr Engineer?"

"Not many."

"I grew up beside a lake in the middle of the Sierra Nevada, but I know nothing about plants apart from a few that can be eaten or used to heal a wound. I can only recognise the tracks of animals that we eat, and I call them by the names that the Indians and the people of our region give them. Not the kind of names you'd find in encyclopaedias. All I know about nature is how to find my way and how to hunt."

"Hunt? You're beginning to seriously intrigue me. As I said, I don't know many plants either, but I do know quite a lot about the soils in which they grow and the chemical elements on which they feed."

She found him attractive, for a reason that was perhaps nothing more than a succession of ideas: the image of roots sunk in the ground, the ballet of pollinating insects, his beardless chin, his face tanned by hours on the bike, which reminded her – among all these pale gentlemen in hats – of the men on the Fitzpatrick Ranch.

"You see, we're learning much more about each other by talking about frozen soils and chemical procedures than about children I haven't had."

"And why is that?"

"Because you won't talk about your passion for your wife the way you'll enthuse over the Parisian subsoil. Conventions, unlike your artificial ice, still have the edge over naturalness."

The waiter brought them the glasses of Armagnac, a carafe of water, a porcelain icebox, and two menus. Jacques thrust his hand into the shards of ice and deposited them on his napkin, then tied the fabric in a knot and handed it to her.

"For the bump on your head . . . some cold from the mountains."

"Do you still feel passion for your wife?"

Again, he had the courage to reply, without hiding behind his Armagnac, without any false hesitation.

"I don't know any more about the names of those things than I do about plants. I don't know if one feels love or passion only for what is new. If the feelings that grow over the course of years can still be labelled passion. But I have feelings for my wife that took years to form. I'm not a literary man, so I hope you'll forgive me if my analogy is clichéd, but . . . I have the impression that my wife and I have become islands in a river. Sandy shores growing further and further apart, changing with the currents, but without ever slipping out of sight of one another. The desires from our first moments have gone, and they've been replaced by others, of a different magnitude and intensity."

"The first moments are all I know."

"They're the simplest ones."

"The least interesting?"

"No, the ones with fewest commitments. As time goes by, feelings bring responsibilities."

"Those feelings moulded by time don't seem to have much to do with love or passion."

This time, he drank. He looked like he needed it, since he couldn't simply walk away.

"Go ahead."

"I'm sorry. This game has gone on long enough."

"Don't apologise. I'm enjoying your company and our conversation. I just didn't want it to become sad. Or banal, if you prefer."

Something had stopped. The bees were buzzing more loudly, there were more customers at other tables.

"Let's order some red wine and you can tell me how you freeze the earth."

It was too late.

"Forgive me, Aileen, I'm not brave enough to keep playing with our feelings. As you said earlier, they run through us, not over us."

Jacques stood up.

"Don't worry about the bill, I'll take care of that. I'm glad your fall wasn't serious and that you're feeling better. Thank you for your sincerity, but I fear that your solitude might cause our meeting to take a dangerous, irrevocable turn. I regret it, for both of us. Goodbye, madame."

He quickly shook her hand, left his glass half-empty on the table, and turned to leave.

Aileen rummaged in her knapsack and pulled out her father's pipe. She stuffed the bowl with tobacco, lit it with a match, bit down on the mouthpiece and licked it with the tip of her tongue, as if to taste the remnants of Arthur's saliva, his words, one last piece of advice. But Arthur knew no more about feelings than she did about plants. In that regard, too, her father had taught her nothing more than how to be waterproof. Jacques Huet was permeable. As with Marguerite Durand or Séverine, she pushed away those who attached importance to what frightened her. Commitments, communities, responsibilities.

She finished her glass, then Jacques'. She believed – or wanted to – that she could sense a presence, somewhere in the park's foliage. A presence that was there only for her. Someone watching her. Aileen Bowman's very own stalker. Joseph, perhaps, who could have followed her here. The failure of the meeting with her cousin had hurt her. And vexed her. In revenge, she had ruined the pleasure and truce offered by the engineer.

And now here she was, inventing a mysterious admirer. So that someone, at least, would notice when she left the restaurant, alone.

II

Every day, she noted down images and observations from the Exposition, which then filled columns in the *New York Tribune*, for readers on the other side of the world who were no longer interested in it. Then she strolled around Paris, sometimes seeing a vegetable market as a choreography of extras, the way that ancient buildings standing next to plaster imitations seemed to blur the lines between real and fake. Her nights spent writing further accentuated her impression that the capital had become a backdrop that she could paint, whenever and however she wanted, with her words, attempting to dig articles of substance from that hollow material. It was similar to the Women's pavilion, for which she'd had such high hopes: its architectural elegance had come at a disastrous cost, putting a strain on the budget for the exhibitions inside. In the basement, there was an "educational exhibition on ablutions and hygiene", which turned out to be a shopping arcade where women came to make purchases. Wax mannequins from the Grévin Museum illustrated the daily stages of a woman's life. On the ground floor, in a reading room, books by women authors were for sale, with paintings by female artists displayed on the walls. The arts and letters were flanked on one side by a patisserie and on the other by a restaurant. On the first floor, there was a theatre hall with a capacity of four hundred, where plays written by women were supposed to be staged; instead, the only performances – put on three times a day – were by shadow puppets. The irony of those stiff, stereotyped, manipulated silhouettes prancing around in the penniless Women's pavilion drew a bitter laugh from Aileen.

At the stand for the Smith Premier Typewriter Company – arms manufacturers who had converted their factories to produce weapons for writers – Aileen rewarded this pacifist conversion by buying a Smith Premier No. 2 typewriter. It was the best model on the market and weighed only twelve pounds. It came in a portable wood-and-leather box with handles. She spent two days fighting the machine before she finally understood the way it worked and managed to type correctly, slowly at first and then with growing assurance, until in the end she could type faster than she could write, producing page after page of articles that already looked like they'd been published in a newspaper.

It would soon be June. The scaffolding had almost completely vanished. The inauguration parties were over and the Exposition was now fully open. Belated visits by lesser-known kings and presidents were the occasion for modest processions, and the press and public made do with those. With politicians and diplomats shuffling off stage, it was now the publicists who had their time in the spotlight. There were blaring advertisements for incredible new products: a revolutionary locomotive in the railway section, an electric light bulb guaranteed to stay lit for a thousand hours, a dynamo powered by the wind, chemical fertiliser with unparalleled productivity. After the bombastic, idealistic speeches, it was now time for negotiations, and the most important visitors were the millionaire captains of industry, here to make deals. There were no parades for them, just meals on the first floor of the Eiffel

Tower, or in the great Celestial Globe, or at the best restaurants in Paris' chic neighbourhoods. Scorning the Exposition became the favourite activity of the city's snobs. The establishment was back in its antechambers, the discreet, velvet-lined rooms from where it drew its mysterious power. They bargained and negotiated in low voices while, behind the 400 feet of bay windows of a temporary building by the Seine, the Exposition devoted itself to one of its greatest pleasures: conventions. Two hundred and fifty of them had been planned. The list of subjects under debate was too good to be true. Social economics, protection of working-class children, profit-sharing, trade unions, training, houses for workers, institutions for workers' intellectual and moral development, an international peace convention ... The Palais des Congrès was a gigantic advertisement for the advancement of the human race and its preoccupations: safeguarding mountain pasture, the kingdom of Siam, the global shortage of timber, oral hygiene, the colonisation of Siberia, accident insurance. The world's fair was a list, a list of lists, through which Aileen strolled as through the city's streets, and which she consulted as she would a map, with its sections standing in for neighbourhoods: remuneration of labour, large and small businesses, building societies and cooperatives. Large and small farms, agricultural credit unions ...

Behind this ambitious accumulation, she sensed an anxiety intrinsic to all lists; it was like a whole civilisation trying to defeat insomnia by drawing up a to-do list for tomorrow. The sheer number of these crucial objectives was dizzying, overwhelming; inevitably, there would not be enough money and time to put them all into practice.

She went back to Vincennes.

Pawnee Bill's Show was supposed to keep performing until July, and then the troupe would leave Paris for a tour of Europe, followed by England in the autumn, before returning to the United States in December. Aileen had attended a show, seen the sharpshooting demonstrations, the rodeo, the showjumping and reconstructed battles. During the great parade and the battle of the pioneers against the Indians, she had looked for Joseph among the actors but had been unable to spot him. He must be spending more time drinking in his tepee than perfecting those absurd stunts. But he and his horse were still there.

Several times, she had gone close to his tent. At first, she had hidden herself, to take Joseph by surprise. Later, she'd abandoned such ludicrous precautions, feeling certain that he was already aware of her presence. So she would lean her bicycle against a tree and sit there, watching him, sometimes taking notes. They had found a suitable distance – about 100 feet – and each could observe the other without being too close. It was far from ideal, but she couldn't just ignore his presence. As for Joseph, he must have found the arrangement acceptable, otherwise he would have chased her away on the first day.

Sometimes Joseph would paint episodes from his past on the tepee, while Aileen wrote. There was nothing innocent about this compromise: they were monitoring each other. Aileen wanted to make sure that he didn't do anything crazy. Joseph wished to verify that she wasn't giving up, that her emotional declarations were not just vain promises. It was an arm-wrestling contest, in preparation for the departure of Pawnee Bill's Show, a struggle over what conclusions they should draw from their meeting once they were alone again.

There were times when Joseph and his mustang weren't at the camp, and nobody there knew where they'd gone. Aileen was the only one who regretted the half-blood's absence, although it did give her an opportunity to take a closer look at his tepee and his mobiles.

Sometimes the mustang remained in the corral even while his master was absent. The paintings on his black coat changed in accordance with Joseph's moods. There would be more or fewer inverted hands, and occasionally a splash of white and green would appear, a sign of fleeting calm. Other times, the horse would be all red and lightning bolts for a whole week.

And perhaps there were other times when the opposite was true: she didn't go to Vincennes, and Joseph sat there waiting for her.

In the streets of Paris, Aileen would turn around whenever she heard the echo of hooves on cobbles. When she didn't see anyone for several days – neither Joseph, nor Julius, nor Marguerite – she would find herself wondering from how far away a person might be able to view the window of the room where she stayed awake to write. That square of light and the person who was spying on her – that presence she continued to imagine to stave off her loneliness, the stalker's face changing with her moods – became the point of departure for the erotic scenarios she dreamed up as she masturbated. She would touch herself while sitting at her desk, sliding off the chair, framed by the light from the window just as she was framed by the composition of the nude that Julius was painting on rue Copernic.

When Joseph went into hiding, Aileen would go to the velodrome, hoping to see Jacques Huet again. She wanted to show him how she'd finally managed to master her bicycle, which she rode proudly around the capital, cutting through parks, following unpaved paths between her apartment, the post and telegraph office, Vincennes, and the offices of *La Fronde*. But she didn't see the engineer again. Maybe he was avoiding the woods. One day, she thought, when enough time has passed, he'll come back.

That was the entirety of her life in Paris. One sunny afternoon, when she couldn't write, she rode her bicycle to the artist's studio, pedalling across the city to scatter behind her in the warm air the idea that was pursuing her.

Julius was at his easel, but he wasn't alone. Mary Stanford stood on the models' stage. And it wasn't her first visit: her portrait was almost finished. The artist had deliberately kept the young woman's visits a secret from Aileen.

Mary was wearing a fashionable black dress, sober and elegant, but beneath it she wore no corset, so her flesh pressed voluptuously against the fabric instead of being restricted. She didn't look as young as she had before. Beneath her collarbone, the dress had been cut with scissors and the fabric hung down in a triangle. One breast emerged from this nest of silky threads, the brown nipple erect.

Neither the artist nor his model seemed disturbed by the journalist's arrival. Aileen sat in a chair and drank some absinthe. She became absorbed in the spectacle of this alchemical transformation: from a woman of flesh and blood, to a woman of canvas and paint. An artificial replication similar to the hollow buildings of the Exposition. But here, through the intermediary of Julius' eyes and hands, something real appeared on the canvas. The image of a woman who was not Mary Stanford, but the idea she'd had of herself, the idea of becoming a free being, in the torn mourning dress of her youth. Julius, a child of fragile women, lent her the strength, the good health and sensuality necessary for this transformation. She had shed her old skin and the canvas was her new skin. The flesh of that breast, escaped from its fabric prison, looked more real than painted. On the corner of the stage, on an easel covered with a sheet, stood the portrait of Aileen, still unfinished.

"When are you going back to Pennsylvania, Mary?"

"In two days. Eugene is done with his business meetings and I can't persuade him to stay any longer."

"I'm sorry I never replied to your message. I hope this doesn't seem like a weak excuse, but I've been doing a lot of writing."

"It's okay, Julius explained all that. And I found my way here without you anyway."

The journalist raised her glass to the painter, who gave a brief complicit smile. Aileen looked at Mary's breast, then caught her eye. The young woman didn't even blink. Aileen remembered their dinner on board the *Touraine*, their silent glances across the table as the conversation droned on in the background.

"What will you do with your portrait, Mary?"

"The same thing as you: give it to Julius. I can always imagine it somewhere in France, on the wall of someone's living room or hidden away in some rich man's study. Maybe next to yours? I find that idea . . . amusing."

That word gave little indication of the excitement that Mary Stanford felt at the idea of leaving this scandalous painting behind her, a secret from her husband and the state of Pennsylvania.

"You saw Julius' portrait of me?"

Without pausing in his work, the artist gave a little bow, apologising for his betrayal of their secret.

"Yes," replied Mary, blushing slightly at this guilty pleasure.

"I, too, am amused by that idea of our portraits hung side by side. In two days, you said? That doesn't give me much time to enjoy your company. What is your husband doing tonight?"

Julius smiled as he heard the warm invitation in Aileen's absinthe-sweetened voice.

"I'm afraid Eugene isn't available. His partners are giving him a send-off in a gentlemen's club tonight. A party for American men, with Cuban cigars and French champagne."

Julius put down his palette.

"I think it's finished."

Mary came down from the stage without covering up her breast. Aileen went over to the easel too. The painting had a good balance of colours and dimensions, with a dignity that stood in equal measure to its sensuality and provocativeness. Mary's arms hung by her sides, a posture that was simultaneously natural and arrogant. The torn dress gave the impression that she'd just been in a fight and was daring her opponent to attack her again. The backdrop was a sad, bare, blackened hill, studded with oil derricks. Mary slid her arm under Julius' and leaned her shoulder against his.

"It's perfect."

"You and Aileen will make a beautiful diptych."

Mary turned to the redhead from the *New York Tribune* who'd written that article that had made her husband so proud.

"Are you going to work on your portrait tonight?"

Julius was quicker than Aileen to respond.

"I can have some food and wine brought up for the three of us. We'll have as much time as we want."

Aileen still hadn't rid herself of the idea that had been pursuing her. On the contrary, it had become almost inevitable since her decision to come to the studio that day. Even on her first visit here, when she'd fled the Grand Palais and Royal Cortissoz, the idea had been there, waiting for her, like one of the ingredients that gave the paint tubes their scent. Time to quit. Aileen would soon put an end to her career as a journalist.

She moved behind Mary, kissed the nape of her neck and, cupping her exposed breast in one hand, felt her shiver.

La Fronde, 15 June 1900
A column by Mme Alexandra Desmond

THE FRUIT OF MY LOINS

An army of navvies, quarrymen, bricklayers and riveters, solid men from the poverty-stricken region of Brittany, have ripped up my streets and avenues, and dug holes as deep as buildings pointing down towards the centre of the earth. They have passed under the houses, the monuments, the parks and the roots of trees, driving out moles, mice and worms, brushing past the much older tunnels of the catacombs, bumping into the foundations of churches, crypts green with mould, subterranean aqueducts engraved with Roman numerals. The ground falls in on them or gives way beneath their feet when they dig into the water table, the forgotten quarries where I was born, and prehistoric caves. My loins have been eroded by the gonorrhoea of centuries and the stubbornness of men.

Huge stakes are planted in the unstable clay, concrete blocks that will support the tunnels' metal frames. They've turned rue de Rivoli, avenue Kléber and place de la Nation into immense trenches where they've smashed the rock with pickaxes and set up hoists. Trenches, shields, maps and – everywhere – the enemy, water. The Métropolitain is a war.

A new means of transportation to unclog the streets on their surface. Because I have become a non-stop traffic jam. The people in charge of my logistics – politicians and technicians – have given another of these Bretons, an engineer, the task of adding this new organ, a system of arteries for millions of travellers. The man in charge of this herculean task, the wonderfully named Fulgence Bienvenüe, and his army of earthworms soon finished the first line. Six others are planned. They will radiate in all directions, to my outer edges. A new digestive system, from Vincennes to Maillot. Or a throat, rather, for my human nutrients, as they enter my vaulted intestines, the sewers.

On Quai de la Rapée, they are building giant dynamos for M. Bienvenüe's train. While the electric powerlines run along my streets to illuminate the night, somewhere below them other cables will light up the bulbs on routes that will never see daylight. Whoever goes down into the building site of the Métropolitain says goodbye to blue skies forever.

Some future lines will run on bridges over roads, others under my sister the Seine. Fulgence Bienvenüe's engineers will freeze its subsoil by injecting it with icy brine for long enough to put in place their waterproof steel tanks. They're going to freeze the arse off my shifty, prudish sister.

The Métropolitain was designed so that no other train from outside Paris, no other railway companies or other countries, could pass through it. If an enemy lays siege to me, my people will be able to move around safely inside me.

Fulgence is not a lover like Gustave, divided between the duty of his mission as a builder and his lust for glory. Fulgence is an engineer's engineer. Bony and preoccupied, he has only one arm – the other one had to be amputated after he fell onto the train tracks during the inauguration of a new line and a train crushed it. You have to hang around him for a long time before you discover his charm. This man gave an arm for his work. He may lack poetry, but he is nonetheless capable of heroism. And that's without even mentioning those new sparks and the warm sensation in my loins . . .

I now have a new symmetry, like some anti-podes, an inverted world beneath my feet: artificial rivers of passengers. But down there, deep in my guts, anxieties are nesting. The engineers will conquer new spaces that were previously considered beyond reach. The subsoil, and soon the sky. I can see some of them trying already, from the top of my tower, making wings so that they can take off into the air. They keep crashing but they won't give up.

And yet Fulgence ought to know, this man who lost his arm to a machine, that inanimate objects, in the hands of animated beings, can veer out of control.

Perhaps I'm worried because the navvies are digging up too many old memories. Their work is often interrupted by curators from the museum, by excavations. Sarcophagi here, skeletons and armour there. Investigations, long closed by time, are opened again. Smells rise up from disturbed graves. In the strata of the soil, machines break the seals of sediments. The history of so many defeats, a few rare victories, so many betrayals and crimes.

For Fulgence, the past is the greatest obstacle. He has dug up whole underground mountains that nobody even notices: millions of square feet of rubble carted away and camouflaged on the surface in filled ditches, dykes, in ballast and backfill.

What I like about Fulgence, when his machines

cease roaring, is the silence of his tunnels. We can speak down there. From one Métropolitain platform to another, under the vaulted ceilings, 50 feet apart, a man and a woman can whisper to each other and be understood, as if they were side by side. Even in the middle of a crowd. The geometry of tunnels overturns Euclid's axioms: the words of a woman and a man do not follow the straight line traced by their eyes; they fly up and touch the elliptical vault above before reaching the other.

Once the trenches have been refilled, there is no sign, on the surface, of this subterranean flux. Except for its hot breath, through the ventilation grids. All you see of the Métropolitain from above are its mouths. My heart races for another artist, the inspired architect M. Hector Guimard, who surrendered to the obvious: those mouths should be plants. Wisteria, vines and lily of the valley sink their roots into the electrified, mineral subsoil of the Métropolitain, and a cast-iron vegetation grows upwards. Hector has added flowers to the letters of the Métropolitain, tulips, with pistils of electric filaments.

Deep in my subterranean antipodes, I have a hanging garden of mechanical cultures.

12

For the *New York Tribune*, Aileen telegraphed a didactic version – turned into an interview stuffed with figures – of her *La Fronde* column.

At forty-eight, Fulgence Bienvenüe already looked like an old man. The absence of his left arm, in the empty sleeve of his suit, drastically slimmed his tall figure. She questioned him among a swarm of engineers and subordinates. He divided his time between them, the journalist and the workers that he greeted. She, too, was distracted, on the lookout for Jacques Huet, the geologist engineer.

They walked through the tunnels of Etoile station, below the Champs-Elysées, which would soon stop at the Exposition. A triple station, at the junction of the current Line 1, some sections already being built of a circular Etoile–Nation–Etoile line, and a third line heading towards Porte Dauphine. Aileen quickly lost all sense of direction and distance. After visiting for an hour in the heat and dust, with the magnetic weight of the earth pressing down on her head, she started to feel ill. Bienvenüe, a pale habitué of the underground dark, accompanied her back to the surface. She asked about the frozen soil and mentioned an engineer she'd heard about, who was in charge of the project.

"M. Huet?"

"Yes, I think that's his name. Do you know if I could meet him, for an article?"

"When he's not underground, M. Huet usually works at the design office of the Compagnie du Métropolitain, on boulevard Haussmann. Would you like my secretary to arrange a meeting for you?"

"Oh, there's no need. I was planning to follow the whole of Line 1 on my bicycle anyway. I'll just make a quick detour to boulevard Haussmann."

She had freewheeled down avenue de la Grande-Armée, the breeze cooling her face. At Porte Maillot, she'd taken notes beside Guimard's canopy over the station entrance. The long sweep of the Champs-Elysées was funnelled through the Arc de Triomphe, then went along avenue de la Grande-Armée, before it reached Maillot and left behind the scar of Route Nationale 13 amid the forests of Neuilly. She stared at this line of dried earth and the vehicles moving away from the capital. Her last memory unstained by Paris went back to Le Havre, when she'd felt intimidated, on the threshold of the European continent, by the promises she'd made to herself. The first one – finding Joseph – had taken her weeks and had not gone at all the way she'd imagined. She now saw him only rarely at the tepee. He kept disappearing for longer periods, and their meetings didn't help, offering no answers to the uncertain future of the ranch or of Joseph himself. She had stopped writing, too, since his absences had grown longer.

Aileen worried that her second promise – to visit the village in Alsace – would have the same result.

It was annoying to have to ride up avenue de la Grande-Armée; she was impatient to reach her goal. After the Arc de Triomphe, she let the slope of the Champs do the work for her, before turning onto avenue Matignon. It took her only a few minutes to find the building she was looking for, on the corner of boulevard Haussmann and rue d'Anjou.

The offices were modern-looking, with glass walls on both sides of the corridor. Behind standardised furniture and high drawing desks, employees watched her walk past as if she were parading for their entertainment in her cyclist's outfit. One self-assured man came out of his cubicle to ask her what she was looking for, then pointed the way to M. Huet's door.

Jacques had his back to the corridor and was sitting on a stool at his drawing table, in front of the windows. Aileen knocked on the glass, took a step back, and forced herself not to adjust her clothing behind that transparent door, which forced them into a silent, embarrassing exchange of looks, watched by Jacques' colleagues. He opened the door before his hesitation could make her visit look any more suspicious.

"Hello."

"M. Huet?"

"Yes."

She held out her hand.

"Aileen Bowman. I work for an American newspaper. M. Bienvenüe suggested I come here to meet you. I hope it's not a bad time?"

"How can I help you, Mrs Bowman?"

He let go of the journalist's hand, too quickly or too late, he couldn't tell which. He'd been careful with his voice, hamming up the proud swagger that his colleagues would expect. He kept a tight rein over the pleasure he felt, pretending to be slightly irritated by the inconvenience of her arrival.

"My editor is interested in the method of soil-freezing that you're developing. But if you don't have time now, perhaps we could arrange a meeting when I could interview you?"

He hesitated as best he could, while two men from neighbouring cubicles came out to smoke in the corridor.

"Will it take long?"

"Fifteen minutes. Thirty at most."

"Well, if M. Bienvenüe thinks it's a good idea . . . why not? And we may as well do it now, since you're here. There's a café across the street. Could I meet you there in a few minutes?"

Aileen thanked him and went back down the corridor, feeling the weight of men's eyes on her bottom, as heavy as the layers of earth above the metro tunnels. Jacques shrugged and shot a complicit smile at his envious co-workers. He pretended to draw a few lines on the map he was working on, before throwing his jacket over his shoulder.

He could be seen at a table in the café, behind the painted letters and arabesques on the window, in conversation with the redheaded journalist, who was taking notes. Each of them drank a glass of white wine, he more slowly than she did, and as he made his way back to his cubicle, responding to his colleagues' banter, the woman drank a second glass.

The dance hall called La Galette was located beneath two mills, the last survivors of a neighbourhood of artisans ruined by industrial flour production. They'd been left in place because, in addition to the small amount of flour they produced, they were also a tourist attraction.

By an ironic and erroneous role reversal, the mills in that café were compared to Don Quixote's – standards to rally romantics and drinkers – whereas Cervantes' mills had been the representatives of a new era that, with a movement of their mechanised arms, knocked the old knight and his old-fashioned ideals into a ditch. The princes of intoxication confounded Don Quixote and his mechanical enemy, industrial flour production.

Artists, lackeys and workers came to dance under the mills' large wings, immobilised for the night. The bourgeoisie, for whom the dance was merely a sort of extension of their daytime life, came to mix with the working classes and enjoy their authentic talent for having fun, a compensation for their fate.

At Jacques Huet's table sat some artists who were not exhibited at the Petit Palais. Jacques introduced them quickly, speaking directly into Aileen's ear to make himself heard above the music, voices and laughter. There were writers, poets, sculptors.

"Pablo is a young painter who's just come from Barcelona for the Exposition. Next to him, that's Casagemas, another Catalan; he's in love with a dancer from the Moulin Rouge. Poor man can't get over it. Nobody really knows if they have any talent, but they certainly have no shortage of revolutionary theories about art. Pablo adores the Métropolitain. He wants to visit the tunnels in construction. You should talk with him about that."

The room was lit up by a panoply of lamps. On their little stage, the musicians in the orchestra played rhythms that Aileen had never heard before. The dancers launched into new moves with each song, some of them alone, others in couples or even lines of ten or twenty. Around the dance floor was a barrier of red-painted planks, separating it from the tables where people played cards or chatted while sipping cheap wine made from the vines of Montmartre. At the tables of the rich, champagne corks went flying, attracting girls whose smiles and expert hands paid for their dresses. It was a weekday night, so the dance hall wasn't packed, but it was lively enough for the atmosphere to be good, the sound loud, and anonymity guaranteed. Because a scandal here was riskier than at a brothel. The whorehouse where Julius had taken Aileen was reserved for the upper classes; here, all the people of Paris came together. In fact, the real transgression was the amalgam of classes normally separated by the social order.

The artists at the table, ordering rounds on the engineer's tab, swore that Impressionism – Renoir, Monet and Pissarro – was dead and buried. That they were the future. The place was like a bigger version of the New York basements where Aileen used to meet artists and other women. Fanatical painters and businessmen in love with idiotic dancers, grandiose theories, drunken tears, noisy breakdowns and – everywhere – the crackle of sex. There were also men fleeing their home lives, like Jacques, who greeted the other regulars, drank a lot, left his sentences unfinished, and did all he could to defuse the danger of Aileen's presence. She asked him, her voice too loud:

"Does your wife know you're here?"

Her question was not an attempt to provoke. Aileen wanted to know whether Jacques shared his despair with someone who – unlike this gathering of young boozers – genuinely cared about him. The engineer's face took on the expression of self-mocking sadness that she had seen in Vincennes.

"Let's get some air."

There were stairways and terraces on the little hill, overlooked by the mills. From the slopes of Montmartre, the illuminated streets flowed towards the centre of Paris.

"I read your columns in *La Fronde*, written under your French pseudonym. I like the way you make Paris speak. All those transformations, those events too numerous for us to have the time to register them. Pablo mocks us for our slowness. He thinks he's the fastest painter in the world. Do you have a high place in New York like the Eiffel Tower where you can escape the rush of time?"

"You think my columns are really about me?"

"Are you saying they're not?"

"The tyrants' whore?"

"No, not that part."

"The engineers' mistress?"

He laughed.

"Definitely not them! Even their ambitions are dull."

She waited for the joke to be forgotten.

"I don't care if your wife knows where you are, but I do think you should talk to her. Nothing to do with our meeting."

"Our meeting? I wish I lived in a world like yours, where discussions like that are natural. Or that I had your talent for inventing another story that would tell mine."

"It's not that complicated. Find a suitable starting point. After that, it will all flow naturally."

"A starting point?"

"Where does the story of Jacques Huet and his wife begin?"

He thought for a moment.

"The story of his future wife."

"See? You've found it."

She took his arm and they left the Moulin de la Galette, then walked slowly down rue Lepic.

"It was a union of two families. In fact, it had all been decided long before. We were part of a plan drawn up before we were even born."

When Jacques talked about family homes in his country, his descriptions evoked presbyteries. Silent places built to protect their inhabitants from the outside world, inhospitable refuges, long buildings made of blue granite with narrow windows and heavy slate roofs to shelter them from strong winds. The Huets moved to Paimpol in the early 1860s, in the département of Côtes-du-Nord redrawn after the Revolution on land belonging to the region's bishops. His father, an artisan weaver, had a small workshop with two employees, in addition to his wife and himself.

"The Breton nobility, deprived of the taxes they used to levy on their land and goods, but still powerful. They hate the Republic and everything that comes from outside. Change, mechanisation, modernity . . . these things threaten their closed system of privileges. The big landowners did everything they could to slow down this transformation of Brittany. With the same efficiency as the industrial innovations they so feared, they drove the region into poverty. The forges, the slate quarries, the sail factories and the weavers' workshops all closed, one after another. All those activities that the nobility despises. They abandoned all that to their former subjects, a few of whom got rich and became the aristocrats' most hated enemies: the industrial bourgeoisie. The class into which I was born."

Jacques' father, with the aid of a Parisian relative, was among the first weavers to embrace modernisation. Within a few years, the widespread poverty providing him with cheap labour, his small business had grown into a factory employing fifty people, then a hundred.

"My mother was able to stop working, and to stop having miscarriages. I was born in 1866. For appearance's sake, in that society where wealth was considered tasteless and humble origins a source of shame, my parents decided that their eldest son would become a man of the cloth. It was also during that period that they bought the large house in Paimpol from a ruined shipowner. They paid in cash."

Jacques had gone to a seminary, but, at seventeen, instead of going to a theological university, he'd enrolled in a preparatory class. He would have made a terrible priest, so he decided that his sole objective was to be accepted by the Ecole des Ponts in Paris.

"What made you want to become an engineer?"

"I don't know ... An accumulation of ideas, almost all of them false, that I had about this profession and about Paris. The weaving looms in my father's factory fascinated me. And, looking back, I think maybe – although I never formulated it this way in my mind – I had an urge to make, to invent, not just to earn money and follow in my father's footsteps, to perpetuate a new form of lineage and domination similar to that of the nobility. That's what I think now, but at the time my greatest desire was just to get out of Paimpol."

"Were your parents disappointed?"

"Yes, but they couldn't stop me. They tried everything they could, though, and when the time came for me to leave, they organised a party on the Ile de Bréhat with members of another bourgeois family they knew, the Cornics. They were just as crafty as my parents. Their daughter, Agnès, was my age. She was the trap they set for me. What interested them was the Cornics' wealth: they'd made a fortune trading in foreign cotton. Agnès and I were both only children, so we had to carry all the hopes of our families on our shoulders. Agnès had been raised like a princess on Bréhat. It was one of the most beautiful parts of the region, and she had no intention of leaving her family home. I left. To please our families, I agreed to Agnès' request that we should write to each other. For a long time, reading her letters, I thought I'd been right about her. That the lessons she'd learned from her parents were the bars of her prison cell. You see, bourgeois families like the Cornics and my parents are convinced that the education of their children is their best defence against the prejudice they encounter. But they're wrong. Aristocrats, whose status runs through their veins, despise nothing as absolutely as education."

During the five years that followed Jacques' departure, the courtship of the Huet and Cornic heirs continued along the same wait-and-see approach. Their parents pressured them. Their shared resistance gradually brought the two young people closer. In summer, when Jacques went back to Brittany, the crossings between Bréhat and the mainland, sometimes difficult due to high winds, gave their meetings a touch of romance.

"And then one day, as we were walking ahead of our parents after the two families had eaten lunch together, Agnès spoke to me while staring straight ahead. I realised then that I'd been wrong about her. While everyone else was expecting me to return to Paimpol after I'd graduated, she asked me to take her with me to Paris. I'd thought she was a hopeless case, but in fact she'd just been biding her time. She'd been waiting to find out if this pretentious, arrogant young engineer was up to the task of helping her escape that island prison."

At twenty-five, Jacques received his degree as a geologist engineer. His reputation as an innovative student led to him being immediately hired by Chagnaud, a major firm specialising in public works. With his career prospects looking bright, he asked Agnès to marry him. Their secret pact – to satisfy their families' demands while at the same time escaping them – was sealed on Bréhat, at the local church of Notre-Dame-de-Bonne-Nouvelle, one bright and breezy day.

"Were you happy?"

"Yes. Agnès . . . Agnès inspired desire. We made a handsome couple. We still do. But Paris was a bad idea. Despite what we thought at first, Agnès wasn't ready for it. Perhaps she'd spent so long on her tiny island, living a life of confinement, that her mind had narrowed to fit within its parameters. But it was partly my fault too. I always worked too hard. Agnès didn't feel at home here, after summoning the courage to leave her family. In the end, she reduced her experience of Paris to the dimensions of Bréhat."

Jacques described the small Breton community that Agnès surrounded herself with. He detailed all the parties they held in their apartment, the visits from friends and relatives, not to mention all his professional obligations. They still loved each other, he said, for what they were, but without the joy of imagining what else they might have been.

"We had the courage to accept our responsibilities and our

mistakes. We did that together. But our relationship is not equal. Agnès loves me in a different way. Maybe because she depended on me to get out of Brittany. She feels a gratitude towards me that distorts the balance of our feelings. She wanted to pay back that debt by giving us a child. As soon as we moved to Paris, it became an obsession."

He was going more slowly now, as if afraid of reaching his destination too early. Aileen squeezed his arm encouragingly.

"We have all the time we need. Go on."

"You didn't plan all this, did you? Fainting in the stands of the velodrome, I mean?"

"No. And now I want you to tell me about your child. Please."

Jacques' expression darkened. He took a deep breath.

"After we had lived together for three years, Agnès still wasn't pregnant. The doctors couldn't give us a reason. She went back to Brittany for the summer. Her mother reproached her for not being able to satisfy her husband, putting her infertility down to some imagined dissolute life in Paris. Embarrassed by her mother's pestering, her intimate advice, Agnès asked me if we could stay in Paris the following summer. The city was quiet, and I had more time and less work. We spent several enjoyable weeks together. The following October, Agnès finally told me she was pregnant."

Jacques fell silent, as if he regretted having said too much. Then the muscles in his arm and the contact of his hip against hers grew tenser.

"We never again shared the simple happiness of those few weeks. That summer, we had freed ourselves from something. Mentally, but physically too. Our lovemaking had been more joyful. We weren't doing it to make a child, to give our parents an heir, or to repay a debt. We dared to make love purely for the pleasure. Then there was the pregnancy, the birth, and after that Agnès started going to church more often. Her desires were no longer strong enough to vanquish the taboos of her education, just strong enough to make her unhappy. She became a mother, but she was barely a wife anymore."

Agnès gave birth to a daughter in April 1893. Alice.

Every summer since then, she would take the little girl to the family home in Brittany, and Jacques would join them for one week in August. Agnès hated Paris now, and Jacques went out more and more.

"Our relationship has hardened. Our differences, however imaginary or unimportant, have grown more solid because we didn't fight them. That emotional drift . . . it's like a tide going out, exposing the ugliness beneath. It worries me when I hear Alice begging me constantly to let her go back to Bréhat, the magical island, the island of princesses. Agnès' parents have always blamed me for stealing their daughter from them; now they're doing their best to turn mine against me."

In a further attempt to avoid spending time at home, Jacques started cycling, riding for miles on end to empty his mind and tire out his legs. Since the opening of the Exposition, he'd been going to the Vincennes velodrome to train.

"Then I saw you fall off your bike and get to your feet, looking annoyed, on the dusty path, and you were the first woman to make me laugh in a long time. When I realised that, it made me sad."

They had reached Aileen's apartment building. Her head was spinning and buzzing. She imagined a tidal wave crashing over the island of Bréhat, sweeping away the Cornics, their granite house and all their possessions in a deluge of foam and debris and dragging them down to the bottom of the Channel. She stepped away from the engineer so she could look him in the eyes. He was pale in the electric light supplied to rue des Saints-Pères and the apartment building.

"I'm sorry if this sounds like a cliché, but would you like to come upstairs for one last drink? Everything around here is closed, and I don't want to let you leave in this state."

"Nothing between us is a cliché, I promise you that. But the conclusion of my story was so depressing that I feel compelled to go home and see Agnès."

Jacques held out his hand. Aileen held it and wouldn't let go. She pulled him gently towards her, stood on tiptoes in her boots, and kissed him on his hairless lips. Their mouths didn't open. She felt him smile. She grew smaller as her feet flattened themselves against the pavement.

"A little negotiation with the possibilities. To prove that we're alive."

"Your old knapsack smells of horse."

"All those hours on the bicycle don't change a thing. I'm a horsewoman."

"Good night, Aileen."

"Good night, Jacques."

Jacques took off his shoes in the entrance hall of their apartment. Agnès had fallen asleep in the large armchair in the living room, her body shaken by the spasms of a bad dream. He sat on the floor next to her. After a few minutes in his presence, Agnès' nightmare dissolved and her body grew calm. Jacques wanted to yell at her. That being part of a couple should not guarantee a good night's sleep, but rather the madness of insomnia. He mastered his anger, out of fear that it would disturb Agnès and bring back her bad dreams. He tucked the shawl more neatly around her shoulders, turned off the light, walked past the door of his daughter's bedroom, and went to bed. He was only two hours away from daybreak. He would be tired tomorrow for the visit to the construction site; he would feel ill underground, in the damp air of the tunnels.

He washed his face above the basin in the bedroom. The water in the bowl was white with soap, slimy between his fingers. He could smell Agnès' perfume, her beauty cream, her make-up.

Beneath all great tiredness lies a refusal to sleep. He floated on the surface of consciousness.

Through the window, he watched as the early dawn mists took possession of the Saint-Martin Hospital. Through their silver swirls he saw a man on horseback. The silhouettes of rider and animal were a darker black than the shapes of the tree trunks and the lawns. For a moment, they were still. Perhaps a policeman making his rounds. The man pulled on the bridle, the horse turned and disappeared into woodland. Jacques envied him: to have the whole city to himself, to be able to mount a beast and spur it to a gallop.

13

The horses slept standing up, swaying from side to side like drunkards. All was grey in the salty air of dawn. Only the black mustang was awake. He'd washed away his paintings that night.

He led his horse by the bridle across the camp of Pawnee Bill's Show. He was wearing the hat and the black suit with its long jacket stolen from the costumes trunk; he would have to put them back before the show began. On the horse's back was a discreet English saddle, chosen from among the Mexican saddles inlaid with silver.

The most difficult thing, each time, was convincing the mustang to walk like a white man's horse, trained for men and women who didn't know how to ride.

He knew the ways by heart, but Paris always scared him. He was too white to be an Indian, too red when he wanted to pass for a white man. In broad daylight, he was barely more discreet than a black man and he preferred to leave the mustang at the camp. He mounted the animal only at night, or when he was leaving for a few days.

The shoes he'd taken from the trunk that night were too big for him. Sometimes they were too small. The trousers were too tight around his buttocks. He rolled his shoulders and the tension on the reins made the horse lift its head; it was nervous on the cobbles of place de la Nation. There were people on the pavements and more traffic on the road. The first workers and shopkeepers were already up.

For him, the hardest thing was to look at this world through a white man's eyes. The eyes betrayed far more than they concealed. He was red inside.

He worried that he was late. Forcing himself not to use his spurs, he urged the mustang into a gallop along boulevard Diderot. His chest tightened at the idea that the horse might career out of control, that this journey might have no end, that he might never see the tracks of his own world again or smell the cold air of its winters, the warm summer scents of its plants. But he had also sworn, when he embarked for the Old World, never to return to the reserve again to be fed like a baby bird by white men. That was the direction indicated by his downward-facing hands. His duty. This thought came as a relief. His stomach didn't hurt anymore. He had fasted for four days, as he did before every expedition into the city. His stomach had stopped clamouring for food. The dizziness he felt was caused not by hunger but by time coiling around itself. On the warpath, past and future are identical; they lead to the same place. Time, for Indians, is not the same as it is for white men, cut into slices by their clocks. Red time turns like smoke inside the tepee, from top to bottom and from bottom to top, spreading and shrinking, all at once. Time is a snake, the first spirit to have inhabited the earth, which moves by rubbing its belly along the ground, advancing in waves – hence the idea of lying on the ground in Paris, to dream about it while looking up at the sky? He used to do it back in America, with his father Pete Ferguson – the white man who tried, staring at the evaporating clouds, to forget the time he'd been taught to count.

The people who slept on the pavements of Paris were all madmen or drunkards. Before going off on his expeditions, Joseph would wean himself off alcohol.

White men believe that they brought the grandeur of cities to the savage worlds of the red men of America, the yellow men of Asia and the black men of Africa. Maria, his Indian mother from South America, told him about the ruins of even greater, higher, more magnificent cities than the cities of white men. She described pyramids, temples that would have towered over cathedrals, sewers and public baths, fortresses covered with gold on mountain peaks so high that the air was thin there, about paved roads that ran for hundreds of miles, through forests so thick and vast that the white man was seized with fear. He himself had seen, in the United States, the remains of cities as ambitious as New York. On the banks of the Mississippi, what some had taken for mountains, incongruous in that landscape, had been man-made elevations. In New Mexico, there were stone buildings ten storeys high, cities still standing in whose streets you could lose yourself for a whole day. In Colorado, there were cities clinging like wild beehives to the cliffsides of mesas; on the tepees were drawings of trade routes connecting millions of men. But after the Spaniards' diseases had killed off the Indians and turned their cities into ghost towns, the new Americans had passed these remnants without even seeing them: white men do not see what is not white, Joseph repeated, hoping that this rule would apply to him too.

In his head, he heard his mother's voice, describing those ancient civilisations in Xinca, a linguistic family shared by the great Aztecs and the Paiutes. Joseph could speak the language of an entire continent. English and French were not even understood by all the inhabitants of England and France.

On the Pont d'Austerlitz, he stopped to look at the boats propelled by steam engines, which moved effortlessly, terrifyingly, against the Seine's current. The pilots and passengers probably imagined that these movements were magical. White men looked at but did not see the black smoke that poured from the chimneys, the dreck left behind by all this mechanical innovation. The steam horses were as greedy as children and they vomited half of everything they swallowed. White men were obsessed by money, but they didn't understand the cost of such things.

He followed the river along the docks on the southern bank, passing moored barges, then set foot on the Pont des Arts. In the shadow of its arch, the horses were tied to iron rings cemented in the stone. A young groom stabbed a pitchfork into a wheelbarrow full of dung and soiled straw, then threw the muck into the water. The boy froze for an instant, recognising the little man on the handsome black horse. This man with his strange-coloured skin who talked to his animal in a sorcerer's language and couldn't speak French. The groom knew what he had to do. The man in the black suit knew the prices and he handed the boy the money it cost for him to look after the horse for a day. Every time, the mustang made the workhorses nervous. The boy had told his master that the coloured man scared him, but the master didn't care as long as he got the money. And he paid well, this sorcerer with his shining eyes, in his clothes that were too big for him. He always gave an extra coin for the boy, who watched as his strangest customer walked away.

The sun rose along the buildings. Joseph soon found the street where his white sister lived. He knew the number of steps it took to reach her floor, knew which windows belonged to her apartment, knew how to slip into the inner courtyard without being seen by the woman who looked after the building. He knew how to climb onto the roof of the house across the courtyard, so he could get within a few feet of his ranch sister's lodging. She stayed up late at night, writing her articles and her story of the Bowman family.

The first time he followed her here and waited for her to leave the apartment, he'd wanted to break a window and steal her papers. She'd come out, then gone back inside just in time to prevent him, and she'd started writing again. Joseph despised himself for being curious about what the white sister thought of him, the words she would choose to describe him. So he stayed where he was, mired in his shame, watching as she leaned over the white paper and darkened it with her pencil. His white father had told him that people of his race used words not to say things but to hide them: "They have so many, it's impossible to know what's true and what's lies. They even write whole books of made-up stories – novels – as another way of talking about reality. The characters in the stories imitate real people, and the readers like to believe in them so that they can feel fear and joy and imagine themselves as heroes. These are the words that hide other words: lie-words."

Joseph loved his white father. It took him a long time to realise that Pete was half-mad and respected because of that by the Indians. He loved his white father and he was ashamed of him. But the real madness – the one that the people at the ranch said was in him – was his mother's. Maria Bautizada, the uprooted.

Joseph loved his mother and he was ashamed of her.

What he'd realised too late about his parents was that their love for each other was much stronger than the humiliation they suffered, much stronger than what the rest of the world thought of them. Joseph didn't understand the forces that produced this feeling. Was it something he needed? Was love necessary for the warrior as it was for other men? Was it a weapon or a weakness if your life was spent fighting? All he knew was that there were several different kinds of love. Love of war, love of bodies, love of beautiful things. But his parents' love for each other, was that what his ranch sister had brought him as a gift?

While he was on the roof of the neighbours' house, spying on Aileen Bowman for the first time, she'd turned her chair to the window and looked out at the night. Joseph thought he'd been caught. His white sister could track animals; she knew some of the red man's tricks. But she hadn't stood up. From the brightly lit room, she could see only blackness . . . or her reflection in the windowpanes. She'd unbuttoned her trousers, slid them off her thighs, slipped one hand between her legs and the other under her shirt. Joseph had crawled to the very edge of the roof.

White women smell bad and are ugly: that was what young Indian boys were taught. But he knew that red men liked white women. That they were proud to possess them. But they couldn't be accused of preferring their white blood to their Indian blood. If he had a white woman as a slave, she and Joseph would look like a couple, not a master and his possession. In the white sister's world, too, they would soon find a reason to hang them both. Like his parents, rejected by two worlds, who died frozen together by the cold, which – that winter – was merely a lie-word, concealing the poverty-stricken reserve, the insufficient rations, the absence of game, arable land, blankets. The cold that had killed his parents was, in fact, the name of a crime. And the scene of the crime was that very same tepee where he'd once hidden to catch a glimpse of his ranch sister's naked body. He remembered his mother's hands as she tattooed that pale, pale skin, touching it, covering it, as if to forbid it to him.

On the slippery slates, his face reaching out towards the window, Joseph had heard Aileen's final sighs.

She had stood up, holding her trousers in one hand, and turned off the light.

Since then, he had gone back as often as he could. He was on his way there now, but he had missed the night. Too late yesterday, they had raised new backdrops for Pawnee Bill's Show. He'd rushed to leave Vincennes at the hour of the wolf, in the hope that he would at least see her before she left the apartment.

The roof was only accessible at night. In the day, he waited in the street to follow her.

She came out of the apartment building. She looked dazzling in the sunlight, with her red hair that can only be produced by mixing two white people. Aileen pushed her bicycle beside her as she wove through the crowds. He became a shadow in her wake.

She straddled her two-wheeled machine and rode along the road, her knapsack on her back and her old hat buffeted by the wind. He started to run, keeping his eyes on her red curls. If he wouldn't ever see the tracks of America again, his muscles could consume all the energy in his body. He ran, without pacing himself. The only waste, the only smoke, was what poured from his mind, spiralling upwards into the pillars of the sky.

Aileen came to a halt at the top of a large avenue of luxury shops, with the triumphal door towering over it: a strange door, with no walls around it, a door that opened onto nothing. She shook hands with a one-armed man, surrounded by other men in long coats, who were standing in front of some metal balustrades in the shapes of plants.

Joseph watched her disappear underground, accompanied by the men in black frock coats, like the ones worn to sign peace treaties. He walked over to the mouth of the Métropolitain and sniffed the scents rising up from those damp galleries, that world of rodents, foxes, snakes. Unsure where Aileen would re-emerge from that subterranean labyrinth, he stayed where he was to keep an eye on her bicycle.

When she reappeared, an hour later, his ranch sister was pale. She let the slope of the boulevard sweep her along on her bicycle away from the centre of Paris. Eyes fixed on her, he began to run again, in those absurd leather shoes that hurt his heels.

At the gates of the city, she took notes as she contemplated the dusty road that ran through dense forests.

He didn't need to run to keep up with her when she rode back up the slope towards the city. But at the top of the hill, she changed direction and began moving more quickly again. Joseph didn't know these streets and it became important not to lose her. His strength failing, he had to draw on new reserves. The warrior can find within himself what other men do not know they possess. His running grew more erratic as his legs tired. He bumped into pedestrians. Coach drivers yelled that he was a madman. Finally, she stopped in front of a building and went inside. In a stone corner, he collapsed. Old alcohol sweated through his pores as he caught his breath, never taking his eyes off the bicycle, that animal that consumed its rider's energy as it advanced.

His white sister re-emerged a few minutes later and crossed the street to a café, one of those places with glass walls, dark furniture and polished brass. She sat at a table behind the window and, when she took off her old hat, her red hair mingled with the red-painted plants on the glass. Something in her had changed. He couldn't read the expressions on her face. Tension, impatience and anxiety were the lie-words that didn't say what he was seeing. She turned towards the street and other emotions flickered on her furrowed brow, in her quick eyes and mobile lips. Joseph followed her gaze and saw the man with pale hair coming out of the same building, crossing the boulevard, forcing himself not to break into a run, just as she forced herself, behind the window, not to wave to him.

The man sat opposite her. Joseph's vision blurred.

Their conversation didn't last long. The man came out again and disappeared into the building, and Joseph waited for Aileen, who didn't leave the table. She drank another glass of alcohol. The edges of Joseph's vision were drowned in translucent waves. A warrior doesn't cry. He waited, unblinking, for the water in his eyes to be dried by the wind.

At last Aileen got back on her bicycle and Joseph, heavy-legged, wove after her. When he recognised the neighbourhood where she was staying, he stopped. She was going home. He took a wrong turning. His heart wanted to lead him somewhere else. He let her vanish at the end of a street and the smoke from his mind, which had risen on the heat from his dreams of possession, fell cold onto his shoulders.

Joseph went back to the river and picked up his mustang, paying no attention to the groom, who wanted to give him his money back since the day wasn't over. He sat in the saddle and rode towards Vincennes. After a few feet, he pulled on the reins and the horse stood immobile on the dock. The boy watched as the strange man turned his horse around. He shivered as they passed, the man's dark eyes staring somewhere into the distance.

Joseph had not forgotten the way. He retraced his footsteps. In one of those back alleys where he'd learned to find shade at all hours of the day, he and his horse melted into darkness. He had a perfect view of the building and, that evening, he had no trouble recognising the man who'd spoken with Aileen. Joseph had recovered his strength. He wasn't hungry. The warrior's belly is always full. War is his food.

The man with blond hair went first to the café and had a few drinks with some colleagues. Then he stood on the pavement and waited for a hackney cab, which took him away. The sun began to rise up the buildings' floors. Joseph dug his heels lightly into the mustang's flanks. He was a horse rider in a suit, surrounded by the late-afternoon crowds and traffic jams. Everybody saw what they expected to see. He followed the carriage to a distant part of town, on a hill that rose above the rest of Paris. The man paid the driver outside an arched doorway garlanded with lights. Above, the immobile arms of a windmill reflected the pink gleam of the setting sun. He found a shadow even darker than the last one, where he could hide for the evening. His heart beat more quickly when Joseph saw his ranch sister arrive a few minutes later, in another cab. She went through the garlanded doorway.

When the sky was darker and the streets less busy, Joseph

took off his suit jacket, drew his cutlass from the holster at his belt, and sliced the jacket into four pieces. Lifting his horse's feet one by one, he wrapped each one in cloth. Paris was too silent now for them to go unheard once the hunt began again.

Aileen and the blond man came out of the building together. Behind them, Joseph heard muffled music and laughter.

They walked at the rhythm of two people who are listening to each other. Joseph followed. He was no longer afraid of losing them. He could smell the odour of alcohol coming from the man, the odours of leather and clothing from his ranch sister. Sometimes he had to stop, to let them get a little further ahead. Either they were slowing down or he was speeding up without realising. His curiosity kept overpowering his caution, taking him closer to them. Not that he needed to hear them. They were saying the same things that all men and women say when they first fall in love. Foolish nonsense. Lies to make them appear more than they are. Made-up secrets. They were manufacturing a love from cities, poetry, unmanly feelings. Women's rubbish. Had he moved close enough to hear them, Joseph would not have understood a word of the French they were speaking to each other. But he knew.

There were too many lights outside the apartment building on rue des Saints-Pères, so he had to keep his distance. But he could see, beneath the electric streetlamp, his white sister stand on tiptoes and pull the white man towards her so she could kiss him. Joseph's vision blurred again. Instead of going upstairs with her, though, the man left and Aileen went back to her apartment, alone.

Joseph hesitated. He wanted to be happy about this separation. It had all been a misunderstanding. Inconsequential. The clerk wasn't right for his ranch sister. Everything separated them.

How could he have imagined that Aileen might like this man, as soft as a woman?

The man went home. She went up to her apartment. Perhaps she would write that night. Turn her chair towards the window. Because she knew. She must know, deep down. Nobody can be followed like that, for weeks – nobody who knows Indian tricks and the art of hunting – without guessing. She must suspect that he was out there, on the roof, on the other side of her window. She knew there was somebody there.

Joseph's cheeks and scalp suddenly went cold.

And what if, tonight – when she pulled her trousers down, arched her back against the chair, slid her fingers through the thick red hair – she would be thinking about that other man?

Joseph turned to the far end of the street and saw the man walking away through darkness. Joseph mounted his horse. Hooves muffled by the sliced-up frock coat, the mustang and his rider passed under electric streetlamps, appearing and disappearing like cinematographic images, silent and in slow motion.

In the park, the horse nibbled grass, then stopped eating; it didn't taste good. The horse was trained for war and could fast if need be. The mustang decided to feed on the patience of its vigilant rider.

Joseph stared at the windows of the man's apartment. The man's figure appeared behind a raised curtain. He must have seen Joseph on his horse. Joseph decided to stay there for a moment, long enough for the man to register his presence, and perhaps to start feeling afraid. Then he squeezed his thighs together and the mustang, obeying his order, carried them into a cloud of mist that was swelling in the first glimmers of daylight.

14

Two days later, Jacques Huet was sitting at his desk and going through his work correspondence when he found a letter personally addressed to him. His anxiety mounted when he saw who it was from.

Since his evening with Aileen Bowman and their conversation, which had lingered on the subject of Agnès, there had been a strange presence in his apartment, between his wife and himself. Questions that had, before, been dissolved in the air were now solidified into the form of Jacques' ghostly double. A shadow that followed him around, murmuring the thoughts that he muzzled, that his wife would, in the end, hear too. At home, Jacques would turn suddenly, imagining a creak from the floorboard, imagining Agnès coming up behind him. In the street, he would jump at the sounds of voices, thinking he was being spoken to, mistaking perfect strangers for acquaintances, as if everyone in Paris was angry with him. His double dogged his footsteps, as if about to yell into his wife's face the question that would betray him: if they had nothing to hide, why did he and Agnès live so guiltily?

And now Aileen had sent him a message.

He wanted to throw it in the bin, but he didn't. He opened the envelope, unfolded the page.

Dear Jacques,

I worry about the consequences that your confessions must have had on you, because they have had an effect on me. I feel so saddened by the fate that years of marriage have had on you and your wife.

So I am going to make a suggestion. You can do whatever you like with it. But whatever you decide, please don't doubt that I am sincere.

You are making a mistake when you go out alone and seek, at those artists' tables, the happiness and enjoyment lacking in your home. While the Montmartre dance halls may not be to your wife's tastes, she has as much need as you do for another Paris beyond her little entourage of Breton friends. Don't let her wither away for false reasons. Your daughter will grow up. After years of being a mother, your wife will soon become your wife again.

I have an artist friend in Paris whom I am sure you would like. Come, with Agnès, to have dinner with us. That way, she will be able to share another world with you, and not the world of your work. We will be among friends.

Sometimes, simple things, at the right moment, can have significant effects. Like talking to a stranger about something that has, for a long time, been weighing on your heart.

Think about it.

Affectionately,

Aileen

That evening, Jacques did not say anything to his wife. The American woman was crazy. She wasn't content to play with words, like the drunkards in Montmartre; she wanted to meddle in reality too. She wanted to meddle in his marriage. With her trousers and her riding boots and her "artist friend" (the combination of those two words enough to give Jacques disturbing dreams). She wanted all four of them to go out for dinner? In Paimpol, even saying hello to a woman like Aileen Bowman would be enough to earn you the opprobrium of the entire town.

The next morning, Jacques was so angry that he couldn't concentrate on work. His rage was directed towards all those bigots who would not let him go out to dinner with his wife and Aileen. Besides, Aileen herself had included a male friend in this invitation. As a precaution. For the sake of decorum. To reassure Agnès? It wasn't his wife's reaction that prevented him from accepting, but the reaction of the rest of the world. The world he lived in. The world he'd chosen. The world he'd fought so hard to reach after leaving behind the equally suffocating world of Brittany. He was also angry with Aileen, for her naivety and the way she was offering a solution to problems that she herself had created. But he was lying to himself. His anger was really at himself. What problem did he have now that had not already existed before he met Aileen in the Bois de Vincennes? For the rest of the day, his frustration alternated with bouts of sadness and flickers of resolution.

That evening, as they were dining with the windows open, the background noise of the city and the June heat seeping into the apartment, Jacques began to speak, in the most neutral tone he could manage. He'd answered a few questions, he said, after being asked to do so by M. Bienvenüe in person, from an American journalist, a woman. She was writing an article on the Métropolitain, which would perhaps include a few lines on the work he was doing. Agnès was interested.

"In which newspaper?"

"An American newspaper, in New York. And perhaps in *La Fronde* too."

"*La Fronde*? But isn't that a newspaper with a . . . um, a strange reputation? Is it a good thing for your name to appear in its pages?"

"I'm not worried. It's true that some of its articles have been criticised for their excesses, but it also publishes a lot of serious journalism, which is increasingly well thought of."

"Is it true that only women write for it?"

"I don't know."

"And that American woman works for *La Fronde*?"

"As well as for her newspaper in New York. She speaks perfect French."

Agnès' curiosity had been piqued by the mention of *La Fronde* and the female journalist, so Jacques changed the subject. How long had it been that he'd believed his wife incapable of accepting more than he suggested? Was she too timid, or was he too cowardly?

The next day, at the same table, he put things to her this way:

"I got a letter at the office today, from that American journalist I was telling you about. It's a little strange, but she wants to invite the two of us to dinner at a restaurant to thank me for answering her questions. She's also inviting an artist friend of hers, another American, who lives in Paris."

"The two of us? With an American artist?"

"She's a little . . . how can I put this? . . . original."

Then, leaning towards his daughter and his wife, he added in an amused tone:

"She always wears trousers and riding boots."

He laughed loudly. So did Agnès. Little Alice looked up from her plate.

"Does she ride around Paris on a horse?"

"No. She dresses like a horsewoman, but she actually rides a bicycle!"

All three of them laughed. Jacques started eating again.

"I'll decline politely. Never mind if she doesn't publish my interview. It's not important."

Agnès didn't say anything. They finished the meal in silence. As she cleared the table, Agnès told him that she thought it was perhaps a bad idea.

"What's a bad idea?"

"Turning down her invitation. What if M. Bienvenüe doesn't understand?"

"Hmm, I hadn't thought of that . . . But I don't know this woman, never mind her artist friend. I don't want to put you through that meal."

Agnès stood up tall.

"It's for your work."

"Well, at least the restaurant is supposed to be good."

"Then we'll enjoy a delicious meal."

She went into the kitchen and Jacques, watching her rigid back, wondered what expression she had on her face at that moment.

"You're going to eat dinner with the woman who wears trousers?" Alice asked.

Jacques didn't hear her. He was hoping that his lies, when laid out next to each other, would form a virtuous chain. That something good might finally emerge from this web of deceit.

The restaurant was new, but very good. It was on rue Mesnil, very close to place Victor-Hugo. The benches were upholstered in Empire-green leather. Trellised panelling and a low ceiling gave the place an intimate feel, in contrast to the large brasseries that were currently all the rage. The hangings on the walls absorbed the echoes of voices, and you felt comfortably isolated from the other tables. The paintings that decorated the restaurant were mostly modern, Impressionist, and Jacques Huet wondered if it was Julius Stewart – who invited him and Agnès to sit down – who'd chosen this restaurant. Jacques had heard of Stewart's paintings. He knew quite a few artists, of course, but not many who'd been successful. And he'd never before shaken the hand of a millionaire. A little intimidated, he became muddled as he introduced his wife:

"My wife, Agnès. Agnès, this is Mr Stewart, a famous artist. It's an honour to meet him. Mr Stewart, we are enchanted to make your acquaintance. Miss Bowman didn't tell us . . ."

The famous artist, whose wealth freed him of the obligation for exaggerated formalities, gave a simple bow and held out his hand to Agnès.

"The pleasure is all mine, madame."

Agnès was wearing her prettiest dress. It was also her most expensive dress, but it had been chosen so as not to appear to be her most precious possession. A strategy that befitted her natural modesty – and one of the first Parisian lessons that she had learned: trying too hard to appear a certain way, in this world of appearances, was the surest sign of poor taste. Julius didn't care about Agnès' dress or her provincial manners; he was delighted by her face and her figure, and no longer regretted accepting Aileen's strange invitation.

They sat down and, with a single sweeping gaze, Julius gave Jacques a simple smile, and Agnès a smile of pleasure, before noting the grain of her neck, the shape of her mouth and the strength of her eyes. Then he hailed a waiter, who went away to fetch the bottle of champagne he'd ordered.

"I apologise for Miss Bowman. She's running a little late."

"I saw two of your paintings at the Grand Palais, Mr Stewart. I'm an admirer of your work, and of your colleagues from the American school. M. Sargent in particular. Henry Tanner too. And Thomas Eakins."

Julius tore his eyes away from Agnès. He wondered if Jacques' enthusiastic tone was intended partly to make him stop staring at his wife.

"You only like American painters who live in Paris?"

"I know the work of French artists too, of course. I have met M. Monet and M. Renoir a few times."

Jacques felt stupid, dropping the names of artists that Julius probably didn't care about. The arrival of the champagne distracted them for a minute. Julius raised his glass.

"To new encounters and surprises."

Agnès took a sip of the sparkling wine and asked the first questions that she had prepared for the evening:

"Have you been friends with Miss Bowman for a long time, Mr Stewart? Did you meet in America or here in Paris? Have you lived here long?"

"Which question shall I answer first?"

Jacques, embarrassed, echoed Julius' laughter.

"We became friends recently. But, as is sometimes the case, our meeting seemed fated. What about you, M. Huet? Aileen tried to explain to me what you do, but I'm afraid it went over my head. You're freezing the subsoil of Paris, is that right?"

Julius stood up before the engineer could respond.

"Ah, here she is."

Jacques imitated him and the two men froze. Agnès, looking up while trying not to let her curiosity show, followed their gaze. Because, while the famous artist intrigued her, it was this journalist – the mysterious, trousers-wearing Miss Bowman – whom she was most impatient to meet.

Aileen had taken a deep breath before opening the door. She was a little nervous, but above all she was struggling to breathe. She quickly looked around and spotted them at the back of the room, both men standing tall: the blond engineer, all dressed up, and Julius, with his black beard and his butcher's shoulders. They made a perfectly odd pair. Jacques Huet blinked while Julius seemed unsure whether to laugh or applaud.

After prevaricating for so long that she made herself late, Aileen now felt certain that she'd made the wrong choice. It would surely have been sufficiently respectable to invite Julius, rounding out the numbers so that Mme Huet wasn't shocked. The decision to squeeze her body into Marguerite Durand's dress had just succeeded in making her look ridiculous. She wasn't even sure she was wearing the damn thing correctly. The collar made her itch, the seams under her arms were uncomfortably tight, and – even after getting rid of the corset – the tightness of the fitted waist and the bra cups were suffocating her. The only thing she liked about the dress, to this point, was the air circulating below, caressing her legs. She was wearing only one slip and no stockings, and her old riding boots were hidden beneath the layers of fabric.

The staring eyes of all the men in the room were putting her ill at ease. The dress showed her bottom less than her trousers did, while the stiff bustier revealed less of her breasts than her badly buttoned shirts, but – once she had got past the novelty of not making everyone around her look shocked and disapproving – she immediately found the dress's power of attraction deceptive and dangerous. Along with sexual desire, it gave men the violent urge to take back that power. There was something repulsively bestial in those looks between the males in the restaurant, each of them measuring up the others, trying to work out which of them – young or old, rich or less rich, handsome or not – could claim possession of such a female. Aileen, in this dress that was supposed to flatter her, was constantly sending out signals of submission, to feminine fashion and to masculine judgment, validating the men's right to turn women into social merchandise. And the only reason she'd succumbed to this ridiculous convention was to appease a stranger, a bigoted woman whose husband she was hoping to steal for a night or two. The most revolting thing, in fact, was the competition that the beautiful redhead, in her pearl-coloured dress, had launched among the other women. They all sat up and whispered something, expressing their hostility, feigning indifference or contemptuously refusing to compete, all in order to make themselves look good in the eyes of the men they were with. Faced with Aileen, they defended their right to be possessed, their value in this green-leather livestock market.

Jacques gave a formal bow, while Julius looked like he could barely believe his luck: not only did he have the delectable Agnès Huet for company, but also this second woman who immediately made their table the most envied in the establishment. Before sitting beside the artist, Aileen held out her hand to Agnès. It was violently obvious that the two women were not prepared for this encounter.

Mme Huet's surprise – at meeting not Miss Bowman, a young American journalist, a woman who looked like a cowboy, but a woman in her thirties, wearing a beautiful dress, hair tied in a brazen bun, without make-up or the faintest idea of the effect she had on men – turned to unbearable embarrassment when Aileen, not letting go of her hand, gazed directly into her eyes for far longer than decorum dictated.

Jacques Huet panicked internally, imagining that this exchange was a gauntlet thrown down between two rivals.

Julius, who knew Aileen's tastes when it came to women and the complex detours of her desires, wasn't fooled. He realised that this dinner would need a wise moderator, a referee, an agent provocateur: all roles that, as an habitué of luxury brothels and society events, he could ably fill.

"My dear Aileen, your dress is enchanting. I would love to paint you dressed like that!"

Then, with an irreproachable sense of gallantry and timing, he turned to Agnès.

"Something I hadn't yet dared ask of you, my very dear Agnès, out of fear that I would appear impolite, but that I will do now. If your husband permits it, I would be delighted to invite you to my studio."

Agnès, blushing deeply, had to force herself not to stare at the table. Jacques observed his wife while he awaited her response. Aileen, left to her own devices, at last had time to examine her properly. The engineer's wife, princess of Bréhat, reduced by her family to a shameful portion of herself, was far more beautiful than necessary. A beauty quite absurd for such a timid being. Aileen imagined that this woman was terrified by her own appearance, which contradicted the degraded image she had of herself. Aileen felt stupid in this dress which distorted the real Aileen Bowman, the rebellious, liberated journalist, heir to forests and waterfalls. She wanted to prove to Jacques' wife that she was not some vain fool; she was *that woman*, the one that she – like Joseph – believed she'd given up being.

Agnès was the woman who doesn't want the right to vote. The woman who is suffocated to death in corsets. The woman who lives in a husband's shadow. Even a husband like Jacques.

Aileen couldn't bear Julius' double-entendres, which she alone could understand, about the studio and the portraits of the two women, spoken as they were in an urbane and lightly mocking tone that showed his contempt for the Huets. Or was it the reaction of the engineer's wife – intimidated but curious, attracted to the idea of saying yes – that she couldn't bear? Aileen swallowed the remarks she wanted to make about Charlotte and the artist's other models and muses, hired by the hour from the local brothel. After all, it had been her idea to organise this dinner and to invite Julius to entertain Jacques' wife, in order to give Jacques and her courage, and – even though she refused to feel guilty about it – to smooth over any anxieties that she might have given the engineer. So she let Julius launch his charm offensive and continued to observe Agnès. With her shyness conquered by a second glass of champagne, the young woman was able to tell the artist that it was a new idea for her, being the subject of a painting. Aileen realised then that her desire to intervene had nothing to do with Julius' half-indecent proposal. She wanted Agnès to notice her. She now wanted this dinner, which she'd arranged for M. and Mme Huet, to be a tête-à-tête between Agnès and herself. Unwittingly granting this wish, Agnès turned to the American woman. She had some questions prepared for her too.

"Do you like Paris, Miss Bowman? You don't miss New York?"

Aileen played along with this game of innocent questions and answers, taking care not to mention her ranch or her wild childhood, because she knew that would make the evening about her. She'd decided to stick to her initial reasons for this meeting: entertaining Jacques and Agnès. So it was their conversations that she and the ever-polite Julius followed and sustained.

She couldn't tell if Agnès realised she was the centre of attention – not only from her loving husband, but from predatorial Julius and bare-legged Aileen – or whether she chose not to notice it. The woman seemed to have none of the affectation, coquettishness and guile common to her gender. When Agnès was surprised, she practically jumped in her seat; when something sad was mentioned, she immediately felt sad; when someone paid her a compliment, she genuinely refused to believe it. As the evening wore on, it became clear that the handsome Huets were enjoying the modern cuisine, expensive wines and eccentric company. From Jacques' looks and smiles, Aileen also understood that Agnès was drinking more than usual. The engineer was euphoric, his cheeks flushed with alcohol, and when the meal was over he kept making toasts. The Huets were taking a simple pleasure from this evening that Julius and Aileen would never be able to share. But she didn't care how banal their conversations were. In the presence of Agnès, that pure object of desire, time seemed to fly for Aileen.

After dessert, the restaurant owner suggested they go through to the smoking room for a glass of cognac. The two men sat in armchairs with cigars, while the women sat on a sofa, a few feet apart, and were finally able to have a conversation uninterrupted by Jacques and Julius.

"Miss Bowman, I envy you your life as a journalist. It seems so fascinating, and you get to travel all over the world. Jacques and I still haven't had a chance to go anywhere. We do talk about it though. He dreams of visiting Egypt."

"You're both from Brittany, if I understand correctly? Do you go back there often?"

"I spend every summer there, with our daughter."

"Do you like Paris?"

"Yes, of course."

"And you don't mind spending all your time at home, without working?"

"I beg your pardon?"

"You don't get bored?"

Agnès controlled the volume of her voice, not wishing to be heard by her husband, but the words came out in a rush:

"I am fully occupied looking after our home. And the little spare time I have, I devote to our parish. No, I certainly don't have time to get bored. That's not how I was raised."

"Don't take my questions the wrong way. If my work as a journalist interests you, I could introduce you to the editor of *La Fronde*. I'm sure you could find some work there, during the little spare time that you have."

Agnès felt herself losing her temper again, even while she realised that Aileen was trying to help her, that the wine was affecting her judgment, that the journalist's question about Brittany had made her uneasy.

"*La Fronde*? What a strange idea! I have never read a single line in that newspaper. Besides, what do I know about journalism? Absolutely nothing."

"You could learn. You're educated, cultivated."

"You don't know anything about me!"

Agnès turned bright red. One hand resting on her stomach, she apologised.

"Excuse me, Miss Bowman. You were trying to be nice and I replied very rudely. I think I'm starting to feel tired. We should go home."

"Don't apologise. You have the right to do whatever you want, including losing your temper. The whole team at *La Fronde* are fighting for those rights. The right for women to say what they think, to practise any profession, and to refuse the roles that their education and their family have moulded them to take. You should read that paper more often and travel the world, instead of going back to see your parents every year and using your spare time to do charity work for your church."

Agnès was stunned, but she still kept control of her voice, polite even in the depths of humiliation.

"What have I done to earn your anger, Miss Bowman? You say you want to help me, but your tone says the opposite. You know nothing about me and now I have no idea what I'm even doing here. Excuse me."

She stood up. Aileen, teeth gritted, didn't move. Agnès told Jacques that she felt tired and wished to go home. They both thanked Julius, who insisted on paying for the meal. They were the last customers to leave the restaurant. As they were saying goodbye outside, Jacques almost overdid it, torturing Agnès by thanking the journalist at great length.

"This meal was an excellent idea. I'm delighted that this article for your newspaper gave us the opportunity to get to know each other better, and to meet Mr Stewart. I hope that, before you leave Paris, we will have the pleasure of returning the favour."

"I'm sure the opportunity will present itself."

"Don't hesitate to get in touch."

"Your wife is waiting, Jacques."

Agnès, suddenly sober, held in her anger but refused to let the journalist have the last word.

"It's very late and we need to collect our daughter. One of our neighbours is looking after her."

With this ordinary, domestic remark, the Huets left. As the engineer waved enthusiastically from behind the window of their car, Julius suggested to Aileen that they have one last drink.

"I think I'll go home, actually, and take off this stupid dress."

"I would offer my aid, but you seem determined to leave me alone tonight. However, I am not going to let you leave before you give me an explanation. Let's forget this strange meeting; just tell me about that dress. You didn't dress like that to please me, and I find it hard to believe that you went to all that trouble to impress some Breton engineer! I'm not sure whom you had the biggest effect upon, the husband or the wife. The beautiful Agnès, whom I would have guessed was a nun if not for her wedding ring, is going to take a long time to get over this encounter with a woman of your kind."

And he burst out laughing.

Without a word, Aileen left. She walked for two hours, in her worn old boots, skirting around the barriers encircling the Exposition and Paris' illuminated centre, until she reached rue des Saints-Pères. Not only did this dress make her look ludicrous, but it meant she couldn't ride her bicycle.

Inside her apartment, she tore off the dress. Buttons and hooks went flying and scattered over the floorboards. Her trousers, shirt and jacket were waiting for her, on the chair at her desk. She looked at the manuscript, which lay there on the desktop, and wondered where her story was going. She kept delving further and further back into her memories, into the biographies of her parents, and now she had no idea when the story would start being about her.

She put on her trousers, depriving her skin of that contact with the air, and walked over to the window, where she buttoned up her shirt, hiding her tattoos. Her desire for Agnès and her anger with her had cancelled each other out during that long walk across Paris. She wondered what had driven her – beyond her usual mistrust – to make an enemy of Jacques' wife. Had she done it to snuff out her impossible desires? Or perhaps, more perversely, to ruin the end of Agnès' evening? Despite her naivety and all the things that the Huets hadn't understood, the evening had been saturated with sensuality and its echoes would accompany them, along with the effects of the alcohol, back to their bed. Had she wanted to darken Agnès' mood to pour cold water on her sexual excitement?

Aileen cursed. If she hadn't acted so stupidly, she'd have been able to keep some of that sensuality for herself, and share it with Julius, or bring it to her writing desk, let the scenarios unfold in her mind, turn her chair to the night and imagine whatever she wanted. Instead of which, she found herself alone, frustrated, staring out at the meagre view offered by her window: the rooftops, with the neighbourhood rats and cats running along them in the dark.

That night, Julius was working on a painting that he'd begun long before and that worried him. He knew the story, but only half-knew the central character: a woman, in a wedding dress, standing there for years amid the painting's backdrop, but still without a face. He'd tried out many different faces – imaginary faces and models' faces, some of them prostitutes, others not – without finding the one that would finally reveal what it was he was trying to say. After the restaurant and Aileen's sudden departure, he had rushed home, realising that the quest for that mysterious face was perhaps over at last. He had frantically prepared his palette and his brushes, then begun to paint, above the strange woman's shoulders, the face of Aileen Bowman. It seemed obvious now, but he hadn't understood until that evening, when he'd watched her walk away. Of course: because this was the first time she'd worn a dress in his presence. During the meal, he'd been too taken with Agnès to give the matter any thought. Aileen was not only the subject of the portrait that they were working on together, but also the answer to this long search.

He ended the night sprawled on the models' sofa, drinking absinthe and feeling perfectly satisfied. Smiling, numbed by the alcohol, he found himself imagining what the Huets had done when they got home. Had their lovemaking lasted longer than usual? Had thoughts of Aileen in her dress infiltrated the engineer's mind as he screwed his wife? Had thoughts of Julius haunted Agnès?

In the bedroom, Agnès still felt ill at ease. She had wanted to get home, but at home she was only ever a hostess being hospitable to her husband, or to a guest. It wasn't her bedroom, but their bedroom: the conjugal bedroom, with all its obligations. Tonight she felt torn between the desire she'd felt all through dinner to be with Jacques and the desire she felt now, to be alone. She wanted to be able to take her time to think over all that had been said, and all that hadn't, about the moments when she should have spoken up or kept silent, and to sort through what she'd imagined, what she'd wanted to believe, what she'd dreamed. They had talked about so many more things than they usually did at Jacques' uncouth work dinners. They'd talked about things that had stirred up arousing memories, making her afraid that she would blush. Seeing Jacques laugh, tasting the champagne and the wonderful food, she'd wanted to make love with him again the way they had done that summer, when she stayed in Paris, when Alice was conceived. To make love naked, in the light, to see Jacques again, and to see herself. That had been so exciting. To finally witness their own lovemaking had led her to pleasures she'd never felt before.

Tonight, during the meal, despite her fear and shame, she'd wanted to feel that pleasure again.

Then, in the smoking room, when Aileen Bowman had become aggressive towards her, Agnès had realised how dubious the atmosphere of the evening had been all along. That artist, Stewart, had been scabrous beneath his veneer of distinction. That journalist had been vulgar and provocative under her show of courage. And they had been the cause, in the false intimacy they'd established, of her inappropriate thoughts. Now, she could see that the sex she'd remembered had been the fruit of moral squalor.

In the carriage that took them home, she'd almost thrown up. She'd drunk some cordial in the apartment before going into their bedroom, where she knew she would have to play hostess to Jacques' desires. Because she could tell, from the way he'd held her hand in the carriage, the way he'd caressed her waist as he helped her down, the way he'd moved towards her under the sheets, that – unlike hers – his desire had not faded. Agnès knew how to avoid frustrating her husband: she would use some oil when she was dry, would lie on her side in his favourite position, and when he caressed her breasts, she would caress his hands to hasten his pleasure. But tonight she couldn't do it, and she fretted over the best way to explain things, trying to come up with an excuse that wouldn't ruin an evening that, as Jacques kept repeating as he nuzzled her in bed, he had thought a great success. So she just exaggerated what appeared to be true: that she'd had too much to drink and didn't feel well. She'd had a very nice evening too, she said, and she was sorry that she couldn't end it the way she wanted. She sensed his disappointment. He pulled back, leaving her side of the bed to her alone.

"I understand."

"I'm sorry."

She forced herself not to say anything negative about Julius Stewart or Aileen Bowman.

"I hope Miss Bowman's article will be good and that M. Bienvenüe will be pleased with you."

"Thank you for coming with me. I'm glad we shared that moment, especially before you leave for Bréhat with Alice. It's been a long time since we laughed like that together."

They both knew that, in fact, it had never happened before. Agnès wanted to talk about what had happened in the smoking room, but said instead:

"Not only did we eat very well, but the company was most entertaining. Do you know what I was thinking, during dinner?"

"No."

She slid closer to him.

"That, next year, we should make that trip that you've always dreamed about, if M. Bienvenüe will agree to you taking a month off work."

"To Egypt?"

"Yes."

Jacques pressed himself against her again and began gently caressing her abdomen with his fingertips.

"Alice is old enough now. Would you want to come too?"

"Yes."

She turned to Jacques and placed her cheek against his chest. Then her hand, which swept lightly across his belly. She hesitated, before moving her fingers under the drawstring of his pyjama trousers and releasing his penis, which she gripped in her hand. He was only half-erect, a remnant of his thwarted desires.

"Agnès, what are you doing?"

As he grew hard again between her fingers, she said: "Don't you want to?"

He ran his hand through her hair and, in time with the caresses that he gave her, she began moving her hand up and down. Then, whether because she felt Jacques' hand pushing her head that way or because she wanted to, for the first time she surrendered to that curiosity. And found a new way of satisfying Jacques when her body couldn't welcome him. She slid under the sheets and took him in her mouth. Jacques shivered with nervousness and excitement.

Her husband's back arched and, while he sighed ever louder, she breathed in the tastes and smells of his penis and thought about Aileen Bowman. Was she the artist's mistress, that woman who'd lectured her about freedom? That American woman's words had wounded her more deeply than she could have imagined. And yet, despite being beautiful and free, Aileen Bowman was a sad, lonely woman: that much was obvious. Agnès had Jacques. If Aileen was Julius Stewart's mistress, was she capable of this? Did she take him in her mouth? Agnès imagined her doing it and, a novice herself, imitated the movements that she thought the redhead might make. She pictured Aileen's naked body as she bent over the artist, then she imagined Aileen alone, standing here, still naked, somewhere in their bedroom, watching her in action. With her free hand, as she swallowed his erection more deeply, she began to caress herself, unseen by Jacques.

Her hands moved more quickly as she sensed her husband growing inside her mouth and, at the same time, felt her own pleasure swelling, sharpening to a point. Tonight, she gave herself the right to that feeling. To prove to the journalist that she could.

15

All night long, Joseph danced, drank, stumbled, sang and ran around the fire. Alcohol transforms thoughts into spirals and leads them where the flames go. Alcohol shows the centre of things around which we orbit, the siphon that sucks them up. He ran out of drink in the middle of the night and tried to borrow some bottles from the camp. They shoved him away and he got into a fight over a few mouthfuls of hooch and some wine. The Lakotas from the show had banished him. But their decisions no longer mattered; they weren't a real tribe anymore, just a bunch of extras. He was the last warrior. They'd banished him out of shame.

He hadn't drunk in search of courage. He knew alcohol did not have that power. Only cowards believed that. What it does is lift you up. Turns you into a spirit, lighter than air. Divine, as the white man says.

Joseph the white man had used up his arguments, grown tired of his lie-words, and fallen silent. Joseph the Indian was now leading the fight. The Ferguson blood wasn't hot enough for that, diluted by peace treaties. His mother and the others had been wrong: Joseph Ferguson was not a split stone. Maria – the exile who couldn't live without her husband, who died with him – had been mistaken on that count. The two Josephs had made a pact, long before, back in their childhood on the reserve, to fight back-to-back, so that they could keep an eye on their enemies on both sides. If peace was the best strategy, the white man negotiated and the Indian was his witness. When hunting, or travelling along the tracks, the Indian led and the white man accompanied him, the beneficiary of his knowledge. But the white man, eager for peace, had listened to Aileen's promises for too long, tolerated her visits to the tepee for too long, with her pitiful looks and the sheets of paper that she covered in lie-words. The Indian had spat on the ground, where the other would have knelt to pick up the white sister's charity: the Fitzpatrick Ranch, that guilty legacy, just one more piece of white trash.

The mustang – now returned to its true colours: yellow, white and red – only had to imitate the way that work horses and city horses walked. On its black coat, there was now no space for the green of healing. It was a war horse.

Joseph no longer wore the frock coat from the theatre of negotiations; he had an Indian blanket on his back, falling over his thighs and his knees, concealing the paintings of war and exposing only a small flash of his dark skin and his moccasins. He felt shame, hiding like this, but it wouldn't be for much longer. All he had to do was reach his destination without being stopped. His arms were invisible under the blanket, and in the sunlight the brim of his hat made a little circle of shadow that obscured his features. He headed towards the camp of human monkeys, on the hill named Trocadéro. His colours attracted attention, but anyone surprised at his appearance there, among the ox carts and horse-drawn carriages, quickly remembered the nearby colonial village. Children pointed at him, ladies raised hands to their mouths, and men reassured them (even if they weren't entirely reassured themselves): "It's one of those savages who are allowed to ride around Paris, an extra from the show." But Joseph wasn't going to the Trocadéro. He was going somewhere close, on avenue Kléber.

At the crossing with rue Copernic, home to the big, bearded man whom his ranch sister often visited, Joseph came to a stop. He'd never managed to slip inside that building to see what they did there together. He didn't care about that. When they were together, side by side, the bearded man and her, two equal forces attracted and repelled them. It was the other one she wanted: the blond man. That straw-coloured hair that, like Aileen Bowman's red hair, could only be produced by the white races. The man in a suit, who travelled around on a bicycle and sometimes rode through the Bois de Vincennes, who already had a wife and a child. A liar and a cheat, just like the ranch sister.

She was what divided the two Josephs. She was his fracture.

And she alone could unite them perfectly, when they followed her tracks through the city, the Indian guide and the white man imitating other white men. She it was who made them climb across the rooftops together, at night, to masturbate over her masturbations, to gather the refuse of her white lovers, the detritus of her feelings for the blond man.

She alone had the power to set the white man and the Indian back-to-back. In their solitude.

Halfway between the triumphal door and the hill of the colonial village, just past the street where the bearded man lived, there was an entrance leading down to the subterranean spaces of the Métropolitain, all metal plants and electric flowers. Surrounded by wooden barriers, it was closed to the public. Only workers could go down there. Joseph steered the mustang towards the pavement and they waited there, beside the stone facade of an apartment building, indifferent to the pedestrians who skirted around them as they stood watch over a bicycle.

When the blond man emerged from underground, Joseph shrugged his blanket off his shoulders, revealing the inverted hands that covered his body.

From the strap of his loincloth, he pulled the club and the dagger, and with his heels he kicked the horse's flanks. The images of plains and mountains that had filled his daydreams while he waited melted into the colours of the city, filaments of greenery dissolving into the grey of roads and houses. He gave the man a small headstart. Joseph had followed him to Vincennes before, so he knew that the bicycle could not escape the mustang, but he didn't want to strike a slow enemy. Joseph had seen the vision of a hunt, of speed, a mighty blow. He – the red painter – was the subject of a representation, a story that would be told to others, whose details, like those of all Indian wars, would have to be choreographed to be understood, for its truths to be remembered.

This man was not just any white man; he was one of those engineers who invent and manufacture powerful weapons for the armies exhibiting their human trophies in the colonial village. He didn't ride a horse but a machine on wheels, designed for those streets and roads that disfigured the landscape, modelling it to their needs just like a railway blasting through mountains with dynamite. Joseph was flying the flag for nature against its new enemy, the white man from the cities of skyscrapers. He had come to scalp the city itself.

When the mustang charged, passers-by looked up, suddenly doubtful. That wasn't the sound of a work horse, nor even a dispatch rider in a hurry. The rhythm of those hooves on the cobbles signalled another intention altogether. Then a cry summoned their attention. It was a war cry, ordering each man in the area to protect his children, to weigh his courage, and – if fear hadn't frozen the blood in his legs – to flee.

Jacques Huet had no reason to believe that this strident cry was aimed at him. But when he turned around, he realised that he was in the path of a bolting horse. He pedalled hard to get away from it, the wheels brushing against the curb. When he looked again, the horse had changed its trajectory. It was still heading straight at him. Losing his balance and almost falling, Jacques made out the man on its back, his arms raised, a murderous look on his face.

For several days now, the engineer had been visiting the construction teams at the Bossière station. M. Bienvenüe had personally asked him to solve a worrying seepage problem. They couldn't tell whether it was a natural waterway, between layers of rock and clay, or a leak from a broken pipe somewhere nearby. Either way, the tunnel was threatened and the digging of a second passage had been stopped. Exiting his office, leaving behind his plans for the tunnels under the river, Jacques had hurried to the rescue. This change in his routine seemed perfectly timed, illustrating, in a way, the ideas for travel with which he and Agnès had been entertaining themselves since the dinner with Aileen Bowman and Julius Stewart. His dream of visiting mysterious Egypt, land of the most legendary engineers in human history. The upkeep of their apartment, the supervision of Alice's schoolwork, the daily shopping routines . . . all these tasks, once so sacred to Agnès, had become secondary chores. As if she was, at last, no longer reduced to her duties as wife and mother. None of these changes was spectacular, but they were no less important for that. Jacques and his wife made love in a different way now. The tone of their dinner conversations had become more cheerful; what they said mattered less than the fact that they were together. A new atmosphere. Like the strange situation he now found himself in – disturbing, obviously, but also almost amusing – of being chased by a horse in the street.

As he twisted his neck to look at the beast, Jacques changed direction without meaning to and crossed to the other side of the road on his bicycle. The animal was still pursuing him. Unwilling to give up on the idea that this was all some absurd prank, Jacques changed course again, slipping between a handcart and the pavement. The horse and its rider imitated him. A top hat flew off the man's head. His face was painted, covered with parallel lines of various colours. In his raised hands he held a thick club and a flash of metal that appeared to be a large knife. For an instant, Jacques was outraged by this macabre dramatisation, which was terrorising the ordinary people around him. Then, hearing a piercing cry, he convinced himself that what he was witnessing was not a game but a fit of genuine madness. He started pedalling furiously, as fast as he could on the cobbles. He was in danger. He had to accept this change too, react, and save himself. Had he sped up too late or was the horse faster than he'd realised? The cry was just behind him now.

The mustang, fully extended, legs outstretched and the weight of its head leaning forward, and the arched rider, chest open to give the battle club as much force as possible, covered the fleeing cyclist with their shadow. The extremity of the club, launched in a semi-circle by the joined forces of horse and man, smashed the engineer's back, breaking ribs and expelling air from a crushed lung. Jacques Huet was knocked from his saddle and his velocipede rolled several feet without a rider before sliding between the mustang's legs. A hoof passed through the spokes of the rear wheel, then another through the metal frame, which resisted the beast's power. The energy of its muscles, halted in their tracks by the steel bars, communicated itself to the tendons and the bones, which cracked. Jacques was still rolling along the road when the mustang collapsed and Joseph hit the cobbles and rippled forward.

Jacques, his senses numbed by the fall, heard various cries: a woman; the horse, wild with pain; a man calling for the police, and another running towards him. His body swelled with substances at war with one another. The hot flow of a need for sleep and the promise of rest. The cold of the pain in his dislocated bones when he tried to stand up. The fear prickling his skin like shards of glass when he saw the painted rider walking in his direction, weapons at the ready. The men who'd surrounded him, eager to help, now fled, abandoning him. Jacques, alone on the ground, raised his hands to protect himself. His vision blurred when the club smashed his forearm and he felt it fall, hanging from broken bones. The man grabbed his hair. His broken hand, the one he still controlled, waved frantically above his head. The blade swung down, slicing through flesh, tendons, bones. He lost consciousness. The blade touched his forehead. He hoped that those people around him would rediscover their courage and save what there still remained of him to save, that they would bring an end to this absurd pain.

16

The surgeon had the arrogance of a man who is never blamed for his mistakes. For him, bad news had only one explanation: fate.

"The wounds in themselves aren't deadly. The policemen who scared off his attacker arrived in time. But he was beaten very severely, and even though none of his arteries were severed, he has lost so much blood that his condition is critical."

His white coat was stained red.

It was only that afternoon, at *La Fronde*'s office, that Aileen had heard about the tragic events blazoned all over the front pages of that morning's newspapers. A man hunted down in the streets by a savage from the Exposition. Then she'd understood that the victim was a Métropolitain engineer. She'd asked for more details. Yes, they knew his name.

The Necker Hospital was the closest to avenue Kléber, though still too far. The surgeon, learning that the American woman was a journalist, had granted her a minute of his time.

"That's all I can tell you. His wife is with him."

"What can you do for him?"

The surgeon flushed angrily.

"That is no longer my responsibility. Go ask those two madmen who want to perform a blood transfusion."

"What's that?"

"A heresy, madame! A scientific nonsense! They'll just kill him even faster."

The patients in the ward sat up in bed to see. Half a dozen journalists were taking notes in the middle of the central aisle and a nurse was doing her best to prevent them getting too close. An illustrator sketched the scene in his notebook. Agnès Huet, sitting on a chair, turned her back on them, holding her husband's hand with one of hers while she used the other to block her ear so as not to hear their overlapping questions. Aileen recognised a journalist from James Gordon Bennett's *New York Herald*. Her American colleague nodded at her, then unexpectedly grinned, pleased to note that Aileen Bowman, the snooty socialist, was here to pick up crumbs too – and that she was late. Aileen told the overworked nurse that she was a friend of the family. Agnès Huet turned around.

"What are you doing here?"

"I heard what happened. I came as quickly as I could."

The nurse, her red face clashing with her white uniform, suddenly lost her temper.

"Get out of here now, all of you! Leave him in peace!"

The men retreated, the cartoonist finishing his sketch as he went, but Aileen didn't move.

"You too! Don't you have any pity? Get out of here!"

"Agnès, I don't want you to go through this alone. Let me help you."

Agnès looked at the journalist and nodded. The nurse moved out of the way. Agnès hesitated, then gestured at two men in white coats. "These gentlemen are from the faculty of medicine in Montpellier. They say they can save Jacques."

She looked at her unconscious husband, his face covered with bandages, then back at the journalist.

"I have to give him my blood."

Aileen addressed the two doctors. "The surgeon told me that a blood transfusion is dangerous."

Dr Jeanbrau and Dr Hédon, who had come to the Exposition to present the results of their research, stood tall. They'd read the stories about the engineer and the savage in the morning papers and immediately set off for the hospital so they could offer their services and take advantage of this heaven-sent opportunity. If they saved the engineer, their procedure would be front-page news.

"Our method of transfusion is perfect. Obviously we can't guarantee results . . ."

"I beg your pardon?"

Agnès put her hand on Aileen's arm and gazed into the American woman's eyes.

"He has a two-in-three chance."

Her response was also a question. She was seeking Aileen's approval.

"A two-in-three chance?" Aileen stammered.

The doctors impatiently repeated their explanations for her benefit.

"Not all blood types are compatible and we are not yet able to identify the different types. The operation poses no danger for the donor, but it may prove ineffective for the recipient."

"Ineffective?"

"That's why, wherever possible, we ask for family members to donate their own blood. So that nobody else feels a sense of . . . responsibility."

Agnès was still pondering that mathematical formula. She shuddered as she realised what they were talking about.

"Responsibility for what? . . . For the death of my husband?"

"I can do it, if you prefer," said Aileen.

Mme Huet flinched with hurt pride, before emitting a brief burst of nervous laughter.

"Certainly not! It's out of the question."

On the verge of collapse, she turned to Dr Jeanbrau.

"My blood could kill him?"

"Your blood could . . . complicate his condition. He is very weak, and it could prove fatal."

"Wouldn't it be better for a man to get a man's blood?"

"Blood types have no connection with the donors' gender, madame; that is one thing we know for certain."

The American woman interrupted them again.

"If you choose two donors, does that increase the chances of success? Could two different blood types . . . work together?"

Around the bed, the tension was growing. Decisions had to be made and they were wasting precious time with these discussions. The American woman kept asking questions. Her solicitude was unsettling. Jeanbrau, the youngest of the doctors, was rendered speechless, and his colleague answered the question for him.

"No, madame. If one of the blood types is not compatible, it will still cause clotting, which would be dangerous for the patient."

"Could you do tests before the transfusion?"

"No, madame. Outside the body, blood coagulates too quickly for us to be able to study it."

"Will Mme Huet be able to give him enough blood without putting herself in danger?"

Dr Jeanbrau raised his voice.

"All these statistical calculations will be pointless if we waste any more time! He'll be dead in an hour!"

This hysterical outburst silenced the others. Agnès looked at her unconscious husband.

"We have to do it, Jacques. It's our only chance of saving you. I'll give you my blood."

Curtains were drawn around Jacques' bed. Agnès' sleeve was rolled up, a tourniquet tied around her forearm, and Dr Jeanbrau slid the needle into one of the swollen veins. A small rubber tube, red like bicycle tyres, connected the hollow needle to a syringe, from which a second tube led to a second syringe implanted in Jacques' arm. Each of these tubes had a tap on it. Leaving the tap on Jacques' side closed, the doctors released the valve on the first syringe, which filled with Agnès' blood.

"Wait! How long . . . How long before we know?"

"We'll have the necessary information within three or four hours, madame."

Agnès stifled her sobs but couldn't stop the tears pouring down her face. She nodded. Once the syringe was full, Dr Hédon closed the first tap, opened the second one, and injected the collected blood into Jacques' body. Each syringe contained 60 millilitres. They performed this operation ten times. More than half a litre. Agnès watched the liquid pass from her arm to her immobile husband's, following its movement through this obscene, artificial umbilical cord. A two-in-three chance.

"We have to stop now, madame. You've done all you can.

If we took any more blood, it would be dangerous for your health."

Agnès began to protest, with the agitation of someone in an advanced state of fatigue. She put her hand on the needle in her arm.

"He needs more. He's still not moving. I can give him more."

Two nurses rushed over to subdue her. Dr Hédon pulled the needle from her arm and a small jet of blood spurted from the vein, staining Agnès' dress. She was helped to a bed on the other side of the curtains. Dr Hédon sat beside her and muttered a few words, repeating that they had done everything possible, that now they must simply wait and pray. His voice was so calm and soothing that the entire ward followed his advice and went back to sleep.

Aileen stayed close to Jacques.

In the morning, Agnès drew back the curtain. Her husband was dead. The American woman was still there, watching over his corpse, her face pale.

Agnès refused to believe that Jacques was dead until his bandages were removed and she could see his eyes. She became hysterical, and in the end the hospital staff gave in to her demands.

For the rest of her life, Agnès didn't know if she'd been right to ask for that favour. Jacques' face was disfigured by the blows of the club and the long wound on his forehead – from one temple to the other – which had been roughly sewn up. He looked no more like her husband than the mummy he had been just before. All she knew for sure was that this unrecognisable creature had died in agony.

Agnès had been asleep when he went to work the day before.

She desperately sought her last memory of him alive, but could not summon a single image in which Jacques' face was so clearly defined that it could erase the monstrosity before her. She vomited.

Aileen had seen Indian warriors fighting before. They seemed to dance around their opponent. Then, amid this almost comic choreography, there were blows, brief and unhesitating, like the movements of a fish swimming slowly around a crumb in the water before suddenly swallowing it and continuing its rounds. The warriors spent their whole lives training to be that strong, quick and light on their feet.

She'd believed, wrongly, that Joseph's blows, like his paintings, would be symbolic. He had followed her. She'd invited him to do that by going to see him in Vincennes. She had led him to Jacques. Then the fish dance had begun, the warrior circling and circling to the point of madness, to the point where he saw everything in his path as a crumb, a stone, a hook.

Not for an instant did Aileen think about talking to the police.

The nurses drew the curtains and they were left alone: Aileen. Agnès, who wouldn't let go of her hand. And Jacques. A two-in-three chance.

17

The *New York Herald*, from its offices on the first floor of the Eiffel Tower, had fired the first cannon blast: "Metro Murder – savage killer still on the loose!"

James Gordon Bennett liked nothing more than a headline that relieved him of the need to read the article below. The French newspapers and international press had echoed this news in chorus and, for twenty-four hours, the terrifying front pages reduced Paris to a silence it had not heard for months. Everybody stayed at home. Train, hotel and boat reservations were cancelled.

Witnesses had described the murderer fleeing into the entrance of the Boissière metro station, so hundreds of Breton navvies, armed with shovels and pickaxes, were searching the tunnels for the "beast" that had killed Jacques Huet. Where else could such a "rat" be hiding? They found no trace of him, but the story of that spectral assassin, haunting the subterranean labyrinth, quickly grew into a Parisian legend.

Little Alice did not say a word when she heard the news of her father's death; she didn't understand what they were talking about and asked when he would be back. Agnès replied that she didn't know, then whispered "soon", and they could hear the madness of hope in her voice, which made her own mother feel sick. M. and Mme Cornic had made the trip from Bréhat, in the company of Jacques' parents, the day after his death.

Seventy-two hours after the charge of the black horse, while battalions of workers were still roaming the tunnels, while dozens of policemen were searching the colonial village, the engineer's body, preserved in ice from the Swiss Alps, was loaded onto a carriage and taken to Brittany.

Aileen paid for her train ticket, then went to the station telegraph office and sent a telegram to Whitelaw Reid announcing her resignation.

They left early in the morning and she hoped that the ceremony would take place at a cemetery by the sea. That there would be a view.

They were all hoping to get some rest during the journey. The stop at Versailles jolted them from dreams too early, but by the next stop – two hours later in Chartres – there had been time for the jolting, creaking train to rock the funeral convoy to sleep. Eyelids were heavier, gazes more vacant. The portion of the journey that followed this – to Rennes – lasted four hours, and they were able to focus on sating their appetites, quenching their thirsts. It was a moment of grace; the trip took them out of time.

In addition to the family and Aileen, there were two Parisian journalists and one of M. Bienvenüe's assistants, bearing a letter from his boss in which the architect of the Métropolitain regretted that he was unable to make the journey in person. Agnès' mother, behind her black veil, quickly fell asleep. Paris had exhausted her. She hated the teeming metropolis. Jacques' parents were also rocked to sleep by the train's mechanical lullaby after two nights spent watching over their son's corpse in their daughter-in-law's apartment. The wealthy artisan couple snored side by side.

Agnès, widowed before her mother, could not sleep; she

was hyper-aware of the shapes and colours of things passing behind the window. Alice, taking advantage of her grandparents' slumber and her mother's distracted state, sat on the bench facing Aileen. She had seen the American journalist at home and at the church; each time, the woman with red hair had been next to her black-haired mother. Aileen Bowman, once a little savage at the Fitzpatrick Ranch, did not believe it was necessary to speak to children: their heads were already full of their own stories, and they could observe, imitate if necessary, choose whatever seemed to them important or enjoyable; the interventions of adults spoiled all those wonders of natural intelligence. So she stared at the girl without uttering a word. Alice's resemblance to her father troubled her once again. It was through his daughter's face that Jacques reappeared to her most intensely, bringing back in a rush all those feelings she had once had for him.

Little Alice, with her father's pale eyes and high cheekbones, under her mother's black fringe, looked at her questioningly: who was she, this woman who seemed to magnetise her whole family – her mother, lost in sadness, her vanished father, whose friend she was, and Alice herself, who was fascinated by her?

In Rennes, nobody wanted the journey to end. The final stage of the trip – three hours to Guingamp – was a painful return to reality. They had to rouse themselves from this torpor as night fell, as the hearse and the other family members waited for them at the station. The stop would be slightly longer than usual, the driver warned the passengers, to enable the coffin to be unloaded without haste.

The dawn departure had been better suited to their journey, noted Aileen, than this dusk arrival. The summer solstice was behind them and the days were growing shorter. It wasn't obvious yet, but the evenings had ceased being a minute longer each day and now they were losing the days' light, little by little.

They drove through the dark streets of Guingamp by lantern light, in carriages whose leather seats were damp with dew. This town was as far from Paris as an Amish village was from New York. In sparsely lit doorways, Aileen glimpsed women in straight dresses, looking like nuns in their black veils, and men with pudding-bowl haircuts, hats held in hands and heads lowered. Their bows were formed by a long habit of submitting to higher powers – in this case, the power of a noble corpse. There were granite crosses at every crossroads, and whenever they saw a garden in front of a building, it was a chapel with candles burning. The Bretons may have been Catholics, but their faith was as grey as that of the Amish protestants, whose credo of resistance to the modern world seemed to apply here too.

Three carriages followed the hearse as it left the town. How slowly they moved, after the speed of the train. And how quiet everything was. Aileen was taken back to the true pace of journeys made with horses, on rutted roads, and she flared her nostrils to breathe in the odours of the countryside: grass, earth, worm-eaten wood, broom and heather. Everything she missed in New York and Paris. The scents were as strong as they had been during her most recent visits to the Fitzpatrick Ranch, for the funerals of her father and mother. Her nose avidly sought out the smell of the earth where bodies were buried. How would Agnès, in her carriage, feel about those olfactory signals of her childhood? Would she pinch her nose or, like Aileen, smile at the nocturnal emissions of the subsoil that was going to swallow her geologist husband?

It was almost midnight when they arrived in Paimpol. Aileen had booked a room in a hotel on place du Martray, close to the trading port where rich families like the Huets had built their houses. They would certainly not be inviting that journalist with her hair like an Irish whore's, even if, for reasons known only to her, Agnès refused to be separated from the woman.

Aileen slept badly in that superstitious provincial town.

The parish priest was young and rather relatively handsome. As on Agnès and Jacques' wedding day, the sky was blue and a warm breeze was blowing in from the Channel. The small Trinity Chapel was built on a rocky outcrop overgrown with bushes of broom and privet; amid the heather and asters trembling in the wind, on the rocks overlooking the sea, the dominant smell was of curry from the helichrysum. The air that brushed against granite tasted clean in Aileen's mouth and nose.

The sermon was incomprehensible. To Aileen, the Breton language sounded exotic and barbaric. She recognised the tone of commiseration and the use of Christian symbols, understood the few words of Latin, but soon started interpreting the priest's message as she saw fit. Forgetting the chapel with its sacred architecture, she accepted the naive offering of comfort. With the demands for submission and the blackmail of eternal damnation lost in this mysterious language, she could let herself float on the musicality of the ceremony. Then, observing the gathered crowd, she remembered that, from time immemorial, holiness had been purchased. After the Revolution, the bourgeoisie and the working classes of France had been given the right to own property, yet they still accepted the idea that their most precious belonging did not actually belong to them: their life was a gift from the Great Creditor in the Sky, who could take it back whenever He pleased. Arthur Bowman had an image to describe this vicious circle. "They," he said, referring to priests, officers and politicians, "lock you in a church, a fort or a country, press a gun to your head, tell you you're safe as long as you don't try to escape, and that if a bullet does happen to drill a hole through your head, it will be for a very good reason." In this province where priests had been protected while in the rest of France they were persecuted, the privilege of taxing souls had not been abolished. Unable to contain her irritation any longer, Aileen left the chapel before the end of the sermon and went for a walk along the coastal path.

She could see the Ile de Bréhat, close enough that she imagined she could even hear what was happening there. That was the Cornic family's exile, the island of princesses awaiting the return of Agnès and Alice. The widow and her daughter would not return to Paris. What would become of them without Jacques?

She didn't go to the cemetery. She lay in the heather to stare up at the clouds and fell asleep. When she returned to Paimpol, the Huet family's guests were leaving the mansion. Aileen asked a servant to find Agnès.

"Where were you? I was looking for you."

"I'm sorry I left you alone, but I didn't think my presence was necessary."

"What are you talking about? You're welcome here. You're my friend."

"Do you have a moment to talk?"

"I don't know if I can leave the house now. My parents-in-law . . ."

"Just a few minutes. I promise I won't keep you long. I'm catching the train tonight."

"Why don't you stay? We'll have more time tomorrow. We could visit my island together."

"I have to get back to Paris. Let's just walk a while. Nobody will notice you're gone."

"I don't know, Aileen. Is what you have to tell me really that important?"

"I think so, yes."

"I'm afraid to talk to you, Aileen."

"Afraid of what they'll think?"

"No, afraid that you'll lie to me, out of kindness, about your departure, and that we'll never see each other again. Sorry, I'm not making any sense. But how can you explain my need for you, when we hardly even know each other?"

Agnès looked as though she was about to faint. Aileen held her arm.

"Let's sit down on that bench."

The light from the half-moon glowed on the semi-circular cobbled driveways and the facades of the pointed houses. From the port, they could hear the wind whistling through the ships' rigging. There was no electricity here: the air was free of that constant Parisian vibration from dynamos.

"What do you think people are expecting of you, Agnès?"

"You mean, in this situation?"

"Yes."

Her reply seemed obvious but was somehow belied by the time it took her to speak.

"That I should be strong."

"Do you feel like being strong?"

"I don't know. I suppose I have to be."

She lowered her head.

"There are so many deaths, everywhere, all the time, that Jacques' death shouldn't be more important than the others. But, for me, nothing could be harder. My life may not be as extraordinary as yours, and I may not be strong enough to bear his loss with dignity, but so what? That doesn't mean I'm weak. It means I loved him."

"Then don't fight it. Surrender to it. Let yourself collapse. You'll have everything you need to help you to your feet afterwards. They doubt you and they're wrong. Mourn what was taken from you and, when you're ready to live your life again, live it. The only mistake you could make would be to blame yourself for Jacques' death."

"My blood was bad."

She squeezed Aileen's hand.

"Your blood would have saved him, I know it would. I shouldn't have refused your help. My blood was too weak. It was dirty."

"You're talking nonsense. Jacques died from his wounds."

"Who was that savage? Why did he attack my husband?"

"You have nothing to feel guilty about. It was just a series of coincidences."

"Nothing is ever just a series of coincidences. There are always reasons, even if we don't know them. Coincidence isn't a real word. It's a word that hides other words."

"Jacques had no enemies. It's just terribly bad luck."

Agnès shook her head.

"It's that Exposition."

"The Exposition?"

"That human beast who attacked him, it's . . . like a spirit rising up in rebellion. Against what, I don't know. All this vanity. That idea drives me crazy – that Jacques' death was punishment for the Exposition's sin of pride. So I won't just collapse, because I have to be stronger than that. As is expected of me. You think I'm a stupid bigot. You're not burdened by guilt; you're free of that weight. And yet you bear some of my grief for me, out of solidarity and friendship. I don't care what they think of you."

"We're friends. They can't change that."

"I can see that my world isn't yours, that you don't like these people very much. But if you were what they imagine you to be – a bad person – you wouldn't be here. You're doing more to help me than my own mother. Because you're not afraid to speak. The only duty she knows is silence."

Aileen stood up.

"Go back to your island. Stay there as long as you need to. I promise I'll come back to see how you are before I leave."

"You won't stay in France?"

"I'm not sure."

She took Agnès' face in her hands and kissed her forehead.

"What they don't expect of you . . . that's the woman Jacques loved."

"The one he was expecting. The one I didn't become."

Agnès' tears slid between her cheeks and Aileen's palms.

"There is no reason why she should die with him."

"You promise you'll come back?"

"Come on, I'll walk you to the house."

"No. I can manage. Go and catch your train."

225

18

Aileen offered no explanation for the hardness of her body while she was posing, but Julius immediately sensed her tension. The symbolic lines of her tattoos crossed the taut lines of her tendons and muscles. The locked nerve connections and magnetic hubs of her joints held in her anger like ropes. An erotic impulse led the artist's imagination into a scenario where the journalist's body was slowly freed from its tethers. But in these conditions, a sexual confrontation would lead only to violence, not to pleasure. He forced himself to stop thinking like that and added some more red to the flesh colour, bringing blood to the skin of his painting.

"I had a letter from Mary Stanford. She sends her regards."

Aileen stepped down from the stage and knotted the belt of the dressing gown around her waist.

"Sorry, I can't do this any longer today. Anyway, you know as well as I do that the portrait is finished. We're just pretending to continue."

"Not pretending, my dear. We want to continue. But it's true that I don't actually need you here to make the final touches. It's just a question of interpretation now."

"Have you heard about Dr Freud's psychoanalysis?"

"Vaguely. He cures hysterical women – is that right?"

"He's invented a new remedy for mental illnesses, based on sessions when the patient talks and he just listens. Sometimes he asks questions to guide them towards certain subjects, and the secret reasons behind their actions. Freud thinks that our dreams are proof of the existence of these secret motives, remade as images, as well as the emotions that we're unable to express."

"It's an interesting way of looking at dreams. I like his theory. Do you think our meetings in my studio are a bit like the doctor's sessions?"

"There are certain resemblances."

"Except that nobody speaks. I don't know what you think about when you're posing."

"It's the painting that speaks."

"So, if I follow your line of thought, this painting will be like a dream, expressing what you don't know about yourself?"

"It's a nice idea, don't you think?"

"But, in that case, my part of the dream will be mixed with yours."

Aileen smiled as she looked at the painted image.

"The interpretation of your dreams is unambiguous, my friend. This nude is truly scandalous."

Julius stopped working and looked up at her.

"What's wrong, Aileen?"

"My stay in Paris is going to end, but – as with our painting – I refuse to admit it."

"If you don't feel ready to leave, there must still be something you're supposed to do here."

Julius poured them some wine and they sat in chairs on the rectangular rug in the centre of the studio. He raised his glass, his gaze sweeping the blank space of the room, a formal, dreamy gesture that acknowledged the emotions floating in the air.

"It would have been hard for me to portray in this picture all the women you've been for me. Journalist. Lover. Studious. Insatiable. Generous. Sarcastic. And my favourite . . . intransigent."

"I'm more and more tempted by compromise."

"And, last but not least, temptress."

Aileen tossed the dressing gown onto the back of the chair and got dressed. Julius smiled, savouring one last time the dazzling mix of red hair, paper-white skin and black tattoos.

"Goodbye, then?"

"Soon."

The small pond in the Congolese village – a round ditch barely three feet deep, surrounded by fences – had become a swimming pool for black children. Smoking pipes, tourists of both sexes watched them dive in and splash about. The visitors enjoyed the coolness of the spot as they rested, laughing at the acrobatics of those little black bodies shining with wetness. Parisians were used to such ethnological spectacles. For the past twenty-five years, visitors to the Jardin d'Acclimatation had been able to see not only animals from all parts of the world, but Nubians, Tahitians, Kanaks and Zulus, all kept in separate cages because it was feared that they might transmit certain deadly diseases. A few of them died of cold every winter.

Waiters from the savage Congo, wearing red chechia hats, brought people glasses of lemonade. The children would somersault like monkeys, then quench their thirst with water from the little pond. A bare-breasted black woman went into the water, gargled some, and spat it out. The savages' nudity was no more shocking than that of prostitutes in paintings. Couples walked arm in arm, calmly contemplating the buttocks and elongated breasts of the black mothers. It was noon and the July heat beat down on the hill. In the fountains of the Champ de Mars, on the other side of the Seine, white children soaked their clothes and a few ladies, after removing their ankle boots, dipped their naked feet into the water. Momentarily, the visitors almost envied the savages in their swamp, before moving away towards the quiet streets of the medina. The Arabs had done their best to embellish the poor copies of houses from their lands. To make shade, sheets were hung over facades with the aid of nails hammered into the latticework. Rugs had replaced doors, allowing the air inside while keeping out flies. Doorways were sprayed with water to settle the dust. Under the high sun, the colonial village was peaceful: no drums, no dances, and the shops were empty. Aileen always came here at this hour, or late at night, when the actors in the human zoo had gone to bed.

She'd gone to the camp in Vincennes as soon as she got back from Brittany. Joseph's tepee had been pulled down by the tribe and none of the Indians would answer her questions. They knew who had killed the white engineer. The Lakotas were preparing to leave with the show and they would never breathe a word of what they knew to a white person. Least of all, she'd realised, would they admit the pride some of the warriors felt at the mention of Joseph Ferguson's act of war, his scalping of the city. Not for a second did she think to denounce them for their complicity. To whom? Presumably in exchange for her silence, they had let her go without bothering her. The half-blood was a legend now, untouchable. In the world of the red men, Joseph was redeemed.

She had sat in front of the circle of ashes in Joseph's hearth, stupidly hoping that he would appear at any moment, bring an end to this pointless game. But he had decided to keep it going. The attack had frozen everything in a musical-chairs moment.

She'd thought she would only have to wait a few months for the start of the twentieth century, but now it seemed like it would never come, as if it had been scythed down, like Jacques Huet, before it could begin. It was only logical that Aileen's search had then taken her to the colonial village, an anachronism, free from the clock-time of the white men, those destroyers of the darkness in souls and streets, those missionary makers of light.

In reality, she wasn't looking for Joseph. She was showing herself so that he could find her. Every day, she followed the line of the metro, from the Champs-Elysées to Trocadéro, passing the Boissière station where the barbarian had fled. The colonial village had become the terminus for this ritual journey. Aileen had not written another word of her manuscript and, against the backdrop of the Exposition, she had begun to wonder about the value of time spent writing. That time, taken from life and used to portray it, now seemed nothing more than a hollow duplicate, like the plaster architecture imitating countries and civilisations. Redundant and vain. A waste of time.

After a week following the Métropolitain and wandering around the village, she spotted the first inverted hand, on the wall of a Moroccan handicraft shop. Now she had only to wait, as she roamed the streets of Algeria, the Ivory Coast, Indochina and French Guiana.

Since that savage, with no identity or nation, had killed the engineer Huet, there had been far fewer tourists here. Policemen patrolled the streets and some of the visitors would nervously ward off the over-enthusiastic extras by hitting them with their walking-sticks. In this world of twenty languages and one hundred gods, demons and spirits, in this temporary little Babel, the rumour spread that an evil spirit was hiding somewhere among them. And that a woman, an avenging spirit, a warrior-queen with red hair, was pursuing him. It was for her that he left those painted hands on the walls.

19

On 19 July 1900, that marvel of French innovation, that gargantuan project, Fulgence Bienvenüe's personal crusade – the Paris Métropolitain – was opened to the public. Without the usual pomp of the Third Republic and the Exposition. Only the next day, very discreetly, did the Minister for Public Works and the police commissioner Lépine travel along Line 1, accompanied by Fulgence Bienvenüe and a few journalists.

Was this because of conflicts between the local authorities, between the Paris city council and the State, between the companies competing for building work? Breton workers going on strike? The discontent of Parisians tired of the detours, the dust and the underground explosions that made their apartments shake? Or because weeks of pompous bellowing from street pedlars had worn away everyone's curiosity to the point where nobody now believed that anything was unique or new? The inauguration of Line 1, three months after the start of the Exposition, took place in a shameful silence. Like a bastard's birth.

Among the small procession of journalists crowding into the carriage, there was the American woman. The one who wore trousers and whom you would see sometimes at *La Fronde* parties, the one personally greeted by police commissioner Lépine. When he'd announced to the assembled reporters that he had granted the authorisation for Miss Bowman to wear trousers, all the men laughed. The American woman was beginning to get a reputation. The same sorts of rumours that had followed her in New York were now giving her a Parisian aura. It was said that she frequented a millionaire artist of dubious morals, that she was rich, that she hung around in Montmartre with other debauched artists, that she had left New York very suddenly. And the way she dressed just confirmed the most persistent whispers: that she was a lesbian. Everybody knew that she was the one who wrote those scandalous pseudonymous columns comparing Paris to a whore. She was a dangerous deviant. Like Séverine, Durand and their lawyer and artist acolytes on *La Fronde*. Some of the journalists would have liked to punch her, to take back what she was stealing from their monopoly. It wasn't the woman they wanted to hurt, but the man inside her. They wanted to fight or fuck the part of themselves that she was appropriating. Their shoulders were tense, all contact cold. Aileen no longer had the strength to confront them. Among the small group of engineers, she kept searching for Jacques' blond hair, his tall frame.

Bienvenüe, the man who had lost his arm to a train, wore a black armband on his empty sleeve. Had someone in his family died, or was he still mourning his colleague Huet? Around that hollow cylinder of fabric, the armband was like a knot in a handkerchief, in memory of the fragility of those who build the invincible machines that kill them. Aileen caught the chief engineer's eye for a second and thought she saw assent there, perhaps recognition, as he was swallowed up by the backs of the other men. She kept walking backwards and found herself on the platform, unsure if she had taken the final step herself or if she'd been pushed. An employee closed the carriage door in front of her. There was a loud whistle and the lit-up train moved away.

"Is something wrong, madame?"

"I'll wait for the next one."

"The next one? There won't be another train for an hour, madame. Service has been suspended during the minister's visit."

"That's fine, I'll wait for the next one."

"Madame?"

She walked towards the stairs that led up to place de l'Etoile, and then froze. The employee watched her. Aileen took a few more steps before turning around. The man was headed towards the other end of the platform. She crushed her felt hat in her fist, held the knapsack to her chest and jumped onto the tracks. She crouched down and her fingertips traced the shape of the inverted hand that Joseph had made with a mix of earth and grease on the reinforced concrete wall. The drawing was barely visible in the darkness. She ran on tiptoes towards the tunnel, as quick and light-footed as an Indian woman.

Beneath the elliptical arch she could still hear the noises of the carriage, sucking up hot air that pulled at her hair. Rats scurried between her legs. She raised her knees as she walked, to step over these obstacles, slowly placing her heels down on the stones of the ballast and the wooden sleepers. Her movements made her look like a tall wading bird or an African dancer. The smells seemed stronger in the dark. The steel rails, the damp concrete, the mechanical grease of the points, the scent of sparks from the granite, the heated copper of the electrical wires. Her pupils dilated and she made out shapes, a few lines, enough for her imagination to fill in the drawings.

She knew the way – Fulgence Bienvenüe had led her along here – and found the barricaded junction leading to the section that would soon carry trains to Trocadéro and the Exposition, passing Boissière on the way. She stepped over the barrier.

She reached the half-built station, now covered in bevelled white ceramic tiles whose corners gleamed like pyrite in a cave. The station made her think of an empty treasure chamber, the pillaged funeral hall of a pyramid. She hoisted herself onto the platform, rubbed the grime from her hands, dusted off her clothes, then laughed at her desire to stay clean.

She walked all the way along the platform, listened, and went back the other way as a phrase of her father's circled her head. He'd never said it about himself, only as a piece of advice: "The lives of free men are not like other men's lives." It had taken Aileen time to recognise free human beings; on the surface, their lives did not seem so very different from those of the others. The differences were only revealed in the face of the inescapable, the necessary, the irrefutable. Where some would be paralysed, free beings had other formulas, other images and choices than those prepared in advance for the circumstances of their lives. But it was in the face of fear that they were most easily recognisable. The greater the fear, the greater the freedom.

After the pearl-like clarity of the station, the darkness of the tunnel again intensified the scents around her as she kept moving forward. She guessed she was halfway between Boissière and Trocadéro, the point where the dark was purest. There was another smell here, in addition to the odours of the metro and the nervous sweat produced by her own body. The complex smell of another person. Familiar and problematic, saturated with information. The animal world, with its overpowering scents, is without solitude, forever filled with messages of love and danger, clues about which way to go to find food, which borders should not be crossed.

He was probably hesitant to appear, to reveal his presence to another. They still had the opportunity to ignore each other, the alibi of not being able to see each other. They could still choose to pass each other by.

He smelled of sweat and meat, alive and dead. The sour musk of fear, like a beaten dog, a polecat caught in a trap. The lives of fugitives are not like the lives of other men either. Danger surrounds them.

"Joseph?"

Joseph Ferguson, capable of madness, was more dangerous than any beast. Madness went beyond animal obligations. The freer the mind, the greater the fear.

"Joseph?"

It was a quick smell, trained to hide, pursue, kill.

"Answer me."

He smelled of blood, the curdled sweat of anxiety. Or was it the smell of the Iron Age?

"Answer me, Joseph."

"You didn't ask anything, white sister."

She breathed in slowly, attempting to filter Joseph's scent from the air she needed.

"I don't have any questions, Joseph. I just want to know."

He approached soundlessly; perhaps he was barefoot, balanced on a rail like a tightrope walker.

"Knowledge is a superior sense, reserved for warriors,

bringing together what non-combatants keep apart. The beginning and the end, victory and defeat, heaven and earth. You cannot acquire that knowledge. You either have it or you don't, white sister."

"You say warrior, they say murderer."

"What do they know?"

"That you killed."

"Someone is dead, yes. But those separations don't exist either. There are only forces, opposed or united. The ignorant believe in mysteries. For those who know, everything is solved. You know nothing about the death that the engineer received."

"I was holding his hand when he died. I know exactly what you're talking about."

"If you don't have questions, did you come here to judge me?"

"No. But those are your painted hands all over the colonial village. You alone killed, even if you think you're acting in the name of another cause. I want to know your reasons. The real ones. The ones that are about us."

"You talk of impossible connections, ranch sister."

"The acts are impossible, but it's possible to feel impossible things. Nothing can stop that."

The heat was more intense. Either he had moved closer or his anger had grown.

"To want impossible things is to be mad."

"Or free. Warriors are not the only ones who can bring together what is separated. Are you free, Joseph, in these rat tunnels?"

"Heritage. Freedom. Words that you still haven't learned to keep to yourself, white sister."

"You want to ban me from saying them? Like you thought you were preventing me from loving that man?"

His yell made her jump. Warm spit spattered her face.

"You already have everything and you want the reward of love too!"

Aileen tripped over a rail and fell backwards, grazing her palms. Above her, Joseph spoke.

"All these wonders that you profess do not have the same meaning when they have to be begged for, negotiated, or taken by force. Once you have been chained, you are never free, only freed. When you have been deprived of everything, loving isn't a source of joy, it's a bone thrown to a dog!"

She needed to stand up. Joseph felt no pity for wounded animals; a defeated enemy had to be killed. The saliva in her mouth tasted of her brother now, of fear and decomposition; she had to swallow it before she could speak.

"The man you killed had nothing to do with your fight. I kept my side of our bargain by protecting you, but you won't silence me."

Joseph's fingers, which had held stones, touched stagnant water and scratched shit – the true odour of the West – tightened around her throat. Lights appeared. Two pale yellow points on his eyes, a brightness from somewhere at the end of the tunnel, reflected by the shine of his pupils but unseen by the eye behind.

"I didn't choose the wrong enemy. You know that as well as I do."

Aileen's skin discharged fear like urine, the liquid impurity of her emotions.

"I didn't love him. I wanted to help him. Like I wanted to help you. You killed the engineer out of jealousy. Out of selfishness. Stop lying. You're in love with your white sister and that is the only secret that I will agree to keep."

The lights in his eyes grew as they came closer.

"That love, too, was stolen, white sister. It is forbidden in the reserves."

Weakened, struggling to breathe, she gasped with difficulty:

"You can't take it back by force. Feelings and memories can't be forced – that deforms them."

"What if it's the only way to keep them?"

"Then they're broken."

Joseph's hands released their grip, but his skin remained in contact with hers. His rough fingers moved along her throat, a chaste caress or a reflex. He spoke more quietly.

"Everything is broken here, in this city, even the warrior's time. The past is shameful, the future a lie. The time of journeys has changed, with trains and boats, but thoughts still move at the same speed. When you reach a new place, you no longer know where you are. I didn't get the wrong enemy. Justice, too, is broken. For me, for the yellow- and black-skinned people in the village, even for you. They want to judge me according to their rules? The righteous who rule our reserves? You say you wanted to help the engineer, like you want to help me? How could you? Nobody could find me, not even you. I had to guide you here. You're mixing up our pasts. They took separate paths and they will never cross again. You obey the orders of your world, the world of white morals, my sister. The only secret I'll agree to keep is the secret of your guilt. I have to help you too. If I don't, you'll never be up to the task you face. So listen, since you came to seek my knowledge. You are not responsible for being born white, but for what you do with your white woman's skin. Like I didn't choose my mixed blood, but I did choose my camp. I chose to be with the Indians, because their rules are not broken. You whites cannot judge me, you can only punish me. The privilege of just sentencing has been taken from you. I will choose my own. What sentence do you want for yourself, white sister?"

His hands slowly moved apart. Cold air slipped between his fingers and the warm damp skin of her neck. Aileen's breath smelled of carrion.

"I, too, have crossed the lines that separated what no longer exists. Pain and pleasure, action and dream. Imprisonment and freedom. I know that there are forces in life that do not work with it, and that if you ignore them – as happened with this naive Exposition and its boasts of progress – then what you will sow is not prosperity but war. But borders still exist, in your world and in mine, borders that cannot be ignored. What you did, Joseph, whatever you may think, was an evil act. You brought fear, suffering and grief. In my world, however broken it is, as in yours, there is no honour in such actions. Your real secret, the most cowardly secret, little brother, is that you killed the engineer instead of killing me."

"You said it yourself. Love can't be taken by force, because that only destroys it. That is what I did."

"By killing an innocent man?"

"You still don't understand. It wasn't the engineer I killed by taking his scalp. Nor was it your love for him. It was your love for me."

Without Joseph's hands around her throat, helping her to stand up, Aileen's legs wavered beneath her weight.

"You reduced us to nothing, Joseph. Nothing more than a murderer and an executioner."

He moved away from her. His smell and heat faded, and without them Aileen collapsed to the ground. Joseph spoke softly.

"That's the sentence that you've chosen? Neither enemy nor accomplice. Executioner? Even that, you wouldn't have managed without me."

From the tunnel came the distant sounds and vibrations of a metro train, shaking and pushing the air towards them. Normal service had been resumed.

"Joseph?"

She knew it would do no good to say his name more loudly.

"Joseph?"

Aileen gave herself a little more time, knees pressed against her chest, to stop crying and catch her breath. Then she groped around for her waterproof knapsack. Between the notebooks, pencils and sheets of paper, the tobacco pouch and the pipe, she found the smooth metal barrel and the grip of the Ladysmith, with its little .22 bullets, so small that nobody took them seriously. Every weapon made is destined to be used. "And everything that lives on earth," her father used to say, "was killed with a .22." Unlike her right to wear trousers, her right to carry this gun was undisputed. Because she was American? Because she'd hunted on the red man's old lands since she was a little girl? Because tracking an Indian was the white man's sport?

Aileen unbuttoned her sweat-soaked shirt and spread it over the stones. She unfastened her belt buckle, dropped her trousers and folded them next to her shirt, then took off her boots. She was used to posing nude now and, revolver in hand, nobody could judge her or tell her no. She was working for white art. She was injustice, ruler of ranches, the legal heir, the tattooed cousin, deserter of her camp, allegory of whiteness.

Her father had taught her to shoot. Her mother had taught her that it was possible to love more than once.

Joseph's smell was sharper now. He wasn't running away. He was waiting for her. They had reached the end of the future line, beneath the installations of Trocadéro and the colonial village. They could hear water flowing, like a small waterfall or a mountain stream. A leak, probably, in the city's unstable subsoil.

The sharp granite edges of the ballast cut into the soles of her feet.

Joseph had stopped. Pupils dilated, Aileen could make out a few lines of his body, enough for her imagination to complete the shape of her target. She aimed at Joseph's back. He was so alone that this was all he had to offer.

"Joseph?"

The first duty of an executioner is not to apologise. To kill without flinching. It is all he can offer: a little dignity. Aileen swallowed her words of love and the apologies she wanted to make to Uncle Pete and Aunt Maria.

Joseph Ferguson waited, closing his eyes to the threat. He knew which side of the world it came from. The white world, behind his Indian back. There was nothing else behind. Nothing else ahead, either, except for the tunnel's black mouth and that promise from the surface of the chiming of water.

20

Aileen left a note on her desk, addressed to the concierge and the maid, containing some money along with a note explaining that she would be back "sometime in the future". Then she stuffed her clothes, smeared with grease from the metro, into her old bag, slid the typewriter into its box, and tied her knapsack shut.

On the train to Strasbourg, she realised there was a dimension missing in what surrounded her, a new distance between her and the objects around her. She had lost her sense of smell. When she realised this, she held her breath as if her head had been plunged underwater, into a dangerous element. Her father, a veteran of the East India Company, would sometimes lose the use of his right hand, the one that had held sabres and pistols, the one that had killed. It grew numb and paralysed after nights of terrible dreams. After a few days, the feeling would gradually come back. Aileen's sense of smell would return in the same way. After her first anxieties, she put the typewriter on the table in her first-class compartment.

The first stop, six hours later, was at the Nouvel-Avricourt station, constructed at the expense of the French after the 1871 defeat. The railway line, for several dozen miles, marked the new border between Prussia and France. Strasbourg and the French village she had promised to visit were now German.

After having her passport stamped, the train set off again and

Aileen started work. Writing time no longer felt like a waste. On the contrary, it was time she had to win back from the other time, devourer of memories and odours.

She spent a night in Strasbourg, where the people spoke German and French, and she bought some ink rollers and reams of paper. The next day, she rented a carriage to take her the last forty miles to Thannenkirch. The roads were excellent and she guessed at their strategic value: in this region with all its tensions, troops had to be able to mobilise quickly.

The village, with its tall, solid, half-timbered houses, built around a church with a long, pointed belltower, was nestled in a small, wooded valley in the Vosges. It reminded her of the German communities on the eastern coast of the United States.

She rented a large room in the village's only inn. The hotel had red geraniums on the balustrades of its balconies and overlooked the fountain in the village square. She started writing straight away.

The memories she'd brought with her had arrived at their destination, and now it was time to unload them. Her nose recognised its first smell: the knapsack on the table, with its odour of stables, her father's smell. The work she had to do began with Arthur sitting beside her in front of a campfire, telling her the story of the ivory powder horn, about battlefields in Africa and India, and then it took in Alexandra's books and advice, Uncle Pete describing the virgin forests of the South, Aunt Maria talking about her vanished civilisation, and then all the stories of travellers and seasonal workers at the ranch, and all the people she'd interviewed during her career, and that was where her work ended. Her memories had found their starting point and the direction of their return journey: America and its vast dreams.

After four days, she took a break and asked the landlady of the inn whether any members of the Buchbinder family still lived in the village.

"Why are you looking for the Buchbinders?" she asked, correcting Aileen's pronunciation.

"I'm a friend of the family."

The landlady gave her a strange look, her gaze resting on Aileen's red hair. She was perhaps ten years younger than Aileen's mother. Had she known her? Looking troubled, the landlady finally said: "Karl Buchbinder still lives on the square. He's the last son."

Uncle Karl?

The woman showed her the way to the Buchbinder house and Aileen knocked at the door. She sensed eyes watching her curiously from behind the flowers on the balconies. Her presence must already have sparked some discussion in the village over the past few days.

Old Karl Buchbinder opened the door. As soon as he saw Aileen, he gasped. Aileen had apologies ready in her mouth. She smiled as she dumped her tons of memories on the old man's doorstep. Without a word, he gestured for her to enter. Karl Buchbinder was too moved to speak, so she asked the first question:

"Are there many of you?"

He tore himself away from his contemplation of the woman's face.

"Buchbinders? I'm a widower. I have two sons and a daughter. Seven grandchildren. My brothers and my sister are all . . ."

He stopped speaking and tears rose to his pale eyes.

"Alexandra? Is she alive?"

"She died almost a year ago."

He wiped his eyes with the back of his hand in a quick, embarrassed movement.

"Ah. Then both my brothers and my sister are dead. There were four of us. Three brothers and Alexandra. With you, there are now nine cousins . . . You look so much like her. Where is she buried?"

"On the land of her ranch, in the Sierra Nevada."

"In America?"

"Yes. That's where I'm from."

"She made it there, then?"

Uncle Karl smiled, proud of his little sister. He rubbed his chin as the questions jostled for attention in his mind.

"And the community that she dreamed of? Are you from that community?"

"No. The community was a failure. At the ranch, she bred horses, with my father."

He asked politely: "Do you have time to tell me? Could you stay for a while? There are so many things I'd like to ask you. Alexandra . . . why did she never write?"

It was the worst of questions and the simplest of answers:

"I don't know. But I can show you what I do know."

"Show me?"

Aileen took the typewritten pages from her bag.

"I'm writing it all. It's in French."

He didn't touch the pages on the table, but he couldn't stop staring at them.

"This is her story?"

"And the story of my father, and of our family over there."

Karl Buchbinder brushed his fingertips along the white edges of the paper.

"You know what Buchbinder means?"

"Yes."

He smiled.

"I'd be very happy to read your story."

"It's very personal. Intimate at times. Maybe a little shocking."

He thought for a moment.

"Are you ashamed of it?"

"No."

"Then, if you trust me, I'll read all of it."

When the time came to part, Aileen didn't want to let go of his hand.

"I didn't even know if I'd find anyone when I came all the way here. It was a symbolic journey for me. I'm very glad to have met you."

The old man blushed.

"I don't know if my children will feel so . . . curious about you. Or if their aunt's story will interest them as much as it does me."

"You think they'd be shocked?"

"Yes, if what you write about is out of the ordinary."

"Then I will trust you with that judgment too. The story is for you. Tell them about it only if you think it necessary."

It took Karl two days to read the first thirty pages, then they began to advance together. Aileen wrote in her room at the inn and, every two or three days, brought him the new pages. In August, she was officially introduced to the other family members at a vast lunch in the Buchbinder house. All her cousins and their children were present. There were white napkins and too much food.

By the time Aileen was approaching her story's final chapter – recounting her journey to Alsace – it was October. In the Vosges, autumn came quickly.

Throughout her stay, Uncle Karl performed his role as her editor and spokesman with seriousness and tact. Filtering out any information that seemed too private, he told the others about the adventures of Aunt Alexandra, who left Europe for the New World. Karl had been right. His children didn't care about the travels of this aunt they'd never met, and they disapproved of Aileen's presence in Thannenkirch. The strange appearance of this American woman disturbed them. Their curiosity was quickly replaced by indifference, then by mistrust and finally by jealousy when – through snatched hints and deductions – the Buchbinders understood that Aileen Bowman, their American cousin, was the heiress to a fortune beyond their wildest dreams. Old Karl was embarrassed by this, but when the two of them were together, he would constantly ask Aileen for more details: about the ranch and its buildings, capturing wild mustangs, or about Carson City. In the family legend, Alexandra was the one who left, but Karl was the one who'd wanted to leave. No other Buchbinder seemed to have inherited this desire.

Aileen left in the first days of winter, as the wind was tearing the last leaves from the trees' branches. She went to see Karl, who was waiting for her in front of a crackling fire, having read the last page of her story.

"It's an incredible story. All the time I was reading it, I kept worrying about what might happen to my sister. Now I know that she was happy. And that your father was a good husband to her. Thank you, with all my heart, for allowing me to learn all of that."

"Who was your favourite character?"

"They're not characters. I can't prefer one to another. They all have something that I wanted in my life, and, at the same time, something that makes me sad. Like your adoptive brother, poor Joseph. So nobody knows what became of him?"

Aileen stood up to answer old Karl. For the first time, she lied out loud, after lying with her typewriter. She tried out her version of history:

"No. He disappeared after his parents' death."

"Will you try to find him, like you came all the way here to find your mother's family?"

"I don't know if Joseph wants to be found."

"And what about your ranch?"

"My ranch? What about it?"

"Will you go back there?"

She returned to Paris a week after the Exposition had officially closed. The capital was slowly becoming its old self again as the attractions were dismantled and the building materials sold off in bulk. It was hard to predict what would remain of it. In the echo of the Palais des Congrès, a few ideas left hanging in the air? The whale of the Grand Palais and its child. The Pont Alexandre III, the big wheel in the Tuileries, and the debts, more solid than any building, from this immense waste that had ruined the ordinary people who had bought shares to finance it. Once the last shopkeepers had packed up and left, it would all be over and forgotten. No, nobody would dare predict what would remain of the

Exposition. The disassembly was the last moment of excitement, an opportunity to get rich quick. It was the time of the demolition men and the cleaners, of unqualified workers strong enough to swing a mallet or wield a claw hammer. From the dome of Creusot's Steelworks pavilion, crane operators brought down cannons and turrets, their red paint flaking off and floating over the Seine.

The first person Aileen visited was Marguerite Durand, radiant and ready to confront a world that, she knew, had not changed at all during the Exposition. The editor of *La Fronde* was impressed by the thickness of Aileen's manuscript. She promised to present it to one of her publisher acquaintances. She reeled off a flood of names, accompanied with little comments on their ages, suit brands and the state of their marriages: Hachette, Plon, Fayard, Lévy or Garnier, perhaps young Albin Michel, who was always on the lookout for new talent.

"Will you stay in Paris?" asked Marguerite.

"I don't know."

"Not everyone at *La Fronde* was a fan, but I really liked your columns. I'd be pleased to keep employing you if that's what you want. I could give you a daily column."

"Thank you. I'll think about it."

"Have you heard from the wife of your friend the engineer, who died so awfully?"

"She went back to live with her family in Brittany."

"Did you know that they found the murderer's body while you were gone?"

"Pardon?"

"That's what the police say, and I personally heard M. Lépine talking about it. A body was exhumed in the Métropolitain during the last part of the work on the Trocadéro line, very close to the crime scene. The corpse had been half-buried under stones between the tracks, but rats had uncovered it. The doctors who examined the body couldn't determine what continent it came from, only that the murderer wasn't white. On the other hand, they do know that he was killed by bullets. Police commissioner Lépine told me there was no absolute proof, because they didn't find the weapons used to kill the engineer, but it is very likely that this man was the killer. The mystery, now, is the identity of the person who killed the killer. And why they didn't report their actions to the police. M. Lépine's theory is that it might have been an accomplice."

"An accomplice?"

"Another savage who must have escaped to the colonial village along with the killer. The theory is that they killed each other. Who knows? Anyway, if you see the engineer's widow, you'll be able to tell her that her husband's murderer received a fitting punishment for his crime."

"I'm not in touch with her anymore."

"Ah. Well, it wouldn't bring her husband back anyway, I suppose."

Marguerite, who was always in a rush, dismissed these gruesome details with an airy wave of her hand, reiterated the job offer she had made to Aileen, and vanished in a fanfare of frills.

Aileen left *La Fronde*, turned into a back alley, and ran to hide herself. She didn't come out again until she had stopped shaking and her stomach had been purged of all its contents.

After three months in Alsace, writing a version of history in which Joseph hadn't killed or died, she had almost come to believe her own lies. Joseph was dead and the rats had uncovered his corpse. She'd broken her nails clawing at the stones of the ballast, but she hadn't managed to dig a very deep hole. Joseph had resurfaced and Paris was no longer Aileen's to enjoy.

Julius welcomed her into his studio on rue Copernic as if they'd seen each other the day before; as if she'd come back too soon for him to have got used to her absence. She had the impression that he wasn't as pleased to see her as he used to be, before. Either that, or she didn't feel as comfortable there as she had.

"Take a seat, Aileen. You look like you need a pick-me-up. Help yourself to a drink, I'll be with you in a minute . . ."

He was working on the background of a small painting, around the sketched silhouette of a man in a hat. Aileen filled a wine glass with cognac and drank it calmly, methodically, to the bottom, swallow after swallow.

"Have you finished?" she asked.

"Yes."

"You don't look very happy to see me. Or is it the painting? You're not satisfied with it?"

Julius' silence lasted a little too long.

"On the contrary."

He abandoned his palette and brush, put away the unfinished canvas, and went to fetch another, larger painting, covered by a sheet, which he placed on the easel. Aileen moved closer and Julius pulled away the sheet.

The frame was even bigger than she remembered it – taller than Aileen herself and more than three feet wide. Her painted body was almost life-size.

She closed her eyes and opened them again to understand what she was seeing. It was hard to make out. Julius had covered his tracks. The viewer's attention was not fixed on one single point but had to shift between the points of a long triangle consisting of Aileen's face, in three-quarter profile, her eyes gazing down at a typewriter which marked the second point, on the right side of the canvas. From there, the viewer's eye was drawn down to the ground, where a dog lay at Aileen's feet, completing the triangle. It was one of those muscular, white watchdogs that Julius often painted with his nudes. An immaculate, domesticated and dangerous beast. Of all the figures in the painting, the dog was the only one looking at the viewer. It was the incarnation of Julius: the uncompromising guardian of his art. At the feet of the woman. The dog's ears were pointing upwards at the centre of the triangle occupied by Aileen's red pubic V. One of the ears cut into the outer line of her thigh like a wedge, menacing the fine hairs of the mons pubis. Julius had painted the outer labia slightly retracted, the swollen clitoris, the vagina's opening. The oblique shadow of the desk, refusing to act as an agent of modesty, carefully avoided this fleshy pink flower, highlighting it by contrast rather than covering it. Its shadow was a response to the dark lines of the tattoos, which formed a painting within Julius' painting, with Aileen's skin as a second canvas.

The woman's genitals were painted the same pink as her forehead and her face, which was frowning with concentration at the sheet of paper that protruded, straight as an erection, from the typewriter. Her sex organs, the biological origin of the world, were not only a place of pleasure but a source of energy and inspiration, the origin of intellectual creativity. The lips of her mouth were closed but looked as though they were about to open, like the open thighs and her other lips, the erect clitoris. The corresponding colours and textures of Aileen's genitalia and face were the true subject of this nude: the inspiration, and the intimate ecstasy that accompanied it, of a woman writer. Not a fainting bourgeois female, not a nymph, not a prostitute.

Instead of directly portraying the wetness of the labia, Julius had evoked it by painting a bead of sweat under Aileen's arm, trickling over her ribcage. The heat of the entire body was expressed through this detail. He had remained true to the little asymmetries of her breasts and had painted them smaller than they were. Not as nourishers of infants, but as sexual objects.

Even more daringly, Julius had chosen to paint the stage on which Aileen was standing. The dog lay on it, and, at the bottom of the canvas, you could see a corner of the oriental rug where their chairs were now arranged. Julius was giving the game away, revealing the artifices of the background and, by doing so, intensifying the reality of the woman's nudity.

Behind the woman, emerging from the ridiculous wooden stage, was the corner of a living-room wall, painted in false perspective, lopsided and vertiginous. The elements of the background had the lightness of objects in a dream.

The flowered wallpaper was the wallpaper from the brothel they had visited. A bust stood atop a pillar, its sculpted face disturbing. Aileen thought about the head of Socrates on display in the Louvre, an honest attempt to represent a great, ugly man. The bust in the painting was of her father, as imagined by Julius: Arthur Bowman as an ancient philosopher-warrior.

There were photographs painted on the wall. Among them

was one of Jeandel's cyanotypes, the one of the woman tied to a plank and the executioner pressing a funnel down her throat. The cyanotype was hung above a glass case of knick-knacks, one of those collections of ethnological objects brought back from scientific expeditions. An engraved Indian pipe, a warrior's sword, a doll in a fringed dress, a yellowed pamphlet for Pawnee Bill's Wild West Show. The glass case was half-open, its doors gaping at the same angle as Aileen's legs.

There was one last portrait on the wall, another painting within the painting – of another red-headed woman who, like Aileen, was staring at the typewriter. Alexandra.

Through the window behind the naked woman, you could see the sun setting over the rooftops of Paris, the Eiffel Tower and the big wheel, over towers and domes with multicoloured flags. Electric lights were visible all over the dusk-dimmed city.

This scandalous painting did not even have a mythological title to rescue it. It was called simply "Nude of the American Woman".

"So, my dear, do you think your portrait will become an even greater legend than 'L'Origine du Monde'?"

"I'm sure of it."

"Do you like it?"

"You've done a lot of work while I was away. I think it's perfect, Julius. And what about you – what do you think of it?"

"I am worried that I will never find another subject to match it . . . but pleased to have stolen it from the artists who will come after me. Do you still want me to keep it?"

Aileen nodded and looked at Julius, the artist, the friend from the tethered balloon.

"I've made my decision now. I'm going to leave. Your portrait will take my place in Paris."

As she put on her jacket, Julius observed the dog in the painting – himself – which looked back at him. He thought about the other Aileen, the one he'd painted and kept secret, in her wedding dress. He no longer knew who – out of the naked woman and the dog – was guarding whom. Virtue over vice, or vice over virtue?

Relieved by the American woman's departure, Julius threw the sheet over the portrait and moved it to the back of his studio.

The crossing to the Ile de Bréhat was a minor apocalypse of wind and waves. Raindrops rattled against oilskins like firecrackers. Swathes of sea swept the boat's deck and poured in cascades from the portholes. Unable to fly most of its sails, the boat took twenty minutes to reach the safety of the port. Night was falling as Aileen disembarked, the blackness of the sea and earth melting into the blackness of the sky. In such weather, the winter day had lasted only a few hours.

She had sent word of her arrival, though she had no idea what sort of welcome to expect. Someone was waiting for her. A man walking towards her, back bent in the wind, clinging to his lantern as if fire were still the most precious thing on the island. He spoke Breton, but she didn't need to understand what he was saying in order to follow him. The oil lamp, hung from the pole on the cattle-drawn carriage, lit their way and the driver dropped her off outside the Cornic house. The wind howled and fought against the figure wrapped in a cape, as if trying to prevent it from reaching the door. Aileen felt like a character in a novel by Mary

Shelley or Bram Stoker, an envoy from the rational world sent to battle natural elements that suddenly seemed supernatural. She banged as hard as she could on the house's front door.

The maid who answered took her coat and asked her to wait.

The house was simply furnished, the doors low, the granite flagstones cold. The light was dim with mourning, and Aileen could tell that this funereal atmosphere had nothing to do with Agnès' return; it was what held these old stones together. Fires burned in hearths, vainly trying to dry out the dampness. In the living room, the maid invited Aileen to sit near the yellow flames.

"Mme Cornic will be here soon."

The rooms were not lit by lamps. Like the carriage driver, everyone here seemed to carry their own light around with them. Everyone except little Alice, who came running, an escapee from the house's slowness.

"Hello, Alice."

The little girl stood at the edge of the fire's warmth. Agnès' daughter had become more cautious in the last few months. She hadn't grown bigger, just older. She didn't reply and, her curiosity satisfied, ran off again, exiting stage left while her grandmother appeared to the right.

"Mrs Bowman."

Mme Cornic invited the journalist to follow her upstairs, to the bedroom that had been prepared for her; the bed was made, and there was an oil lamp and a box of matches on a chest of drawers, but no wood in the hearth.

"We will dine in one hour."

The Cornics were as sparing with their words as they were with their oil.

When Aileen went back down to the dining room, the whole family was there waiting. Three lamps, plus the firelight, gave enough brightness to chase the shadows from their faces. Agnès was thinner. Her gaunt cheeks made her mouth look even wider. Aileen had hoped that the widow's first reaction would betray a distress call, but Agnès' smile showed only fatigue and resignation. She wasn't a prisoner; everything here spoke of voluntary servitude. The austere father, the anxious mother, the solitary daughter. Only little Alice's agitation suggested any curiosity.

Mme Cornic made no effort to start a conversation, and M. Cornic restricted himself to civilities. All other subjects were traps, to be avoided at all costs. Paris, their guest's occupation as a journalist, the island. So Aileen did what everyone does when they are caught in the unspoken tension of a family meal; she talked to the child.

"Do you go to school on the island, Alice?"

"No, I have a tutor at the house."

"Is that fun?"

Mme Cornic answered for her granddaughter:

"The tutor's role is to teach Alice, not to entertain her."

"Are you learning any foreign languages?"

"Foreign languages?"

Mme Cornic grimaced.

"French and Breton are the only languages Alice needs to know."

The little girl cheerfully ignored her grandmother.

"How many languages do you speak?"

"The same number as you – just two. The French I learned

from my mother and the English that my father taught me. Do you speak French or Breton with your friends on the island?"

M. Cornic spoke at last. The subject had woken him from his inertia.

"French, here, is always considered a foreign language. The Republic insists that its teaching is mandatory, but some Bretons refuse to learn it."

M. Cornic, however, as a wealthy, bourgeois man, had rid his French of all traces of a Breton accent. His intervention also saved Alice from admitting that she had no friends: the Cornics' house was an island within an island.

"What else are you learning, Alice?"

"Boring stuff. I wish I could learn English."

"Silence, Alice!"

The little girl obeyed her grandmother. Agnès, a gracious ghost, placed her hand on her daughter's to comfort her. Then she looked at Aileen with the patience of the dead.

"The winter is long on Bréhat. In the springtime, Alice will be able to play outside again and she'll be happy to be back on the island."

"Do you miss Paris, Agnès?"

Mme Cornic almost choked at this. Her husband stared at the food on his plate. Agnès squeezed her daughter's hand to prevent her from leaving the table.

"Our life is here now."

Sadness and weight loss had not consumed all of Agnès' beauty, but no traces of it could be found in her parents' faces, not even if Aileen mingled the two in her imagination. Agnès had been the miraculous product of a union of ugliness, a freak in the Cornics' natural order. It was hardly surprising that her mother would do everything she could to hide, spoil and ruin her. Because beauty provoked desire, it encouraged the twin urges of sex and leaving. First, Jacques Huet had stolen away Agnès, and now there was a new danger at Mme Cornic's table: this American journalist, whom her granddaughter and her daughter would not stop staring at.

The words left Aileen's mouth and broke the monastery silence before Mme Cornic could blot out their horror.

"It is possible to have more than one life."

Aileen looked Agnès straight in the eyes as she said this. Then she looked at Alice.

"I'll write that for you in English, if you want. It can be the first sentence you learn."

The grandmother attempted to regain control of the situation.

"Please don't bother, madame. It is late and Alice must go to bed. In fact, it is late for all of us and you have had a long journey."

Aileen took a notebook and a pencil from her pocket, wrote a few words, tore out the page, folded it in two and handed it to the child, who fell upon it as if it were a sweet that she feared someone was about to steal from her. The grandmother cried out:

"Alice!"

The little girl freed her hand from her mother's and ran off. Agnès smiled indulgently at her daughter's impudence. Or perhaps it was a smile of apology for Aileen, excusing herself for not being up to this visit. Aileen pitied her. She wasn't sure she'd be able to contain her rage much longer.

"I'm happy to see that you're well, Agnès. Thank you for this meal and good night to you."

Aileen went up to her room and didn't sleep. The next morning, when Mme Cornic informed her that Agnès wasn't feeling well, Aileen asked to say goodbye to the little girl.

"I'm afraid Alice can't see you either. She is busy with her homework. M. Cornic sends his regards. I wish you a safe journey back to Paris, Mrs Bowman."

"I'm not going back to Paris. I'm leaving for the United States."

"Ah. Well, in that case, *bon voyage*."

"Please pass on my regards to your daughter. Take care of her."

"I know what I must do, madame."

"Really?"

Mme Cornic slammed the front door shut.

No carriage or driver was waiting for her outside. Aileen walked a mile and a half to the port, in the half-light, under a sky whose slate-grey clouds were like a mirror image of the town's rooftops. The return to the mainland was calmer than the journey to the island had been.

Every train station has a hotel, and the same is true for jetties. In this case, it was an inn, in the village of Ploubazlanec. She rented a room there, with a view of the docks where the boat to Bréhat was moored. She slept, read books and, from her lookout post, watched the skies as they passed above the island, the wind blowing the clouds and the clouds shrouding the sun.

Twentieth Century

After the Paris Exposition of 1900, Julius LeBlanc Stewart painted more and more high-society portraits. His nudes became rarer, the women in his paintings less fragile, more austere. The natural lighting of his pictures was still praised, along with the strength and ingenuity of his colours, but his work had lost its power, the sensual provocation that had brought his career its first success.

In truth, although nobody knows exactly why or when it happened, Julius had entered a new phase of his life; after his days as an unruly rich artist, he returned to the origins and principles of his bourgeois education: religion. A profound spiritual crisis, precipitated by the guilt of having wandered for too long along the wrong paths. The Paris Exposition was, for him, a particularly bitter memory, and the shame of it gnawed at him. Perhaps, too, as his sexual urges faded with age, it became easier and easier to disapprove of them.

A few weeks after the departure of the American journalist, he took out the painting of the woman in the wedding dress. For a long time, she had been faceless, and then she had become Aileen Bowman.

He had thought that version of the painting perfect, but now he was starting to have doubts again.

In the velvet salon of a brothel, clients and prostitutes were in the middle of an orgy. Amid this whirlwind of flesh and champagne stood a prostitute in a lace wedding dress, staring directly at the viewer. She was as pure and solemn as the people around her were cowardly and debauched. In one hand, she held a bouquet of flowers; the other was leaning on a table that had been set for a banquet: white tablecloth, gleaming silverware, sparkling glasses. The men were bourgeois, red-nosed drunkards. The women were laughing, vulgar whores. The bride – a promise or a sacrifice – wore a determined expression. On the wall hangings behind her, the decorative patterns were mixed with an apparition of Christ on the cross, a gentle force radiating from Him. One might believe that the woman's moral battle, in the midst of this filthy whorehouse, had been won, and that Christ was there to bear witness to her victory. But the hand that the woman was leaning on the table was a vile thing: its three fingers long, pointed, and without any knuckles, as though it had been replaced by one of the devil's cloven hooves. It was the image of temptation that still held her in the grip of the pleasures around her and the abundance of the table. And it was at this hand that Christ, head lowered, nailed to His wallpaper, was staring.

In this physical monstrosity, there was a seed of doubt that Julius had never been able to remove.

Not only had he taken years to find the right face for his white lady, but he had painted five or six different versions of that hand, human or diabolical, before deciding, out of honesty and respect for his doubt, to abandon it to the demon. The battle for virtue was never won. The hand of this corrupted muse with Aileen Bowman's face would remain hideous.

After taking out the canvas, Julius collapsed. He'd understood that the journalist's face could never illustrate his moral fable. As sinful as she was, Aileen Bowman refused to be saved. But then, remembering the evening when, coming out of the restaurant, he'd first thought of using Aileen as the model for this painting, he had a new idea. Julius took up his colours and his brushes again and, hardly daring to believe it, gave a definitive face, without any doubt whatsoever this time, to the virtuous prostitute. He kept some of Aileen Bowman's features, but added some from a second woman, whom he had never forgotten. The widow of the murdered engineer, who had eaten dinner with them that night, and whose exciting, saintly face still haunted his memory. Agnès Huet.

The red hair shaded into Agnès' black; her blue eyes and her mouth were softened. The two women, fused together, evolved into a complex feminine dialectic, generous and violent, attractive and pure, that perfectly embodied the questions Julius wished to pose to his viewers. The two united faces gave birth to the most desirable of whores, or the strongest of mothers among all those that Julius had ever painted. The painting also received its final title: "Redemption".

After this epiphany, Julius would paint only religious subjects, in which the women became monolithic saints, irreproachable amalgams of suffering and pleasure.

In 1915, he enrolled in an ambulance brigade of the French Red Cross. Julius couldn't bear the horrors that he witnessed on the front, and after having a complete nervous breakdown, he sought refuge with some friends in London. He would stay there until the Armistice in November 1918.

Upon his return to Paris, to the apartment on rue Copernic, his strong figure seemed to have been drained of all its life force.

At sixty-three, Julius had become a hollow tree. He surrounded himself only with men now: friends, most of them artists.

On the morning of 5 January 1919, moving slowly and breathing heavily, he paid one last visit to his studio. He didn't paint, but, after a long meditation, he took out from under a pile of dusty canvases one particular painting that he had taken care to keep hidden. Julius contemplated it with tears in his eyes, his bony fingers clinging to the wooden frame, then carefully packaged it. Concentrating hard, he wrote an address on the package that he hoped would be enough, then called for a courier. That was his last choice as an artist. Afterwards, he returned to his bedroom, where he died an old bachelor.

The euphoria that Eugene Stanford felt when he got back to Titusville, Pennsylvania after his trip to France was fully justified. He had perfectly anticipated the future: in the course of the following decade, Standard Oil would be transformed from a large family business to a disturbingly powerful, international economic force. After diversifying around the turn of the century – buying up gas and electricity companies, pouring millions into the railways to confront the lighting crisis – the company was ideally poised to capitalise on the rise of the internal combustion engine. In 1908, Rockefeller would weep with joy when he saw the first Ford T factory. A new world was beginning, one that would run purely on oil. Standard Oil's unscrupulous methods, its army of spies, saboteurs and henchmen, added to its price-war strategy, would elevate the company to a degree of monopoly unseen since the days of the old India Companies.

But on his return from Paris, the fate reserved for Eugene

Stanford, husband of the young Mary, was not as happy as that of his employers. In Titusville, Mary Stanford began to rebel. All that mattered to her was escaping her marriage before she became pregnant. So, as a first step, she asked her husband to sleep in a separate bedroom.

Mary did whatever she wanted. She painted and wrote and went more and more often to New York to attend art exhibitions and plays. Naturally, Eugene suspected that she had a lover there. In the art galleries of Manhattan, Mary would sometimes bump into Royal Cortissoz, who grew ever more shrunken and intransigent.

One day in 1902, perhaps because he was lonely, Eugene Stanford enthusiastically welcomed a reporter from *McClure's Magazine* named Ida Tarbell. Not only was Miss Tarbell interested in the oil industry, but she was from the area herself: the daughter of an oil man in Venango County, twenty miles from Titusville. She was Eugene's age and, as a professor of geology and botany, had dedicated her life to her career, never marrying. Ida was writing a series of articles on the oil industry for the New York-based magazine that employed her. With Mary absent, Ida visited Eugene several days in a row, and listened as he told her everything he knew about Standard Oil.

It was said afterwards that, in doing so, he sounded the death knell for the company's complete domination of the market; in any case, he certainly lit one of the fuses that caused the ensuing explosion. After noting down his confessions, Ida Tarbell disappeared and Eugene never saw her again. Two years later, she published a book that became a massive bestseller: *The History of the Standard Oil Company*. As a side note, she revealed that her own father had been ruined by Rockefeller's dirty tricks.

Following the book's publication, Standard Oil, already in the sights of the Supreme Court, was attacked from all directions, leading to its dissolution, in 1911, for violating anti-trust laws.

If Eugene Stanford was partly responsible for this, then so was his wife Mary, for abandoning him. She herself attributed that honour to the woman who had opened her eyes in Paris, enabling her to discover a new world of freedom and creation: Aileen Bowman. To illustrate this story, Mary would describe the day she nervously accepted the journalist's invitation to visit the studio of a Parisian artist on rue Copernic.

Eugene, having been fired by Standard Oil, did not try to argue with Mary when she suggested, in 1906, that they should separate. Since divorce by mutual agreement was illegal in the United States at that time, most couples seeking to split up would turn to adultery. There were many lawyers in New York who specialised in that business: they prepared all the paperwork and provided the services of photographers, actors and actresses, often prostitutes, to play the lovers' roles. Mary explained to Eugene that they wouldn't need to spend money on an actor – a photographer would suffice. Flash. Lawyer and judge. Divorce. In return for Eugene's understanding, Mary wouldn't ask him for any money. For several years, she'd been receiving grants from a feminist foundation based in San Francisco that helped support women artists.

Mary had chosen to paint, and she did that until her death in 1964 at her Manhattan studio, at the age of eighty-four, having proved that there is nothing better for a long and happy life than sex and creativity.

*

Royal Cortissoz was obstinate enough to die in 1948, living proof that bile, too, was an effective preservative. He died in his Manhattan apartment after years spent proclaiming that Picasso, Matisse, Van Gogh and Mondrian were mental degenerates who would soon sink into oblivion.

Alice Huet lived long enough to have several lives. The first lasted from her birth until her father's death. As an adult, she was lying when she said that she remembered him perfectly. Only one photograph of Jacques Huet remained, posed in front of a tunnel in construction, among a group of men in black suits, his face a grainy blur. He had been an engineer on the first line of the Paris Métropolitain and he'd been murdered by a madman. One of those savages who were exhibited during the great colonial exhibitions of the nineteenth century, exhibitions that continued until the Second World War. As an adolescent, she discovered that talking about this family legend immediately brought her attention. Later, when she realised what a tragedy Jacques Huet's death had been for her mother, she stopped treating it as a sort of spotlight beam. She was seven when her father died, so she ought to have retained some clear memories of him, but in fact she had none at all. This amnesia was unnatural and suggests that the tragedy had a profound effect on her first life, the shortest and most decisive of them all.

Alice Huet's second life began at the same time as her mother's, during a crossing on a boat that – in contrast to memories of her father – she would later recall vividly. Before, everything was vague; afterwards, it became clear and sharp.

One short crossing, from the Ile de Bréhat – where her whole family lived – to the Breton coast, on a freezing winter day. Her mother held her hand very firmly and yelled when Alice wanted to see the water rushing past the boat's sides. So where could she go on this boat? But her mother didn't want to let her go. Alice had another memory, preceding the ones from that brief journey, of a dinner in a dark room. When Aileen Bowman handed her a piece of paper, containing, she said, some words in English. Her grandparents were there and the whole scene had the feel of a bad dream. Aileen's message was not in English. Alice read it in her bedroom, and afterwards was never able to forget it.

Alice, this message is for you and your mother. I will wait for you on the other side. Come and find me.

When they disembarked from the boat, Aileen was standing on the jetty, in her trousers and her old hat. In the minutes that followed – or at least that is how Alice would remember it – the three of them boarded a carriage, then a train, arriving in Le Havre where, almost immediately, aboard an enormous ship, they sailed away from France.

As a child, Alice had a simple explanation for why they became a family: because all their names began with A. Her grandmother Alexandra, whom she had never known; Aileen; her mother Agnès; she, Alice; and even her mysterious American grandfather, Arthur.

As a young woman, she read Aileen's manuscripts and drew from them three important lessons: that everything is natural for someone growing up in a world that others consider to be monstrous or absurd; that memories are lies; and that children never know who their parents are because the adults who teach them not to lie are, themselves, the greatest liars of all.

The episode of the departure from France, on a transatlantic liner, proved the truth of all three of these rules. Alice remembered it neither as an escape nor as a scandal, but as a wonderful adventure. She recalled her mother and the American journalist having fun together and being as happy as she was aboard the ship. Lastly, she believed what Aileen Bowman had told her: that she was her aunt, who had come here to play with her and to take her mother and herself on a holiday.

Aileen's autobiographical writings were never published in her lifetime. Other than Aileen's uncle, and the editors who rejected them, her manuscripts were read by only one other person: Agnès. Then Alice, when they decided that she was old enough to understand that the letter A was not sufficient explanation for their life together.

Patiently and recklessly, Aileen and Agnès helped her to uncover falsehoods, to recognise true freedom and understand its price, to track down the lie – a crucial ingredient in all truths – and reduce it to its most honest dimension. What Alice realised, long after leaving home, was that, in this new land of self-conquest, her mother, guided by Aileen Bowman, had advanced alongside her.

The challenge was to love, and – as Aileen explained – their love was dangerous: for them, it was natural, but for everyone else it was scandalous and monstrous.

"But I'm a redhead, so don't worry. They'll burn me first."

The most important lesson Alice retained from all this was never to believe that anything is impossible. Faced with prerequisites and preconceptions, with anything pre-empted, premeditated or predicted, free human beings find a new way. Sometimes, to provoke narrow-minded guests, Alice would present Aileen Bowman's life as a riddle: "Ladies, how would you go about luring a young Catholic widow into your bed? I'll give you one clue, and this applies to you, too, gentlemen, if you were trying to seduce a young widower: the best thing is to have enough money to buy them."

On the liner, Agnès Huet had slept. The sea mists cocooned her and her restful state – eternal in Bréhat – became the first step towards her transformation. Her porcelain skin – a translucent white through which you could see the blue veins at her temples and around her eyes – thickened during the crossing, to the point where she was able to walk in the sun, when it appeared and when Aileen took her out on the deck. When Agnès needed to be alone, the American woman looked after little Alice in her cabin.

The first precaution Aileen took, when they arrived in New York, was to organise their departure as quickly as possible. After a sheltered childhood in Bréhat, and her sad, violent expulsion from Paris, Agnès wasn't ready to cope with such a vibrant city. They sent a telegram to France to inform M. and Mme Cornic of the situation. Agnès didn't flinch when she wrote the message.

On the train, Aileen explained that the United States was so big that nobody had yet been all the way around it, and little Alice announced that she would remember everything she saw through the window; that way, she wouldn't need to come back. Because she was going to travel all the way around this country.

"I don't know if that's possible, Alice. The United States is twenty times bigger than France, you know, and three million times bigger than Bréhat. Can you imagine visiting three million places as big as your island?"

"On a train, yes."

"Trains can't go everywhere, though."

"How many years is three million days?"

"Just over eight thousand. Why?"

"Because it takes a day to walk around Bréhat. So it's impossible."

"What about on horseback?"

"Yes! How fast can a horse gallop?"

"Five times faster than a person walking."

"So how many years would it take to visit three million Bréhats on a galloping horse?"

"You have to divide eight thousand by five."

"I can't."

"The answer is one thousand six hundred years."

"That's still way too much!"

"Yes, but in Paris, I saw an automobile that went five times faster than a galloping horse . . ."

"So you could divide one thousand six hundred by five?"

"Yes."

"How many is that?"

"Three hundred and twenty."

Alice became sad.

"That's still too long. Nobody can live more than a hundred years."

Aileen looked at the child.

"Then you'll need several lives. For example, your mama's life, plus yours, plus mine."

Alice thought about this idea.

"Or an automobile that goes three times as fast."

Alice watched the landscape rush past the window for as long as she could before falling asleep, and Aileen began weaving her dreams again. She was thinking about the only place on earth where she would be able to take care of Agnès. The place that her journey to Paris had brought her back to. The fated place. Arthur Bowman's prison. The broken dream of Alexandra's community. Joseph's paradise lost. The island-sized Fitzpatrick Ranch would be their refuge.

There, Agnès would watch clouds move across the mirror of Lake Tahoe. Aileen would ride horses, go hunting, and take Alice with her. That little girl's intrepid spirit must never be stifled by prudence. Aileen would put walnuts and almonds in her knapsack, teach Alice to set up camp and start a fire to shelter herself in the snow. They would bring back the red meat of wild-caught game.

One year after Alexandra's death and Aileen's fear that she would forget how to speak French, two Frenchwomen were bringing the language back to the ranch. There were three of them now, in the middle of the Sierra, who could speak that magic tongue.

In the house on the lake, Aileen removed the dust sheets from the furniture. As soon as Agnès and Alice were settled in, she began to prepare them. In the white silence of winter, beside the frozen lake, they continued to rest but they also started to move together. The first step: Aileen taught English to mother and daughter. She placed cards on all the objects in the house, with the English name of each object written upon them, and in the evenings she read from books which she translated sentence by sentence.

The second step was for Aileen to separate from the ranch, so that she could mourn.

The most difficult discussion, with the two other shareholders in the ranch – her uncle Oliver Ferguson and his wife Lylia – concerned their nephew, Joseph Ferguson. In the deed that formalised the transfer of her shares, Aileen had to convince them to add a clause, valid until their deaths and hers: if Joseph Ferguson should ever return and demand his inheritance, one third of the ranch would be his. Lylia started to scream. Uncle Oliver tried to negotiate his nephew's inheritance. Fifteen per cent? Twenty? Twenty-five? But Aileen would not give in. Uncompromising, she haggled over a dead man's rights.

"A share equal to ours. And when you and I are no longer alive, your children will become sole proprietors. They can make war on each other for as long as they want."

From the shares bought from Aileen, they deducted the value of the house by the lake, its barns and 250 acres around the property. The buildings represented only a small part of the transaction; the cattle and the 12,350 acres of breeding land, on the hillsides of the Sierra, were the true prize. For a long time, the mountain lands had been nothing more than Arthur Bowman's personal obsession, while the house was merely Alexandra's romantic dream – Lylia hated that house, and now lived in a small palace in the centre of Carson City. Oliver and his wife, with an eye on the future, were only too happy to draw a line under the dirty origins of their fortune. They also made no trouble when Aileen asked for thirty horses – stallions and mares – chosen from among the best animals on the Fitzpatrick Ranch. If the lakeside property had been one of her own fingers, Lylia would have bitten it off to get rid of it.

And so those two ideological bodies – the utopian dream of Aileen's parents and the American dream of Oliver and Lylia – were separated like warring Siamese twins. With no way of knowing whether either would have a heart enabling them to go on living. Whether this mutually agreed amputation would lead to their deaths, to the utopia becoming a skeletal ghost, to the evisceration of the American dream.

Joseph Ferguson, with his mixed red and white blood, signed and sealed this agreement with a cross marking his absence at the bottom of the deed.

The next negotiation was with Agnès. Aileen had to convince the widow to sign her name, too, at the bottom of the document, making her and her daughter co-owners of the Fitzpatrick Ranch, each with a share equal to Aileen's. Once lawful prisoners on their island, they now had the opportunity to be free of the past for good.

Agnès Huet, breathing mountain air after a life by the sea, recovered first her strength and then her curiosity. She wanted to understand why this woman, Aileen Bowman, whom she hadn't even known six months before, would offer her a house and so much land – Alice had calculated that their ranch was thirty times bigger than the island of Bréhat – here in America.

Had she been more experienced in life, Agnès might perhaps have worried about such a mad idea, suspecting that there was no such thing as a free lunch. That the journalist's wealth was not enough to explain her generosity. That there must be deeper, darker reasons behind this dream. But Agnès, princess of the island, had the gift and the naivety not to think in those terms. Her whys became whos: who was Aileen to do this for her? A perfect Christian, rejected by the Cornic and Huet families?

In this environment, Aileen's choice of clothing no longer seemed shocking. Nor did her directness of tone and manners when she spoke to visiting neighbours or day labourers on the ranch. She was still the unmarried, childless journalist who wrote obscene columns in a rabidly feminist newspaper in Paris, who drank, hung out with artists and cursed. But here, amid cowboys and trappers, she was the most sophisticated person around. Did she think she was a man? No. She was still, here, despite everything, even more than before, a woman. She might play boyish games with Alice, but she was as attentive as any tutor or mother. Her personality combined all the qualities that Agnès had always thought of as being essentially masculine and essentially feminine. All her worries about Aileen were soothed by Aileen herself.

Driven by curiosity, she began waking up earlier and earlier, walking further in the snow around the lake, and working harder at her English, perhaps imagining that part of the solution to the mystery lay in that language. But a more pertinent question troubled Agnès: if Aileen Bowman was a subversive, a madwoman, or even a simple eccentric, why did she accept her help and her gifts so unhesitatingly?

Because she thought her life had ended in Bréhat.

Because this place was more beautiful than anywhere she'd seen or been before.

Because she'd just made the first real journey of her life.

Because, here, her questions were answered.

Because she was no longer lonely, and had someone in whom she could confide. A woman who reassured her like a man. Or a man who knew how to answer her like a woman.

Because she had the right to be beautiful again in the way she wanted to be, without either displaying it or hiding it. Beautiful in the way Aileen was beautiful: hair hanging loose, hands dirty.

Because when she wanted to learn to ride, she could choose a pair of trousers from Aileen's wardrobe. Because the frozen ground of the corral, which had frightened her so much to start with, no longer bothered her. And because her body had grown harder; because she now felt sure that a fall wouldn't break her.

Because, here, her memories of Jacques were welcome. Time had not stopped in a period of pure mourning; life was mixed with grief to the point where, in a single day, she could remember her dead husband and laugh.

When she woke up crying, her dreams haunted by Jacques' disfigured face in his hospital bed, Aileen would come and sit at her bedside. In her bedroom. Not the one in Paris, not the one at her parents' house. The first bedroom she'd had where she felt no need to lock the door, where Aileen knocked before entering and Agnès welcomed her without embarrassment.

On the evening of 31 December 1900, the three of them waited together, in front of a clock whose accuracy was doubtful, for the twelve chimes of midnight that would announce the new century. Wrapped up in blankets, they went out on the terrace, where Aileen and Agnès drank home-made alcohol. This electrified century that Aileen had gone looking for in Paris now began amid wild nature, under a moon reflected by the white mountains and the frozen lake. Little Alice nuzzled between the two women, who hugged each other under the blankets.

Aileen was careful not to spoil the evenings with her sad thoughts, but the addition of that 1 in the year 1901 seemed to erase all the promises of 1900. Time had not been suspended by those two zeros; its mechanics ground on. The first year of the twentieth century did not seem like a blank page to her, but like the start of a dark countdown.

That spring, when they could begin swimming in the lake, Aileen would sometimes enter Agnès' room without knocking, to bring her coffee or ask her something or just to talk, while she was waking up or sleeping or getting dressed.

The trees drank thirstily from the warming earth, and the mountain turned green in the space of a few days. The sun hung higher in the sky above the ranch for longer and longer each day. Perpetuating a family tradition, Aileen would leave the sleeping house at dawn, a blanket over her shoulders, let it drop onto the grass, and dive naked into the luminous water. Sometimes, when Aileen went back to her bedroom after this morning dip, Agnès would already be awake and – sheltered by mountains and the 250 acres that separated them from the rest of the world – be the only one to see her. Then, one morning, Agnès too went out onto the terrace wearing only a blanket, let it drop next to Aileen's, and dived in to join her friend.

"How do you manage to stay in so long?"

"You have to swim, otherwise you'll turn blue and sink like a stone."

"Let's stay here where we can touch the bottom."

"Don't be afraid. You're a good swimmer."

"It's the only thing my father ever taught me. I learned to swim on the beach at Bréhat, when I was Alice's age."

The little girl had been the first one to start calling Aileen *tu* instead of *vous*. This little linguistic intimacy, impossible in English, had been adopted without discussion, as if it were the secret code of the world they were building. Agnès had never called either of her parents *tu*. Jacques was the only person she'd ever used that form with. As for Aileen, she had only ever said *tu* to her mother.

"My parents used to swim in the lake half the year. It's not like the sea here: it's as if the water is always the same. When I swim, I feel like I can almost touch them, like the lake tastes of them."

Aileen swallowed a mouthful of water and smiled.

"Try it."

"I daren't."

They both laughed. Aileen stopped swimming and let her feet descend until they touched the bottom.

"Go ahead, taste it."

Agnès stood too, suppressing a shudder when the mud, warmer than the water, oozed between her toes.

"I know it's stupid, but I'm embarrassed. Let's get out."

As soon as she stopped moving, the cold took hold of her. She crossed her arms over her breasts: she couldn't stop staring at Aileen's, which were distorted by the movement of the clear water, and she wanted to hide hers. Her lips started to tremble while Aileen's turned purple, their shape unchanged against her white skin. Aileen smiled and bent her knees and the lower part of her face disappeared below the surface. Then she stood up, her cheeks full and round, and took a step forward. The tips of her breasts brushed against Agnès' arms, her cold lips pressed against hers. Agnès closed her eyes and opened her mouth and Aileen filled it with lukewarm water, thickened by saliva.

Because this place was the most beautiful place she'd ever seen,

And this woman the most beautiful she'd ever known,

She drank the lake of dead parents,

The taste of the pure water that flows between the legs and lips of lovers.

On the terrace of the house by the lake, woken that morning by the sound of birdsong, little Alice watched her island mother and her ranch mother kiss each other on the mouth, then she went inside to find some bread in the kitchen.

Alice Huet's life was long enough to contain several lives. After distant Paris, the phantasmagorical island of Bréhat and the Fitzpatrick Ranch of her childhood, in 1910 she moved to San Francisco with Agnès and Aileen. They had a house there. Other women – writers, union leaders, journalists and artists – came to seek aid from their foundation, a feminist organisation promoting artistic expression among women, championing their social and political emancipation through creativity. In San Francisco, Aileen and Agnès were simultaneously important people and objects of curiosity, energetic bourgeois women with enough money to buy themselves some privacy, although they could never completely escape the malice and puritan outrage of others.

Alice left this house – a stronghold, always full of people – early, with a list of goals in her pocket. First among them being to find a university and a fast vehicle.

The rumours of war in Europe were so loud that they could be heard in San Francisco, Carson City and even – crossing over the peaks of the Sierra Nevada – at the Fitzpatrick Ranch. When Aileen heard about the death of Rudolf Diesel in October 1913, she was moved by the circumstances of his last days. For a while, the newspapers speculated about a possible crime, a murder motivated by industrial espionage. The reality, crueller and less exciting, was that Rudolf Diesel had committed suicide by throwing himself into the sea from the deck of a ship transporting him to England. Before leaving Germany, he had left his wife a suitcase full of cash – all the money that remained to him. Aileen remembered walking with him through Paris, how charming and nostalgic he had seemed. Depressed and sinking under debt, this sombre pacifist had chosen to end his life in the middle of the North Sea. She imagined him floating in the cold water, the waves filling his mouth, the last sound that he heard before he sank below the surface being the internal combustion engine of the ship as it moved away. Meanwhile, in England, Germany and France, the ministers of war equipped their battleships and armoured vehicles with Diesel engines. The great military mobilisations began a few months later. Rudolf Diesel was a victim of the countdown, thought Aileen.

In 1917, at the age of twenty-four, Alice became the first woman to earn a degree in civil engineering from the University of California in Berkeley. Her ambition was to build roads and bridges.

Her two mothers regularly returned to the ranch. There, far from the city, they dreamed up new plans, wrote, rode horses, swam, and – protected by the borders of their property – were free to love each other.

In the summer, Alice would spend a month with them at the house by the lake. They were rich and, when the United States decided to send troops to fight in Europe, safe from the war.

"You're a woman, but that doesn't change anything," Aileen declared. "If you were a man, you would have deserted. In 1864, in the middle of the Civil War, your grandfather Arthur was hiding deserters at the ranch."

In 1919, the young engineer Alice Huet-Bowman, as she now called herself, was hired to participate in the construction of the most perilous section – along the cliffs of Big Sur – of the future California State Route 1, which would one day connect San Francisco to Los Angeles. That same year, Alice bought an Indian Scout motorcycle, equipped with a 12-horsepower, 606 cc V-twin engine, which could reach speeds of up to 45 mph.

That summer, after loading her bike onto a train, she then rode it along the thirty miles of tracks separating the Truckee station from the ranch. She arrived three hours later, covered in dust, after two falls and two flat tyres. Agnès and Aileen advised her to jump in the lake, then they took care of her grazes. Aileen declared that this motorcycle couldn't be any harder to ride than a bicycle, nor any more dangerous than a horse. She asked Alice to close her eyes. The young woman did as she was told and Agnès, who had just finished bandaging her hand, burst out laughing.

"Aileen has been talking about nothing else for days!"

Alice heard her come back onto the terrace.

"You can look."

She blinked as she saw Aileen pointing at something. Following the direction of her finger, Alice discovered a painting fixed to the cladding of the house. She stood up and walked over to the canvas and her gaze wavered for a moment, unsure where to look first. It moved from the head of the white watchdog to the woman's genitals, then from the typewriter to her face. When she turned around, Aileen had stepped back and was standing next to Agnès.

"Where's it from? Who painted it?"

Aileen held Agnès' hand.

"It arrived in the mail this winter. It was painted in Paris in 1900, when I was there covering the Exposition."

"When you met each other?"

Agnès was blushing. She still blushed at some of her partner's extravagances, or when her feelings and desires bumped against what remained of her principles from another life. She pressed herself against Aileen and slipped her arm under hers. The small victory she'd just won over her old morals, combined with the exhibition of the nude in the light of the lake, had tightened her guts with exhilaration.

"The night I met Aileen for the first time was in a restaurant in Paris. I was with your father and she came with an artist named Julius Stewart. He's the one who painted this picture. Almost twenty years later, he mailed it to the *New York Tribune*. Someone there found the address of the ranch and sent it on."

Aileen asked her what she thought. Alice leaned close to the canvas, examining the backdrop behind the woman's naked body. She noticed the tiny painted copy of Jeandel's cyanotype and raised her eyebrows.

"What is that?"

Agnès blushed again. Aileen smiled.

"The best entertainment on offer in Paris that year."

Alice continued looking: the flowery wallpaper, the false perspective, the Indian knick-knacks in the half-open glass case, the typewriter, the woman's pose and her magnificent nakedness, the stage and the revealed presence of the artist's studio; all of this in the composition proved that the picture told the truth, and all lies of artist and model had been hidden, guarded by the large white dog, a sphinx to the painting's pyramid.

She smiled at her mothers. The two women shared the same sun in San Francisco and at the ranch, the same water when they swam in the lake, the same food, the same beds, the same work. Their faces were similarly tanned, their eyes and mouths had the same pattern of laughter lines. They were dressed the same way, in shirts and trousers. Agnès' dark hair and eyes had lightened in the mountain sunshine, while Aileen's red hair had lost some of its blaze and darkened; after twenty years together, even their eyes seemed to be merging into the same colour. Aileen was fifty-four, Agnès a little younger. They were still beautiful women, but already they contemplated the image on the canvas with the indulgence of nostalgia. The lies and secrets had been brought back to their most honest proportions and now they could live with them.

Alice told them about bridges over the sea, machines that could drive holes through the cliffs of Big Sur, hundreds of prisoners from Folsom Prison hired at 35 cents per day to carry out the most dangerous tasks on the construction of the California State Route.

In the morning, they threw their blankets over a tree stump and went swimming together.

A handful of such summers remained to them. In later years, Alice would visit two old ladies.

In the spring of 1937, the vast work of constructing the California State Route was completed. Alice Huet-Bowman, whose reputation had already seen her offered employment all over the country, straddled a new model Indian Sport Scout, this time equipped with a 24-horsepower, 1200 cc engine, which could reach speeds of 80 mph. By stopping at the dozen petrol stations along the road, she was able to drive all the way from San Francisco to Los Angeles in a single day using an internal combustion engine. Journalists and photographers immortalised her departure. The beautiful and intrepid Alice, the heroine of the day, was forty-four years old. Her goal was to cover the 465 miles between the two great Californian cities in fourteen hours, driving at an average speed of 35 mph.

She finished the trip in twelve hours and thirty minutes, setting a new record, on her bright red Indian, at an average speed of 37 mph. While she was making this journey, a telegram was sent from Carson City to San Francisco, and from there to Los Angeles. It went faster than she did and was waiting for her on her arrival.

At the Fitzpatrick Ranch, now a part of local folklore, lived the heir of the Bowman family, Aileen, and the Frenchwoman now prudishly described – since they were old – as her "companion",

Agnès Huet. The "ladies of the lake" had gone swimming there every day for forty years. The legend was that they were one hundred years old when they died, and that they drowned on the same day. To ensure this legend's continued ability to fascinate, it was even said that one of them died trying to save the other.

In reality, they were only in their early seventies, and while it is true that they grew old together, one of them fell sick before the other. The order doesn't matter. Either way around, their decision would have been the same.

When she arrived from Los Angeles, Alice found the house perfectly tidy, the wardrobes empty apart from her own summer clothes. On the dining-room table, in front of the windows that overlooked the lake, she found Aileen's typewritten papers, all neatly ordered and categorised: her complete rejected works, which she had, in the end, written only for the three of them. Against the tabletop leaned Julius Stewart's painting, the "Nude of the American Woman".

From her mother, Agnès, there was only a brief note, scrawled on a page torn out of a notebook.

You shouldn't be fooled by the disparity in length between the two women's writings. They had equal weight for Alice. Agnès' message had been held in place by a box of matches, so it wouldn't blow away in the wind.

We've had our share. All the love and the lives that remain are for you.

Alice knew that her mother had cancer, and that it was Aileen who'd nursed her; that it was Aileen, that day, who'd taken the oars of the rowing boat that transported them out into the vastness of Lake Tahoe. But Alice would never have dared guess who, on the day of their death and throughout the rest of their lives, had saved the other from drowning.

Now the lake tasted of them.

Alice piled up the papers by the edge of the water, put the painting on top, and waited for nightfall. She lit a match and used it to set fire to her mother's short message. Agnès's words, in turn, burned all of Aileen's lie-words, those novels that had the feel and look of truth, and the flames devoured the nude of the woman with red hair.

ANTONIN VARENNE was awarded the Prix Michel Lebrun and the Grand Prix du Jury Sang d'encre for *Bed of Nails*, his first novel to be translated into English. His second, *Loser's Corner* was awarded the Prix des Lecteurs Quais du Polar and the Prix du Meilleur Polar Francophone. *The Canvas of the World* is the final volume in a thrilling 19th century historical trilogy that began with *Retribution Road*.

SAM TAYLOR is an author and translator. His translations include works by Laurent Binet, Leïla Slimani, and Riad Sattouf.